Alex [illegible] the *New* [illegible] he critically acclaimed serie [illegible] former Marine Ryder Creed and his K9 dogs, and the international bestselling Maggie O'Dell series.

Published in thirty-two countries with over six million copies sold, Kava's novels have been on a multitude of international bestseller lists. She is a member of the Nebraska Writers Guild and International Thriller Writers. Kava and her pack of Westies divide their time between Omaha, Nebraska and Pensacola, Florida.

Alex KAVA
Lost Creed

Sphere
An imprint of
Little, Brown Book Group
Carmelite House
50 Victoria Embankment
London EC4Y 0DZ

An Hachette UK Company
www.hachette.co.uk

sphere

SPHERE

First published in Great Britain in 2018 by Sphere
This paperback edition published in 2018 by Sphere

1 3 5 7 9 10 8 6 4 2

Copyright © S.M. Kava 2018

The moral right of the author has been asserted.

A CIP catalogue record for this book
is available from the British Library.

ISBN 978-0-7515-7223-0

Typeset in Sabon by M Rules
Printed and bound in Great Britain by
Clays Ltd, Elcograf S.p.A

Papers used by Sphere are from well-managed forests
and other responsible sources.

To Linda and Doug, Hunter and Buddy.
And also to my boy, Scout,
the original inspiration for this series.

We are made of all those who have built and broken us.

ATTICUS

Lost
Creed

Prologue

SATURDAY, OCTOBER 13, 2001

Rest Area along Interstate 85
Georgia/Alabama border

Lester Darnell told his wife it wasn't safe to be on his mobile phone with all the lightning strikes. Truth was, he just wanted to eat his Big Mac in peace without her yammering on and on about her day. His back was stiff, his jaw clamped tight and his eyes bleary from too many hours keeping his rig between the lines while the rain beat down and the lightning snaked overhead.

He kept the truck engine running but shut off the windshield wipers. That squeak-swish sound had started to grate on his nerves like nails on a chalkboard. Tonight that was what his wife's voice reminded Lester of, too. Sometimes he really did believe their marriage worked only because he was gone and on the road for six days out of the week.

Lately, his wife had been nagging him to sell his truck and take a warehouse job at one of the trucking companies. He'd been hauling product long enough that a couple of the local places had offered him a job. Less pay but he'd be home every night, and his wife was itching for them to start a family. But Lester couldn't wrap his mind around the idea. He'd be trapped inside a building with no windows for eight hours a day loading and unloading trucks. Just the thought of being cooped up made his chest ache with anxiety.

Despite nights like this, he preferred to be on the road. He could breathe fresh air, not stale warehouse dust mixed with diesel fumes. There was a rhythm to his day, watching the sun rise and set, driving under the moonlight. He could make small talk and meet new people if he wanted, or he could keep to himself and not be bothered. Actually, he liked the solitude, listening to talk radio or the occasional audiobook.

Tonight he was tuned in to the football game – Alabama Crimson Tide taking on the Rebels of Ole Miss. Fourth quarter with Alabama in the lead, 24-20. Didn't matter that neither team was ranked. This was a rivalry that would have all these ole southern boys glued inside their trucks until the end. All Lester had to do was glance around once a team scored, and he could see which team they were cheering for by their grimaces or their smiles. It didn't matter how hard the rain came down, because in their minds they were miles away on the sidelines. As soon as the game ended, they'd be back on the road again.

That was the best part for Lester. He took breaks when he wanted. Ate when he wanted. What warehouse job would let him do that? He was his own boss, confined only by a delivery schedule. And he had fine-tuned that over the years to give himself plenty of time. Except for days like this. The downpours had put him behind, so he was short on sleep and cranked up on caffeine. He'd put off stopping for food and needed the Big Mac and fries more than he needed the shut-eye.

From the looks of the rest area he and his fellow truckers

weren't the only ones taking a break. The place was crazy, the steady hum of eighteen-wheelers in every slot with a half dozen RVs in between, the snowbirds escaping early this year. On the other side of the building, the car parking lot looked just as full. Smeared amber and red lights blinked as vehicles backed out and were immediately replaced by the headlights of a new set of travelers.

There was a steady stream of people entering and exiting the building's lobby. Some jogged, others cut through the grass, all of them trying to avoid getting drenched. Lester had stopped here many times. It was one of the bigger rest areas. Inside was a nice assortment of vending machines that even included hot coffee. The lobby had a set of glass double doors on this side of the building and another on the other side for the car parking lot, so no one had to trek all the way around like some of the smaller places.

Lester turned up the volume on the radio. There were still several minutes left. These truckers would be parked and inside their rigs until the very last second. Lester wanted to pull out and get back on the road before that. But first, he wanted to eat.

He unwrapped his sandwich and tried to pace himself. In between bites he noticed a little girl. She walked to the restrooms with her head down, arms crossed tight across her chest. The rain had let up a bit – a steady drizzle replaced the downpour.

His eyes darted back around to the trucks and RVs. A couple of guys and one woman hurried around the girl, but no one seemed to be accompanying her. She looked too young to be alone – maybe nine or ten, but what did Lester know? His wife always pointed out that he had a lot to learn about kids. Besides, the girl didn't look scared. Instead, she marched from the truck parking lot and up the winding sidewalk, not glancing back or waiting for anyone. She looked like she was on a mission.

Shouts from the radio.

'*Manning's pass is complete to Joe Gunn. Touchdown, Rebels.*'

Lester reached for the volume. But he turned it down, not up. He wanted to eat in silence before he had to listen to those windshield wipers again.

He finished his sandwich and fries but was still hungry. He reached for the bag of raisin oatmeal cookies his wife had baked especially for him. She did take good care of him. He'd call her back once the rain stopped.

He checked his watch. The game would be over very soon. He worked the lid off his Thermos and started to fill his stainless steel mug when he saw the little girl coming back from the restrooms, only now there was another girl walking beside her.

At first, Lester thought he was seeing double. Through the smear of the windshield the pair looked like twins, both with long brown hair, parted down the middle. They were about the same height and stature. The only difference was that one marched – again, with her head down, arms wrapped tight across her chest – while the other practically skipped along with a book tucked under her arm.

He saw several headlights flicking on. Game be must over. He started putting everything into place, getting ready to roll. He wanted to get back on the interstate before the others, or he'd be stuck in a long line on the entrance ramp.

Lester looked up just in time to see the girls disappear

between the trucks. As he buckled up and shifted into gear, he wondered how he'd missed seeing the other little girl going up to the building.

Days later, when he heard on the radio that a little girl had been taken from a rest area in Alabama, Lester Darnell would wonder if it was one of the girls he had seen. But quickly, he'd dismissed the notion. After all, he hadn't seen any adult with them, let alone forcing them along.

And besides, they looked like sisters.

16 YEARS LATER

1

WEDNESDAY, OCTOBER 18, 2017

Florida Panhandle
K9 CrimeScent Training Facility

Ryder Creed watched the black Labrador named Scout bound over the pile of broken concrete blocks. When he came to the makeshift ladder, the dog climbed the rungs without hesitation.

A little too fast. But Creed pushed the thought out of his mind.

The dog had enough puppy in him that everything was still fun. Creed didn't take his eyes off Scout, despite being totally exhausted. He'd gotten back before sunrise and hadn't slept yet. He and his best disaster-search dog, Bolo, had spent three days working an explosion site in east Texas. Bolo had scraped and cut his pads searching the rubble. They'd found two people alive. Creed worried there might be more and didn't want to leave until other handlers and dogs arrived. But he knew not to push his dog's limits. As soon as another handler and dog made it to the scene, Creed hightailed Bolo home.

Now, Creed kept his focus on Scout. The dog had stopped at the top of the ladder and glanced down at his handler, who stood beside Creed. But he hesitated only for a few seconds.

Then the dog navigated the narrow beam that was ten feet off the ground and stretched for six feet before coming to another ladder.

That's when Creed noticed the slight grimace on the handler's face.

In a quiet and casual tone, Creed said, 'Don't do that.'

He chose his words carefully because Scout knew 'stop' and 'quit,' and Creed didn't want to distract the dog.

To his credit, Jason Seaver, the young handler, didn't look over at Creed. He kept his voice calm as he said, 'Sorry. Makes me nervous.'

Creed waited for Scout to finish treading over the beam, which he did with zeal. The dog was revved up and anxious to show off. Creed couldn't help but smile. Scout was fourteen months old. He was a bit of a hotdog, an energetic jackass, but that drive was one of the characteristics that would make him an excellent scent detection dog.

'If you're nervous, he'll sense it. Why does it make you nervous?' Creed asked Jason when the dog had cleared the second ladder and was back on the ground sniffing out the canisters Creed had buried in the second pile of broken concrete.

The rubble reminded Creed of the explosion site and his concern for Bolo still nagged at him. He looked back over his shoulder toward the driveway, watching for Dr Avelyn's black Tahoe. She was their on-site veterinarian, but she also had a thriving clinic of her own in Milton. Still, she had already texted Creed that she'd check out Bolo as soon as she could get away.

'What if he falls?' Jason finally answered with a question.

Even though the two men stood side by side, neither turned to each other as they talked, not taking their focus off the dog. From the corner of his eye, Creed could see Jason rubbing his arm. Despite the shirtsleeve covering it, Creed knew it was the place where Jason's new prosthetic joined his amputation site. The high-tech addition was only a couple of months new to the kid.

Funny, Creed still thought of Jason as a kid even after watching him grow and mature into a decent dog handler over the last year. Both men were in their twenties, Jason at the beginning, Creed at the end. In fact, Creed would turn thirty in a few months. Age didn't matter to him. He measured time differently than others. Like how many years since his sister, Brodie, had gone missing. It would be sixteen years this month. He knew the exact date despite how much else had happened in those years in between.

Life goes on. He hated that saying, but it was brutally true.

Once upon a time, Creed believed there couldn't be anything worse than losing your eleven-year-old sister and not having a clue as to where she was. But Afghanistan proved him wrong. He'd joined the Marines as soon as he was old enough and learned quickly that he had only replaced one hell with another.

That was one thing he and Jason had in common. They were both war veterans, having served in Afghanistan: Jason in the Army, Creed in the Marines. Both had returned home early after being blown up. Both damaged in different ways. And now it occurred to Creed that both of them had been lucky enough to be saved by dogs in one way or another.

'He won't fall if you train him so well that he doesn't even think about falling,' Creed told Jason. 'Make sure it's second nature to him. Then believe in him. Believe in him so strongly that he can feel your confidence radiating off your entire body.'

Right at that moment, Scout sat down at a crevice between the rocks and lifted his right paw. He looked over at Jason. Not exactly at Jason, but at the handler's pocket where he knew his toy – his reward – was.

'Hurry up. Reward your dog,' Creed told him as he checked his diver's watch. Scout had found the scent in record time.

Jason yanked the rope toy from his pocket and tossed it to the dog who caught it in mid-air despite the awkward pile of jagged concrete. And when Creed saw Jason wince, the kid shook his head before Creed could say a word. This time, Creed couldn't blame him and glanced, again, at the driveway. He felt a surge of relief when he spotted the black Tahoe winding its way up the long drive.

Scout came racing to the two men, prancing and shaking his head so the rope slapped around, the knots hitting him upside the head. Jason held out his hand for the dog to give the toy back. When Scout relinquished it, drool dripped from his mouth in long strings as Jason slipped him a treat.

'What did you just give him?' Creed asked, his tone still calm.

'Just a little training treat.'

'I told you, you can't use food as a reward.'

'It's not food. It's just one of those tiny little training treats.'

'He doesn't know the difference. To him, it's food. You can't have him alerting to someone's discarded fast-food wrapper.'

'I don't give it to him when he alerts. I give it to him when he gives me back his reward toy.'

'He needs to give it back to you with only a command, not another reward. The rope toy is the reward. That's what you want him to be excited about. Not a treat.'

Creed stopped when he noticed the dog's head cocking from side to side. Scout recognized the words 'treat' and 'reward.' It didn't matter what tone was being used. This was a conversation they shouldn't be having in front of the dog.

'Let's move on,' he told Jason. Now that Dr Avelyn was here, he needed to relax. Focus on the work at hand.

And he could see that was exactly what Scout was waiting for. He wanted another chance to earn his rope toy. The dog was staring hard at Jason's pocket.

'I've hidden a surprise for him,' Creed told Jason and pointed to the woods. But the idea of a surprise brought another grimace from Jason. 'You're clenching your teeth.'

'Sorry.'

'Don't apologize,' Creed told him. 'Just relax. He's doing great.'

Creed dug out a plastic bag from his pocket and handed it to Jason. Inside the bag was an extracted wisdom tooth wrapped in bloody gauze. In the woods, Creed had planted another training canister with a second tooth. Both teeth were from the same person. He kept a cache of items like this that friends had given him to use for training – anything from teeth to pieces of bone and even one gall bladder.

'Scout,' Jason called and waited for the dog to stand in front of him. He snapped on a leash to the dog's harness. Then he pulled open the seal on the bag. He held it low for Scout's nose to hover over the top. As soon as his tail stood straight out, Jason gave the command. 'Go find.' And he waved his hand toward the path into the woods where Creed had pointed.

Scout bounded off.

Too fast, again. Yanking and jerking at Jason to hurry up.

By the time they got inside the woods the dog's breathing had changed. His nose poked and sniffed the air as he pulled and plowed through the thick brush, not interested in following any of the existing paths. Jason kept up with no problem. He held on tight to the long leash, wrapping it a couple of times around his wrist for an extra grip just like Creed had taught him.

The kid was shorter than Creed, but he'd put on weight in the last six months, most of it lean muscle from working with the dogs and all the daily chores around the kennel. But Creed noticed Jason still wasn't using his high-tech prosthetic. Almost as if he didn't trust it . . . yet. He kept it hanging at his side like something he simply carried along.

It would take time. Creed knew that, so he didn't say anything. He left conversations about such things to his business partner, Hannah. She had more patience than Creed. And she knew what to say. Hannah was the one who had hired Jason. Creed rescued dogs and Hannah rescued lost souls.

When they hired him, Jason was a recent amputee war veteran with a chip on his shoulder the size of Montana. Hannah said the kid reminded her of Ryder. When she and Creed first met, Creed was belligerent and drunk, a Marine, injured and sent home to recover. Hannah saved him before he picked a fight and took on three drunken patrons in the bar she was tending. In that way, Creed supposed he and Jason were similar. Both had come home damaged and pissed off.

It hadn't been five minutes, and Scout came to a sudden stop. So sudden, Jason almost tripped over him. Creed followed from about ten feet behind. This was a blind hide, which meant that even the handler didn't know the location. That way, Jason couldn't give Scout any hints.

Not intentional hints, of course. This was a tricky business. Handlers and dogs created a deep and trusting bond.

Handlers needed to make sure their dogs didn't get hurt. An air scent dog could get so caught up in following a scent it may not pay close attention to barbed wire, thorns and thicket, sharp rock or flood waters with hidden debris. The handler and dog were a team, and yet, the dog was still expected to work separately. The dog needed to be more focused on finding the targeted scent than pleasing the handler.

The pile of freshly dug dirt was the surprise test Creed had planted. He wanted to see if Scout and Jason had reached that level in their relationship.

Creed watched, backing away a bit so he wouldn't project his own interest on the mound that Scout was sniffing. Jason waited, patiently, never once glancing back at Creed. Not even when Scout looked up to check his handler's expression as if to ask, 'Is this important?'

The dog sniffed more rapidly and did a quick scrape at the ground next to the pile. He danced at the end of the leash, poking his nose in the air. Another eye-roll back up to Jason's face. Then without warning, Scout lifted his leg and peed on the mound.

Creed wiped a hand over his smile.

Scout turned away, ready to go. His nose was in the air. He already caught another scent and this time he yanked hard, almost knocking Jason off his feet.

Jason shot a glance back, and Creed gave him the slightest of nods to let him know that, yes, Scout was right to leave the mound behind. Not only leave it behind but also mark it, so he wouldn't waste any more time with the distracting smell. Creed had buried the road kill earlier. The scent of a dead animal was different than the scent of a dead human, but for a dog, dead animals could smell too interesting to ignore.

This was one of the tests Creed had prepared, and Scout had passed.

Creed followed Jason and Scout deeper into the woods. The canister he'd hidden wasn't much farther. He'd left it in an elbow of a tree. The second test would be for Jason. Would he believe his dog when Scout told him the target was above them?

But the dog was straining at the end of the leash. Scout's nose twitched, and he was starting to pant from pulling so hard. Creed quickened his pace to catch up with the pair. He could see the hair on the back of the dog's neck standing up. Before he could tell Jason to slow down, the kid came to a sudden stop. He was reigning in Scout, adding his prosthetic so he could reel in the dog despite Scout's dancing and growling.

'I hope this isn't your surprise,' Jason said.

That's when Creed finally saw what had Scout so worked up. Less than fifty feet away, a black bear stared at them from between the trees.

2

'Keep Scout close at your side,' Creed told Jason. 'Don't let him go.'

'Of course I'm not gonna let him go.'

What Creed really wanted to ask is if Jason could hold the dog since he wasn't accustomed to using the prosthetic. Was he capable of controlling a frenzied dog in a situation like this? Despite being only a year old, Scout was a solid sixty pounds, and right now, he was using all that weight to yank and tug while emitting a low growl mixed with a whine.

'And keep him quiet.'

'Scout, quiet,' Jason gave the command, but the dog continued to lunge, jumping on his back legs with his front paws pedaling the air. 'Scout, heel.'

It didn't work. Scout still twisted and tugged. Jason shortened the leash, wrapping it around and around his wrist until only about a foot separated him and the dog.

Creed knew that black bears were naturally shy. Loud noise usually scared them enough to turn and walk away. Scout provided enough chaos that should have made the bear leave. But this one was becoming more and more interested. It clearly was focused on Scout.

Creed walked slowly in front of Jason as he grabbed at his belt only to find the canister of bear spray missing. His stomach did a flip, and he bit back a curse. He didn't gear up for training sessions like he did for actual searches. Time for that to change.

'What the hell do we do?' Jason asked, keeping his voice low and casual, but Creed recognized the panic anyway.

'They don't usually attack unless they feel threatened,' he told Jason just as the bear stood up on its hind legs to get a better view of them.

'Damn,' Jason said under his breath, all casualness gone from his tone. 'I'd say he's feeling threatened.'

'This time of year he's looking for some easy food. They triple or quadruple their calories preparing for the cool temps.' As Creed talked he eased himself between the bear and Scout.

'Are we easy food?' Jason asked.

'I meant garbage left out. From what I remember, they're omnivores. Mostly plants and bugs.'

Even as he tried to convince Jason they were okay, Creed began to search the ground without taking his focus off the bear. A fallen branch was about a yard from his feet. A few green leaves sprouted from one end, so it wasn't dried and hollow. It might pack enough punch if necessary. His eyes scanned the trees, making sure there weren't any others. Black bears tended to be solitary creatures, but if this was a female with a cub or yearling, they were in trouble.

'So what's the plan?' Jason wanted to know. 'I can't climb a tree with a dog.'

'Black bears have curved claws. He'd be able to climb up after us.'

'Can we outrun him?'

'We definitely don't want to do that. Could trigger his chase instinct.'

'Chase instinct? For a guy who knows so much about bears you'd think you'd have some UDAP bear spray.'

'Believe me, it just became mandatory gear.'

Then the bear dropped back to the ground, and Creed felt his stomach do the same. He heard a huff-huff. The bear was blowing air through its mouth. Maybe it was trying to scare them off.

Creed tried to remember anything he could about bear attacks. There had been several confrontations in the news lately. He hadn't worried about bears coming around their facilities. His crew was careful about keeping food stored inside as well as locking up garbage cans. But their property stretched over fifty acres, much of it woods and undeveloped. More than half of it they'd left natural with plenty of pecan trees, live oaks and a shallow creek that ran along the northern edge. When Creed thought about it that way, he realized they were probably lucky they hadn't seen a bear until now.

'So what's our plan?' Jason asked.

'You and Scout start backing away. Do it slow and easy. Try to keep Scout from jumping around and whining.'

The bear stood up again, but it still didn't advance. It was sniffing them.

Creed heard the kid suck in air behind him. But he had to give Scout credit. For all his earlier dancing and growling, the dog stayed beside his handler now, shifting and watching, but not barking. It was something Creed insisted they teach their scent dogs. When to bark and when to keep quiet were important tools. Originally, it was a safety measure so a barking dog couldn't alert drug smugglers. Who knew it would come in handy when confronting a bear.

'What about you?' Jason wanted to know.

'Just do what I tell you, okay?' Creed slid to his right and slowly reached for the branch, never taking his eyes off the bear. 'And if he charges, do not let Scout go.'

When Jason still didn't move, Creed added, 'Go on. Nice and easy.'

Creed heard the shuffle and crunch behind him, dog and handler following his instructions. One thing Jason's military training had taught him was not to argue when given orders by his superior. But as Jason and Scout were backing away, Creed could hear more huffs and a snap-clack that sounded like the bear was chomping its teeth together.

And just at that moment, Creed's cell phone started vibrating in his pocket.

It had to be Hannah. He quickly contemplated whether or not there was anything she could do to help. The bear stayed on its hind legs, and now it leaned to the left. It stretched its neck and tilted its head. The retreating dog still held its interest. What the hell was he going to do if the bear decided to follow Scout?

Creed gripped the branch. It felt heavy and solid, and it was long enough to swing, but he couldn't help thinking that it would probably bounce off the bear. A hit with something like this would aggravate more than injure. But maybe it would buy time.

He glanced over his shoulder. Jason and Scout had taken a turn and disappeared down one of the paths. He couldn't see them through the thick foliage. There was more shuffling and crackling in front of Creed now, not behind him. The bear dropped to the ground and stared as if seeing him for the first time. Creed held his breath and wished he could silence the thumping of his heart.

The bear raised its nose and sniffed the air, again, and Creed was certain it smelled his anxiety. Hell, who was he kidding? It could smell his fear.

Then without warning, the bear sat back down and snatched up a swatch of green, what Creed recognized as holly. It kept an eye on Creed but began plucking off the tiny red berries with its lips, delicately taking them into its mouth, one by one. They had interrupted its meal. Would it simply go back to it?

Creed realized he was squeezing the branch so tight that his hand ached. He took a small step backward and stopped. When the bear continued eating, Creed took a few more steps, careful not to trip and keeping his hands – along with the branch – steady and dropped at his side.

By the time he made it to the curved path that Jason and Scout had taken, he was feeling he was home free. The bear kept watching but now seemed bored with him and continued eating even as Creed turned and disappeared from its sight.

His phone vibrated in his pocket, again. He fished it out as he started walking sideways and listening intently. Without looking, he thumbed the phone on and stole a glance. There were several text messages from Hannah. The last one said:

Need you back at the house for a phone call.

He didn't dare drop the branch but managed to tap out a reply and send:

Can it wait?

Her response was almost instantaneous.

No. Sorry. it's about Brodie.

In the last ten or fifteen minutes he feared a black bear might rip him to shreds, but that was nothing compared to what he was feeling right now. Those three words, 'It's about Brodie,' threatened to knock him completely off his feet.

10 HOURS EARLIER

3

Eastern Nebraska

FBI Special Agent Maggie O'Dell didn't like waiting. Especially in the dark. She'd been hopped-up on adrenaline for the last two hours. Mud sucked at her shoes. Sweat trickled down her back despite a cool breeze, a damp cool breeze. Detective Tommy Pakula had already mentioned several times that the temperatures were all over the place.

'Nothing new for Nebraska,' he told her.

It had been ninety degrees less than ten hours ago, so of course, Maggie hadn't thought to bring a jacket. They talked about the weather – low, muffled whispers, a few curses – as though they were old friends chatting. Old friends who just happened to be standing five rows deep in a cornfield at half-past midnight.

A ten-year FBI veteran, Maggie had chased killers through the snow, the woods, even a cemetery, but this was her first cornfield. The stalks were taller than her. The long leaves waved and flapped – half green, half brown – and surprisingly razor-sharp.

Despite a crescent moon, it was pitch black and almost impossible to see any of the others. She was feeling a bit anxious, maybe even a bit claustrophobic. She'd heard about people getting lost in cornfields, and now she understood how disorienting it could be. She couldn't shake the isolation despite being surrounded by a hidden battalion of law enforcement officers.

Okay, battalion was a bit of an exaggeration. It was more like a dozen. Two dozen, if she counted those deputies and state troopers who were three miles away on the closest blacktop, waiting for instructions.

Maggie couldn't help noticing that sounds were different from inside the cornfield. The songs of night birds calling to each other were muffled, but the buzz of mosquitos, amplified. The breeze seemed to be an entity of its own. It wisped through the rows like a ghost riding an airwave. Maggie could hear a gust approaching, a slight moan in the distance growing and getting louder and louder, long before she felt its arrival. And then, it would be only a puff of air, lifting a strand of damp hair from the back of her neck.

The silence and the darkness made this raid unsettling, ominously so, like a calm before a storm. The sound of the wind and mosquitos competed with a distant train whistle. The moon and a sky full of stars only emphasized how truly dark it was. Out here there were no streetlights, no headlights, only two dim yellow stains behind the curtained windows of the clapboard farmhouse.

A few minutes ago, she caught a glint of light in the trees. A stand of evergreens bordered the dirt track that was the driveway. Pakula had seen it, too, and was immediately on his radio telling the guilty officer 'to keep the hell off your cell phone.'

'How much longer?' she asked, swatting at another mosquito. She kept her pair of earbuds dangling, preferring the night sounds and the rustling of the cornstalks to the static of the radio.

'The team's almost ready. They're trying to get a radar read on how many are in the house. Where they are.'

'Heat sensitive or motion?' she asked, realizing it made no difference to her. This wasn't her area of expertise. It wasn't Pakula's either, and he simply shrugged.

Although he was the local head of the task force, the FBI was running the show tonight. Both Pakula and Maggie were part of a nationwide sweep called Operation Cross Country. Tonight's raid was one of dozens going on across the country. But it was Maggie who brought them to this farmhouse in southeast Nebraska. And she hoped like hell it wouldn't be a bust.

Maggie O'Dell had garnered a reputation for putting together profiles of serial killers, serial arsonists, even a terrorist or two. This was her first human trafficker profile. In the back of her mind, a tad of skepticism nagged at her. Elijah Dunn didn't have the rapsheet to match the suspicion. And this quiet little farmhouse, with the closest neighbor eight miles away, certainly didn't look like a place a trafficker would keep his merchandise.

Or maybe it was the perfect place.

Still, the house and yards – even the outbuildings – looked well kept. Maggie had noticed a porch swing in the back and a couple of larger planters with flowers. The property didn't look like it belonged to a criminal.

It didn't help matters that Pakula had asked one too many times if Maggie was sure this was their guy.

She and Pakula had worked together before. He respected her. He had actually requested her for this case. To have him questioning her started to unravel Maggie's certainty.

Their suspect, Elijah Dunn, had been tagged by the local

authorities as a petty thief who got drunk or stoned depending on how much cash he came across. Sheriff deputies who knew him claimed Eli had a few loose screws. He appeared harmless, but they admitted the man was a gifted liar. His file contained only minor infractions: possession of marijuana, a couple of disorderly conducts and one case of breaking and entering. No weapon was involved in the latter and the charges were eventually dropped.

But Maggie hadn't based her profile solely on his criminal record. It was Eli's cyber presence and internet activity that drew her attention. Together with Agent Antonio Alonzo – Quantico's computer wizard – a compilation of cyber ads and posts on the darknet led to email accounts created by Elijah Dunn. His cyber activity added the grist to Maggie's profile. That and a number of other things. Like the fact that he owned a Ford F150 pickup with a truck cab, a new vehicle that he had already driven over 30,000 miles in less than a year. Many of those miles across various state lines.

Eli took good care of his pickup – just like his property – and Agent Alonzo had been able to track all maintenance and oil changes through the dealership's computer records. The dealership happened to have affiliate service centers along Eli's travel routes in Missouri, Alabama and Florida. As an unemployed petty criminal who never had possession of more than a few grams of pot – which probably cancelled out drug trafficking – where did he go?

If he wasn't trafficking drugs or stolen goods, was it possible he was moving some other cargo? Those kinds of details, along with his internet activity, led Maggie to believe the drunk, petty thief was not only a gifted liar, but also a master manipulator. She was willing to bet her reputation on it.

Now, she hoped there was, at least, a computer hard drive inside that quaint farmhouse that would back up her suspicions. If she was correct, they would find an incriminating inventory, along with other darknet ads and posts, emails and possibly text messages on his cell phone.

If she was wrong ...

Damn, she didn't want to think about the consequences if she was wrong.

'They're going in the front,' Pakula whispered.

She could see he already had his weapon down by his side.

Maggie left hers in her shoulder holster. She slipped the earbuds in and followed Pakula between the stalks. When they came to the edge of the field, they were about a hundred feet from the back of the house. She was surprised how much her eyes had adjusted to the dark. Still, from this angle they couldn't see the team approaching the front door.

'What's that smell?' she whispered. The breeze brought a whiff of something that wasn't there before. It was strong enough to sting her eyes.

She could see Pakula noticed it, too.

'Smells like ammonia?'

Then through the earbuds she heard whispered curses.

'Tripwire. Damn it!'

'He knew we were coming.'

Suddenly, someone shouted from the front yard.

'Runner. We've got a runner.'

'Stay here,' Pakula told her. 'Watch the back of the house.'

Then he took off toward the shouting, disappearing around the trees. She could hear other voices coming from the front yard, a crash of wood, maybe even glass. And then a flash of light.

Pakula wasn't gone but a minute or two when Maggie saw movement at the back corner of the house. Close to the ground she could see a shadow in the moonlight.

Someone was crawling out of a basement window.

4

Maggie followed a fence line that separated the cornfield from the backyard. She hoped the noise coming from the front yard overrode her rapid breathing. She also hoped that the dew-covered grass didn't turn her quick steps into a slip and flip onto her backside.

Just as the man was pulling his legs free of the small window, Maggie was at the corner of the house. She had her weapon pointing at his head when she yelled, 'Not so fast. Stay on your knees and put your hands behind your head.'

The man's head pivoted up to look at her. His eyes were wide with surprise. Even in the dim light and through the scraggly beard, Maggie recognized him from his mugshot.

'Good evening, Mr Dunn?'

Slowly he put his hands up, lacing his fingers together behind his head. He didn't attempt to get up off his knees. Then Eli Dunn did something that sent a shiver down her spine. He smiled at her. Not just a grin but a big, bold smile with a look that said she had no idea who she was dealing with.

'Seriously? A woman cop?' Dunn said, shaking his head and still smiling. 'Hell, this *is* my lucky day.'

He made no attempt to resist. Even when Maggie fumbled with the flex-ties, he held still, keeping his wrists together to make it easier for her. He seemed amused by her clumsy efforts. She pulled the plastic tight, maybe too tight, wanting to wipe that smile off his face even if she had to replace it with a grimace.

She was an expert in forensics and profiling criminals, digging into their psyche, dissecting the evidence they left behind and predicting their next move. Usually by the time she arrived at a crime scene there were only dead bodies to process. The killer was long gone. She wasn't used to apprehending and cuffing the criminal.

'Up on your feet,' she told him. 'Slow and easy.'

'So that's the way you like it?'

The breeze chilled her, she convinced herself. Not his words. And she kept her weapon leveled at him. There was nothing clumsy in the way she handled that. She had worked hard to make sure she was an expert marksman. She hunted serial killers for a living, and more than one had tried to turn the table and come after her. She couldn't afford to not be prepared, and yet, when Eli Dunn began sniffing in her direction, there was something terribly unsettling in his gesture.

'You sure do smell good.'

'Let's join the others,' she gestured for him to keep moving to the front of the house. She couldn't tell if he was high.

He held his nose up and sniffed again. 'My alarm system,' he told her, standing in place and watching her face with small black intense eyes, hard and cold, waiting for her reaction. He looked like a scraggly-haired, lanky teenager wanting to impress her with his latest prank. 'Ammonia. That's how I knew you were coming.'

'Mr Dunn, I must advise you that anything you say can be used against you—'

'Course, if I knew a pretty thing like you was out here

waiting for me, I would have invited you in.' He winked at her. 'You and me could have had a real good time.'

She kept her face from showing her revulsion.

'We still could.'

'Let's move.' When he didn't move, she shoved his shoulder.

'Oh, I do like a strong woman.'

'Maggie?'

Pakula came around the corner of the house, and Eli Dunn suddenly dropped his head, chin to his chest. Even his shoulders slumped forward as if he could curl himself into a smaller frame, playing the whipped victim. As Pakula approached, Maggie noticed Dunn's smile was also gone.

'What the hell?' Pakula said.

'Mr Dunn was trying to escape out the back window.'

'Dunn?' Pakula flicked on his flashlight and shot a beam into the man's face. 'I'll be damned.'

They marched him around to the front of the house into the blinding light. Floodlights now illuminated the front yard. Headlights weaved through the trees and up the driveway as more law enforcement joined them. Windows lit up inside the house, one after another as the team conducted their raid. She could hear their shouts to each other as they cleared each room.

Pakula waved to a deputy who took Dunn by the elbow. As Eli Dunn was being led away he looked back over his shoulder at Maggie. In the lights, the toothy grin was bright white surrounded by dark beard stubble. No chance Dunn was a meth user, but she wouldn't rule out that the man was flying high on something else. Those dark, cold eyes convinced her that she was correct about one thing – this man wasn't some petty criminal.

'So if Dunn was going out the back, who was the runner?' Maggie asked.

Pakula winced and tilted his chin toward an SUV with BUTLER COUNTY SHERIFF DEPARTMENT on the side door. Now, she saw that the back door remained open. A woman officer was talking to someone inside. When she got a better look, Maggie was startled to see the skinny legs, knobby knees, and bare feet.

'The kid's tall but I'm guessing he can't be much over thirteen,' Pakula said. 'Fourteen at the most. He said Dunn pushed him out the front door. Told him to run and keep running. He's naked except for his jockeys. I think he's loaded. Or stoned. Barely looked at me when I gave him my jacket.'

Only now did Maggie realize Pakula was in shirtsleeves.

'If you hadn't been in the backyard,' he told her, 'this little stunt may have worked.'

'Pakula. O'Dell.' Special Agent Stevens waved to them from the front door. 'You gotta see this.'

From the tone of his voice, Maggie guessed her suspicions about Eli Dunn were right.

5

The inside of the house smelled like bleach. But Maggie noticed it was distinctively different than the ammonia that still lingered in the air outside. Even if Dunn hadn't told her about setting alarms, this new odor convinced her the man knew they were coming for him. So why hadn't he left? Maybe he had been tipped off about a police raid, but he didn't know exactly when. He knew enough in advance to clean house.

She could tell Pakula and Stevens were thinking along the same lines.

Footsteps pounded up and down the wooden stairs. She heard doors pushed open with such force they were slamming into walls. The team was still clearing the upstairs and basement. Stevens, however, was leading Pakula and Maggie down a narrow hallway to the back of the house. As she followed, Maggie took in everything around her.

The walls were bare, the carpet well worn. Through doorways, left wide open by the advance team, she glimpsed sparse furnishings. One bedroom had only a mattress on the floor, the bed sheets left in a tangled mess. A small bathroom was missing a shower curtain, giving her a clear shot of the open stall with a drain in a concrete floor. The scent of bleach hit her nostrils as she passed, the scent so strong that it made her eyes water.

'The runner was the only one here with Dunn,' Stevens told them as he turned down another long hallway. 'But there're mattresses and bedding upstairs and cots in the basement. All the doors have deadbolts that work from the outside of the rooms.'

He pointed to one of the open doors as they passed, but Maggie wasn't interested in the locks as much as she was in the stark bedroom. A single light bulb illuminated the white walls and plain sheets pulled tight and tucked neatly. Even the pillow was fluffed. This room had linoleum instead of the worn carpet and it was tiny with only enough room for the mattress. Her first thought was that Eli Dunn had created prison cells within the old clapboard farmhouse, utilizing every area – even what may have once been a closet.

Finally Stevens led them through the last door before the end of the hallway.

'It was locked and padlocked,' he told them, explaining why the door was now splintered and hanging by one hinge.

Compared to the other rooms, this one was messy with empty takeout containers on the desk. The worn sofa was too large for the space. A bookcase overflowed with books and folded maps. Stacked cardboard boxes made a leaning tower in one corner. Maggie's eyes darted back to the desk and the clean spot in the center where a dustless rectangle remained after something was removed. Something like a computer, and she felt the disappointment in the pit of her stomach.

None of this, however, was what had drawn Stevens' attention. Unlike every other room in the house where the walls had been left bare, in here, the walls were plastered with photographs and newspaper clippings. A huge corkboard in the middle had obviously not been large enough for the magnitude of its job. It was overloaded, thumbtacks driven through several layers.

'Son of a bitch,' Pakula said under his breath.

The news clippings were mostly yellowed, a few with torn edges, others looked to be photocopies. Some of the photos were blurry and faded or too dark to see the faces. But Maggie didn't need to see details to know the subjects were young, some just children, others teenagers. Both boys and girls. A collage was made of different sizes of Polaroids, glossy colored prints, black and white matte finish, and colored copies printed out on plain white paper.

There were so many of them.

Maggie felt like she'd swallowed acid. She needed to keep focused. Her eyes scanned the room, but she didn't see any electronic devices.

'Did your men find a computer?' she asked Stevens, breaking the silence inside the room. She was still hoping they had already grabbed the laptop computer that had obviously occupied the center of the desk.

He shook his head, but he didn't look away from the wall. 'They can't all be his victims, can they? Is it possible he collects or takes their pictures before he sells them?'

The photos were thumbtacked so they overlapped to accommodate the volume. In some instances all that could be seen were triangles with an eye and nose, a forehead with bangs or only lips with a chin. They looked like pieces of a jigsaw puzzle.

Maggie started to turn away. Had they looked for hiding places where Dunn could have stowed the computer? But something on the wall caught her eye and she leaned in for a closer look.

At the bottom left corner of the corkboard was a Polaroid pinned over two other photos, stabbed through the white edging. The boy and girl had their arms wrapped around each other as they smiled for the camera. But it wasn't the image that stopped her. What grabbed her attention was the bold print in the white area below the Polaroid photo. Someone had labeled the memory in black marker:

BRODIE and RYDER, 10-12-01

One of those names alone would be unusual. Both of them together could not be a coincidence.

Maggie's knees threatened to buckle.

'What is it?' Pakula asked.

Had he noticed that she was holding her breath? Did she look as sick to her stomach as she felt? She pointed to the photograph.

'I know someone named Ryder.'

Both men stared at her. She glanced at Pakula. His eyebrows went up. His hands gestured for more of an explanation.

'His sister Brodie disappeared in 2001 from an interstate rest area.'

This time Pakula turned and leaned into the corkboard. Stevens stayed put, hand to his chin as he tilted his head at the same angle as the photo to read the handwriting.

'She was eleven and he was fourteen,' Maggie told them in almost a whisper.

'Coincidence?' Stevens suggested.

Maggie didn't believe in coincidences. She pointed to the photograph again and said, 'Take a look at the date.'

'10-12-01,' Pakula read out loud then added, 'Holy crap.'

6

Florida Panhandle

By the time he got out of the woods, Creed was out of breath. The back of his T-shirt was drenched in sweat. His heartbeat pounded in his chest. Jason and Scout had waited for him at the edge of the tree line. When the kid saw Creed's face he did a double take then started searching the path.

'Is the bear following you?' Jason wanted to know.

'No, it stayed put. Went back to eating.' Creed rushed past the handler and his dog.

'Then what's going on?' Jason pressed.

This time Creed stopped and turned back. 'Sorry. Hannah texted me. Something about a phone call. I'll fill you in later. You and Scout did good,' he added, knowing Jason needed the kudos but would never ask. Creed was anxious to get to the house, but this was just as important. 'You've done a really good job with him. Scout's ready.'

'Really? You think so?'

'Doesn't mean you let up on the training.'

'No, of course not.'

'Cut out the treats.'

'Absolutely.'

'He's ready to be in the field,' Creed told him, pleased to see a rare smile from the kid. 'When I finish with Hannah, you and I need to figure out how we can bear-proof the kennels.'

'Is that possible?'

'Sure. We just need to be creative.' At least he hoped it was possible, Creed thought as he turned and headed to the main house.

He slowed down his pace. He needed to concentrate and focus on getting his breathing back to normal. He didn't want Hannah to see what Jason must have seen on his face. And he certainly didn't want to trigger the nightmare loop that had played inside his head too many times over the course of the last sixteen years. But he knew it was too late.

He felt the stab at his temples. And then came the rush in his ears, a steady humming sound. In his mind he could already hear the rain drumming on the roof of the car, the football game blaring on the radio, the volume getting louder and louder so it could be heard over the dog's barking.

His dad didn't want to miss the last minutes of the game. Alabama had been ahead most of the game but now suddenly they were on the verge of losing in the last minutes. His dad was already pissed that they had to listen to it on the car radio, instead of watching it at home in his living room. To make matters worse, Brodie needed to go to the bathroom, so their dad pulled into the busy rest area along the interstate.

In his mind, Creed could hear the hissing of air brakes. The scent of diesel filled his nostrils. It could still make him nauseated. He was never sure how that was possible but after this many years, this many times, he didn't question it anymore. He just wished it would go away.

Creed stopped in his tracks. Squeezed his eyes tight and shook his head. The replay of that night including all the sights and sounds and scents came back as easily as if it had happened only yesterday. Creed had started his K9 business in the hopes of one day finding some answers. It was an honorable mission, but gut-wrenching, because every time he helped find the body of a little girl or a young woman it brought back the panic of that night. He no longer believed that anything short of finding Brodie's remains would offer any relief. And even then, how could he possibly find relief?

He went in the back door of the house, entering the kitchen. Immediately, he was struck by the scent of cinnamon and freshly baked bread. Hannah looked over at him from the counter where she was mixing a concoction that filled the air with a heavenly scent that reminded Creed of the holidays.

'She said she'd call back within the hour,' Hannah said. 'You want coffee? I just made a fresh pot.'

'She?'

'Maggie O'Dell.'

He opened a cupboard and pulled out a mug to give himself something to do. When he went to pour the coffee he noticed a slight tremor in his hand and turned so Hannah couldn't see it. Creed had worked with Maggie several times. Last spring they ended up in an isolation ward together after being exposed to the bird flu virus.

They talked on a regular basis though mostly by phone. They were … friends. Was that what they were? Actually, they'd shared too much to be only friends, and there was way too much electricity between them, but that's where they kept their relationship. Creed tried not to think about it. It was what it was, and he had decided that wouldn't change until or unless Maggie wanted it to change.

'What exactly did she say?' Creed asked when he realized Hannah wasn't going to tell him without him asking.

'I don't want you to get all riled, okay?'

She emptied her hands and placed them on her ample hips, a gesture usually reserved for lectures or sermons. But Creed met her eyes and caught a flicker of alarm before she replaced it with concern.

'All she told me was that she had some questions for you about Brodie.'

He held her gaze, weighing whether or not she was holding anything back. The two of them were brutally honest with each other. Hannah was his business partner but in the last seven years she had also become his family, his confidant, even his moral compass. She wouldn't lie to him. She couldn't lie to him.

'What do you think it's about?' he asked.

She shook her head. 'Truthfully? That girl took me completely off guard saying she wanted to ask you about Brodie. I was so speechless, I simply said, 'Okay.' She said she'd call back within the hour and hung up.'

Hannah, speechless.

Normally, Creed would rib her about that, but just then the phone started ringing. Both of them stared at it through three rings. Creed finally crossed the room and lifted the receiver, checking the caller ID and letting it ring a fourth time before he punched the ON button.

'Hey, Maggie, it's Ryder.'

'I'd ask how you are, but I know you must be going a little crazy about why I'm calling, so I'll get to the point.'

Despite clutching the phone and gritting his teeth, Creed smiled at how well she knew him. Hannah was trying not to hover, but she didn't pretend to not be listening either. She stood stock-still, staring intently.

'Do you remember posing for a photo with Brodie on what looks like a light blue sofa with some kind of blanket on the back?'

'My grandmother had a blue sofa. She kept an afghan on the back. It was one she'd knitted.'

'What color was the afghan?'

He closed his eyes and conjured up the image of Gram's living room until he could see the sofa and the blanket. 'It had big blocks of dark blue,' he told her. 'Blue and purple blocks with sort of a salmon color in between.'

Creed saw Hannah's eyes grow wide. Maggie went silent.

'The last time we visited my grandmother ...' Creed said it slowly as if he needed to remember, but actually, he needed to give his stomach time to stop falling. 'My mom took a few shots with a Polaroid camera my grandmother had.'

She was still quiet.

'Maggie?' he finally asked. 'Where did you see that photo?'

'I have it. I'm looking at it right now.'

7

Omaha, Nebraska

The exhaustion was beginning to wear Maggie down. None of them had gotten any sleep since the night before last. Pakula had left a sandwich and a Diet Pepsi for her. She was using the computer and phone in his office while she ate. She had no idea where he was, though she was certain he had probably told her. A quick glance at her watch made her realize she also had no idea when she had last seen him.

She pushed back in his chair and ran her hands over her face, trying to rub away the exhaustion. She hated leaving Ryder with more questions than answers. Now she wished she had pushed to interview Eli Dunn as soon as they had him in custody. Instead, she was trying to be patient while his newly appointed defense attorney and the county prosecutor along with FBI Agent Stevens made 'arrangements' for her to question him. But Pakula owed her a favor. Stevens now realized that he did, too. Elijah Dunn hadn't even been on their radar until Maggie came along.

When the door to the office opened, it made her jump. She was glad Pakula didn't see it.

'You got a minute?' he asked as he dropped into the visitor chair on the other side of his desk. He hadn't looked up for her response, his eyes still reading something on his phone.

When he finally did meet her eyes, he smiled. 'Don't take this the wrong way, O'Dell, but you look like hell.'

'Thanks. So do you.'

He laughed and nodded.

'When can I talk to him?' she asked.

'Last I heard he wants to talk to you. Against his attorney's advice.'

'Really?' The news made her sit up, a fresh hit of adrenaline teasing her with some untapped energy.

'He's calling you "that pretty little cop who tied my wrists so tight she made them bleed."' Pakula shook his head. He wasn't smiling anymore. 'This guy's a piece of work. I don't want you in there with him by yourself.'

'Pakula, are you going soft on me?'

'I'm not kidding. I talked to the CSU team and they're finding some interesting stuff.'

'Is that what you were reading on your phone?'

Now, she could swear Pakula blushed, even if it was just a tad. He swiped a palm over his shaved head ending at the back of his neck as if he was hoping to rub off the embarrassment.

'No, my wife was making sure I knew when our daughter's volleyball game is tonight. I swear there're three every week.' He dropped the phone in his pocket and continued, 'Mr Dunn thought he cleaned up after himself, but the team found a fire-pit in the backyard. They've recovered bones from the ashes.'

'Human?'

'Of course they need to be tested, but they think a couple of them are human remains.'

Maggie leaned her head against the tall vinyl back of Pakula's chair. This wasn't good. 'He wasn't just trafficking them,' she said, but she wasn't really surprised. The first time she stared into Dunn's hard, cold eyes she suspected the man was capable of killing.

'Are they checking the drains in the house?' she asked.

'Already found some possible tissue in the shower drain on the main level.'

The one without a curtain or shower door, Maggie remembered.

'What about the freezer?' she asked.

Pakula stared at her for a few seconds then said, 'Oh crap!' He yanked his phone out of his pocket as got to his feet. 'I'll be right back,' he told her and left.

Within seconds, she could hear him in the hallway giving someone instructions.

Maggie picked up the Polaroid. She'd actually considered not telling Creed, at least, not until she knew anything more. But now after talking to him, there was no doubt that the boy and girl in the photo were Ryder and his sister. She was glad she hadn't interviewed Dunn yet, so she wasn't lying to Creed when she told him she didn't have any details or information.

Earlier that morning, before she talked to Creed, Maggie had called her friend, Dr Gwen Patterson in DC. Gwen was a psychiatrist and criminal behaviorist who consulted with the FBI. The two had worked together on cases involving some of the most twisted serial killers to be captured. But she had spoken to Gwen before she realized that Eli Dunn might, in fact, be one. What Maggie had actually wanted to talk to Gwen about was whether or not she should call Ryder Creed about the photo they found.

Truthfully, she already knew the Polaroid was of Creed and his sister. Getting those glaring details about the sofa and the date weren't necessary, though it would add a level of proof for the investigation. But she also knew what calling him would mean. The avalanche it might trigger. Because she knew exactly what he would say, and she was right. He'd tell her he was coming up and there was nothing she could do to stop him. Still, she had insisted he wait until they had more information.

But before her call to Creed, she had asked Gwen whether or not she should tell him at all, especially since it was bound to hurt more than help.

'There might not be any answers,' she told her friend. 'And there probably won't be any happy endings. Only more heartbreak. He's already been through this more than once. I don't want to be the one to do that to him, again.'

'What he does with the information should be up to him. You can't make that decision for him, Maggie.' And then Gwen said something that only a friend could. 'You care about him. I know you do. Care about him enough to let him make the decision.'

Now, as Maggie fingered the Polaroid photograph, she wondered how she was going to tell Creed that Brodie might be only pieces buried in the ashes of Eli Dunn's backyard firepit.

8

Florida Panhandle

'You need to get some rest,' Hannah was telling Creed as she refilled his coffee mug.

At some point she had placed a sandwich on the table in front of him, close enough to his fist that he should have noticed when she put it there. He hadn't even noticed her making it, but that was no surprise. Hannah worked with her hands when she was stressed. She glided around her kitchen so effortlessly and smoothly that normally her movements became hypnotic and calmed Creed. Though it didn't seem to be working this time. He flexed his fingers and realized his jaw was clenched. Maybe that's what was causing the throbbing in his head.

'Rye?'

Hannah was sitting across from him now. When he looked up to meet her eyes she didn't bother to hide her concern.

'I know you. You're thinking you'll get in your Jeep and drive straight through. What is it? Fifteen, twenty hours to Nebraska? You just got home last night after working search and research in piles of debris. You're exhausted. Don't go pretending you're not.'

'I've done it before.'

'And I didn't like it much then, either.'

Creed knew she meant well, and he certainly never made it easy on her. Sometimes she knew him better than he knew himself. This was one of those times, because almost instinctively, he wanted to throw his gear in his Jeep, get Grace and go. In his mind he was already calculating how many hours of daylight he'd have on the road.

Dr Avelyn came in the kitchen door, gave them a wave and headed for the coffee. Hannah had made her kitchen a meeting place for their staff and extended the invitation for them to come in and get coffee or whatever fresh baked goods she had for them. Even grab a sandwich. Creed knew she loved filling her kitchen with people and feeding them as if she could also fill their souls with her advice and generous listening. He couldn't count how many people had come into their lives with difficult situations, and they had worked them out while sharing Hannah's food in this kitchen.

Right now both Creed and Hannah were too quiet, and Dr Avelyn noticed.

'Did I interrupt something?'

'Not at all,' Hannah told the veterinarian but her eyes never left Creed's.

'How's Bolo?' Creed wanted to know. He'd forgotten how concerned he was about the big dog. Running into the bear and then the phone call had distracted him.

'He'll be okay. I have some new stuff I put on his pads. It's better than ordinary bag balm. No petroleum products.'

One of the things Creed appreciated about the woman was that she stayed up to date on solutions and treatments, always thinking about the long-term consequences.

'I tried to clean out the debris as often as I could,' Creed said, but he still felt sick to his stomach thinking about the cuts and abrasions. They had spent hours climbing over concrete rubble with sharp pieces of rebar sticking out.

'We should try to get him used to wearing boots.'

'I put some on him, and he wouldn't move. He'd stretch his entire leg and high-step to overcompensate. I worried he might hurt himself.' Creed swiped a palm over his bristled jaw. Hannah was right. He was exhausted. All of his adrenaline had been spent on dealing with the bear, and now he felt completely drained. 'To be honest, I've never used boots on any of my dogs because of that.'

'Well, he has a sock on now, and he's not happy about that either.' Dr Avelyn smiled as she sat down at the table with Creed and Hannah. 'Maybe we could try getting your disaster dogs used to wearing them around the kennel. Just a few hours a day. I have some new ones that are lightweight and not so clunky. I'll bring them tomorrow.'

She looked from Creed to Hannah and back to Creed then said, 'I did interrupt something, didn't I?'

Innovative, smart and perceptive. The young veterinarian always impressed Creed. Dr Avelyn was around his age – late twenties, early thirties. She and another veterinarian had a successful animal clinic in Milton. Several years ago, after too many trips back and forth to that clinic, Creed convinced Dr Avelyn to come out to their property instead. Together they'd designed and equipped a clinic and hospital to take care of their scent dogs along with the others they housed. Not all the dogs in their kennel were working dogs. Some were dogs abandoned and left at the end of their long driveway. The locals had gotten into the habit of leaving dogs they no longer wanted. That was how Grace had come to them. Quickly she'd become Creed's favorite scent dog, despite being a small, scrappy Jack Russell terrier.

But they also had temporary boarders, dogs that Creed and Hannah took care of while the dogs' owners were deployed overseas. One of those dogs, a golden Labrador named Hunter, had recently become a permanent resident when the news came that his owner wouldn't be returning. Hannah had taken the news especially hard. The twenty-four-year-old Army intelligence analyst was the only daughter of one of Hannah's closest friends. Jordan was killed instantly when an Afghan suicide bomber detonated an explosive vest under their military uniform.

Since that day Hunter joined Hannah and her boys in the big house, and he seemed enamored with Hannah, never letting her out of his sight for long. Now, as if summoned, Hunter appeared from under the table. He nudged Creed's arm, asking to be petted. Creed scratched behind his ear where the dog had a splotch of black as if someone had taken a Sharpie and colored in a square.

When Creed looked up he realized Dr Avelyn was waiting for a response.

'You didn't interrupt anything,' he told her. 'We just got a phone call from Maggie O'Dell. An old Polaroid of Brodie and me was found during a police raid.'

Dr Avelyn glanced at Hannah then her eyes met Creed's. 'They just found the photo? How long has Brodie been gone?'

Creed recognized the look. It was one that registered hope.

'Sixteen years this month.'

'Rye wants to pack up right now and go,' Hannah said. 'I was trying to convince him that he needed some rest first.'

There was a long silence, and Creed realized he and Hannah were waiting for Dr Avelyn's response as though it would be a tie-breaker, deciding what he did next. He scratched Hunter's ear with one hand and sipped coffee with the other, pretending he didn't care what either of them thought.

Dr Avelyn took a drink of her own coffee and sat back as if she were examining Creed. His beard was longer than he liked to keep it, and he needed a haircut. If she looked closely she'd probably notice the cut along his jaw. Though it was healing it was still a jagged line of red that even his dark bristles couldn't hide. He crossed his arms almost as if he needed to keep her from seeing the fresh scars on his forearms. The scrapes were nothing. Just a part of working a disaster site, but under her scrutiny he suddenly felt like he did need to get her approval.

Finally she smiled and said, 'You probably could use a butterfly bandage on your forehead.'

He'd forgotten about that one, and his fingers shot up to touch it before he could stop himself. His hair fell over the cut, so it was easier to ignore.

'We should put you on an antibiotic just to be safe,' she told him.

Creed couldn't remember the last time he'd been to a doctor. There was no need when he had a veterinarian who could stitch him up and protect him from infections. He didn't argue with Dr Avelyn and wouldn't get the chance to at that moment, because Jason came in the kitchen's back door, letting it slam behind him. He headed for the coffeemaker as he asked, 'So did you all figure out what to do about that bear?'

The room grew quiet and Jason looked to Creed.

Hannah's eyes grew wide. 'Lord have mercy, what bear?'

9

Omaha, Nebraska

Maggie followed Pakula down the narrow hallway.

'I know I don't need to remind you that guys like Elijah Dunn make up crap as easily as they breathe,' Pakula said.

The whitewashed concrete walls reminded her of a modern-day dungeon. They absorbed sound. No light dared to flicker other than the stark fluorescents overhead. Maggie imagined these walls would absorb the life right out of anyone who dared spend too much time down here.

'You realize I hunt serial killers for a living?'

He glanced at her over his shoulder and shook his head, not amused at her attempt at humor. 'Not the same thing,' he told her. 'Those guys are smart and manipulative. Most of them are expert liars. Guys like Dunn, they're expert bullshitters.'

'What's the difference?'

At first Maggie thought Pakula was pulling her leg just to get her attention. Settle her down. He knew she wanted this interview, and sometimes when an investigator wanted something badly, they could make mistakes, believe things just because they wanted them to be true.

Pakula stopped and turned to look at her now. 'Seriously?'

'Seriously.'

'A liar knows the truth but attempts to hide it. A bullshitter doesn't necessarily know what's true and really doesn't care what's true. That makes it almost impossible to find out what the hell the truth is.'

'So if he just makes something up to yank my chain . . . '

'You might never be able to figure out where that Polaroid came from.'

He stood staring at her as if he was waiting for his words to sink in.

Finally, she nodded and said, 'Okay. Point taken.'

The room looked like so many others she had been in before for other interrogations. Four white walls with a viewing window that showed them only their reflections. There was a long metal table bolted to the floor. Two chairs were placed one on each side of the table – also bolted to the floor. She already knew she couldn't talk Pakula into taking a seat next door to watch and listen through the one-way viewing window. The only way he agreed to help her get this interview was if he stayed in the room.

'Don't worry. I won't make a peep,' he'd promised. He'd made it sound like he believed she could handle it. And yet, he revealed a measure of doubt in the hallway with his lesson on the difference between a liar and a bullshitter. Now Maggie wondered if he was concerned she would botch this opportunity. The realization made her even more aware it could be their one and only opportunity.

The door opened and a deputy nudged Eli Dunn from behind. He shuffled in, his ankles shackled and his wrists handcuffed in front of him. In the jumpsuit he looked smaller, thinner, reminding Maggie of a slump-shouldered weasel.

'Have a seat, Mr Dunn,' she said.

The deputy's hand on his shoulder made sure Dunn sat

down. Then he fastened the shackles to the chair. It seemed unnecessary. Dunn almost looked frail, his skinny arms poking out of the oversized short sleeves. He hung his head so his bristled chin seemed attached to his chest. But Maggie wasn't easily fooled. She knew there were enough episodes of prisoners lunging at their interrogators to justify the extra precaution. Her friend Dr Gwen Patterson had experienced an incident with a prisoner where a simple pencil had become a weapon in a matter of seconds.

'I'm Special Agent O'Dell and this is Detective Pakula.' She avoided first names. Sometimes interrogators used them to gain the suspect's trust. She didn't want Eli Dunn to trust her. She wanted him to fear her. 'Do you remember us?'

He lifted his head and stared at her with hooded black eyes, watching as she sat in the chair across from him. She crossed her arms over her chest and stared back, waiting for his response.

Under the florescent lights his skin took on a sickly pallor. His receding hairline made his forehead protrude. His cheeks looked sunken in and the bright lights accentuated his thin lips as they pulled back and his mouth grew wide with a smile. It was that same smile he'd given her when Maggie accosted him. The full grin turned up both sides of his mouth and made his eyes squint. Like a Cheshire cat, Eli Dunn was smiling at her like he knew something that no one else knew. Either that, or he was mentally unstable and couldn't help from showing it.

'Sure, I remember. I heard you couldn't stop thinking about me.'

He didn't acknowledge Pakula. His eyes stayed on Maggie, so focused, so intent, they felt like lasers that could pin her down in place. Maybe even sting her from across the table.

She uncrossed her arms and pulled out the Polaroid from her pocket. She didn't want to waste any time and certainly wasn't going to let him provoke her. She held the photo up in her fingertips, dangling it with the backside facing Dunn, like a Poker player teasing her opponent before revealing the last winning card. The gesture was enough to get his attention, and his eyes flicked back and forth from the photo to her and back to the photo. Finally, she laid the Polaroid on the table close enough for him to see it without having to pick it up.

She could ask where he got the photo or how it came to be in his possession. She could have eased him into a conversation about it. Instead, she kept to her strategy of hitting Eli Dunn directly and with a question he least expected.

'What happened to this little girl?'

To his credit, Dunn craned his neck to get a closer look. Whether he was really interested or not, at least he was pretending to be. He tilted his head one way and then the other as if trying to trigger his memory. Then he sat back and looked up at her, again.

'Just that one?'

'Excuse me?'

'That's the only one you care about?'

Maggie braced herself and fought to keep her face or any part of her body from showing the sick feeling that slid from her stomach to her knees. The image came to her of all the photos on the wall, so many photos that they overlapped in places. She hadn't expected him to take responsibility for any of them.

Stick to your strategy, she told herself. *Don't fall for his shock and awe.*

'What did you do with her?' She darted her eyes down to the photo and back up to his.

He shrugged, an over-exaggerated gesture that practically touched his ear to his shoulder and left his head tilted as though he was prepared to shrug again.

But then his eyes locked on hers, and he asked, 'What's it worth to you?'

Pakula was wrong. Dunn might have the appearance of low-life bullshitter, but he was quick and smart.

Maggie held his eyes, willing herself to not blink. She didn't glance at Pakula but could feel him watching her. He would be worried that she had lost her edge in this interview, that Dunn had outwitted her.

She needed to keep her face from revealing to Pakula, as much as to Dunn, what her true intentions were. Because this response, this question, was exactly what Maggie had wanted.

10

Instead of answering him, Maggie dug in her jacket pocket, and this time Dunn's eyes followed her hand. She watched him as she pulled out the small notebook. He blinked twice, almost a flinch, before he caught himself.

The notebook was three inches by five inches with a spiral binding at the top and fit easily into a pocket. The black cover showed wear with a splatter of coffee stain – or at least, Maggie hoped it was coffee. The pages inside were filled with hand-drawn diagrams that could have been mistaken as doodles except that each had scribbles next to it. Possibly dates. Some of the pages had only letters and numbers, columns of them. All of it looked like an amateur's code.

Something had been nagging at Maggie since their early morning raid. Eli Dunn's farmhouse looked like it had been cleaned out, the bedrooms stripped down, even the bathrooms scrubbed. The computer and other electronic devices were gone. Someone had tipped him off. He was ready for them.

Pakula had told her the bottles of ammonia had been carefully placed with tripwires that ran the perimeter of the front yard. By Dunn's own admission, he'd set up a trap to alert him by scent if anyone came close to the house unannounced. He even had his decoy drugged and ready on command to burst out the front door. But if Dunn knew they were coming, why hadn't he taken down the photographs and photocopies from his trophy wall? Why would he let them see how many victims there were, let alone give them the chance to possibly identify them?

Why, indeed?

Unless he believed he might get caught.

Did Eli Dunn leave his trophy wall in place to use as a bargaining chip?

Maggie believed that could be the case, especially after the arresting officer found this little notebook tucked carefully away in Dunn's shirt pocket. According to the officer, Dunn didn't surrender it easily and seemed overly concerned about when he could get it back.

Now, watching his eyes spark, not so much with interest as with anger, Maggie realized the scribbles and childlike drawings might be *their* best bargaining chip.

'Interesting collection you have here,' she told him as she flicked the pages, purposely making them sound like she was riffling a deck of cards.

His eyes darted to Pakula then back to Maggie. It was the first time he acknowledged the detective leaning against the wall. Dunn was pretending the notebook was no big deal, but it was too late. Even his body language gave him away. The slumped shoulders were suddenly drawn back. He sat up straight with his chin held high, almost defiant.

'Is this your inventory?' she asked.

She wished she'd had more time to examine the contents. Agent Alonzo had found classified ads on the darknet that he had traced back to Eli Dunn. But the entries in this notebook didn't look like ads. There were none of the familiar phrases human traffickers used to advertise their young merchandise: 'low mileage', 'fresh', 'barely used'.

At a glance, she couldn't make sense of the notebook's hieroglyphics. She was only guessing that the scribbles were related to Dunn's illegal business dealings. Why else would he need to use a rudimentary code?

Somehow she needed to sound interested, but clueless. In Maggie's experience, most criminals were proud of how sneaky and shrewd they were. Some were even anxious to share the details.

'I have to admit,' she told him, pretending to let a hint of admiration slip out, 'this is one of the most elaborate accounting systems I've seen. And believe me, I've seen quite a few.'

She counted down the silence in her head, forcing herself to go slowly. Some people couldn't stand silence and attempted to fill it in. But after several minutes, all she got from Dunn was a slight shift of his mouth as if he were holding back his trademark smile.

'Do you know if she's in here?' She gestured to the forgotten Polaroid.

'Depends,' he said and left it at that.

He was good at this. Too good, Maggie realized.

'What does it depend on?' she finally asked, suddenly frustrated and working too hard to keep from showing it. What she really wanted was to lunge across the table and grab him by his scrawny neck.

'What kind of deal you've got in mind.' He said it so calmly it almost sounded rehearsed.

She tapped the corner of the notebook against the table, and his eyes flitted from hers to the notebook and back, again.

'You need to give me something more than that, Eli.'

He looked directly at her at the mention of his name, and she could see he was pleased.

'How do I know that this is worth anything?' she asked.

This time she slapped the notebook against the tabletop and the whack made him blink as if she had slapped him across the face. 'Maybe you're just a lackey for someone else, and this is just a bunch of mumbo-jumbo.'

'A *lackey*? Mumbo-jumbo?' He said it like he was insulted.

Maggie had to restrain her smile. If this were a boxing match, she'd just landed an uppercut.

'How do I know there's anything in here that's worth a deal to me?' she asked again. 'Are you saying this girl is in here?' She pointed at the Polaroid.

'Depends,' he said, again.

This time she rolled her eyes and sat back, exaggerating her impatience with him. Dunn just stared at her.

'I think we're finished here,' she told Pakula. She dropped the notebook into her jacket pocket, and she pushed out of her chair.

'She might be in there,' Dunn said.

She stopped and waited then crossed her arms over her chest and gave him her best *I don't have all day* look.

He shrugged, but this one was slight, not the ear to the shoulder that he had given her earlier. She held his eyes, watching for a tell, a flicker to the right or left. Sometimes the brain triggered involuntary signals about a lie that even a manipulative criminal like Eli Dunn couldn't always control.

'I just don't remember,' he said.

'Then what does it depend on?' Maggie kept her voice bored as she sunk her hands into her jacket pockets so Dunn couldn't see her fingers gripping into fists.

'It depends if she's one of the ones that got sold or one of the ones that got buried.'

It took every ounce of energy for Maggie to remain

standing when she felt as if she had just been sucker-punched. She avoided stealing a glance at Pakula. In Dunn's eyes she could see a seriousness that wasn't there before, perhaps even a hint of desperation.

Before she had a chance to respond, he asked, 'So what about that deal?'

11

Florida Panhandle

'Black bear sightings are up seventy-five percent,' Dr Avelyn was telling Hannah, Jason and Creed. 'That's just in the Florida Panhandle.'

Creed's mind was racing. They were canvasing the property, concentrating on the area between the trail into the woods and the fenced yard around the kennel. Creed was concerned about his dogs but anxious to hear more from Maggie. At the same time, exhaustion from too little sleep was catching up with him.

There hadn't been any new details about Brodie's disappearance in over a decade. How could someone have that Polaroid and not have been involved in his sister's abduction? Or did they simply find her book that she had with her? He remembered Brodie had been using that photo as a bookmark. Did the book just suddenly turn up in some used bookstore?

Hannah convinced him to wait until morning before deciding whether or not to take off for Nebraska. A dull thrum had started playing inside his head, and he fingered the cut on his forehead as if it were the source. He saw Dr Avelyn notice and realized he had just reinforced her argument for taking a closer look at the wound. Creed tried to ignore her look of concern as he checked his cell phone for the hundredth time. He kept hoping for a call or a text from Maggie. In the meantime, he needed to focus on what they could add to bear-proof their property.

'I think it would be a good idea for all of you to get into the habit of carrying around UDAP pepper spray,' Dr Avelyn said. 'I'll order extra canisters with hip holsters.'

'Is it safe to have them on us?' asked Hannah. 'I'm always worried I'll lean against the counter and the thing will go off.'

'They have security pins to keep them from misfiring.'

'What about Tasers?' Jason asked.

This time Creed answered. 'From what I understand, even a direct hit will only aggravate a bear.'

'You could try singing,' Dr Avelyn told Jason.

'Seriously?'

'They usually want to avoid humans. Loud, unfamiliar noises can scare them off.'

'Yeah, I'm pretty sure my singing would be a loud unfamiliar noise,' Jason said and they all laughed if only to relieve the tension.

'Most of the time, you won't even see them,' Dr Avelyn said. 'They really would prefer to avoid you. But this time of year they're looking for easy food before the weather turns cooler. Your best bet is probably the pepper spray.'

Creed had already made sure that the UDAP canisters were a part of their gear when they were out in the field. He never imagined they'd need them here. He'd always thought of their property as a sanctuary, not only for rescuing abandoned dogs, but also a secure area where nothing or no one could ever hurt these dogs again.

In fact, he and Hannah had put a lot of thought and

technology into the planning for their entire training campus. It wasn't just the kennels. In the last several years they'd added an indoor Olympic-sized swimming pool for water training and a fully equipped medical clinic. He'd installed a state-of-the-art security system that included motion-activated lights and cameras on all the buildings and motion-sensor doors even for the dogs. But lights and cameras wouldn't stop a bear from trespassing.

The fenced yard was constructed with extra gates so they could close off sections. Creed liked the dogs to have the entire acre to run and play and get exercise, but they closed the gates just before dusk until after dawn, restricting the dogs to the interior yard. It allowed the dogs to still go outside and relieve themselves but the closed off section kept them close to the kennel and within the motion-sensitive floodlights.

The building that housed the dogs was more like a modern warehouse condominium. In fact, there was a loft apartment for Creed on the second floor. The area for the dogs had wide open spaces and a high ceiling. Windows started ten feet off the ground and supplied natural light. Though the facility was climate-controlled, those screened windows could be opened with a remote control to provide fresh air.

Inside along one wall were half a dozen traditional crates with beds inside for those few dogs that preferred their own caged-off space, but the crate doors were left open. For the others, various sized beds were scattered around the floor making the area look more like a campsite than a dog kennel.

A commercial kitchen took up one corner section with granite countertops, stainless steel appliances and wood cabinets. Creed remembered the first time Dr Avelyn had seen the facility she thought it looked like something out of an interior design magazine. Creed and Hannah had spared no expense. Even the dog dishes that lined up along the counter were raised to different levels for the different-sized dogs. Unlike most working dog training facilities that dealt with large dogs – shepherds and retrievers – Creed and Hannah's took in a variety of dogs as small as a ten-pound Maltese like Coz and Kramer to a seventy-pound Labrador like Hunter. And Creed's favorite scent dog – a sixteen-pound Jack Russell named Grace.

He looked around for Grace now and saw that she was racing to keep up with Hunter. Hannah had brought the big dog out to the yard to get some exercise. For a long time, Hunter would simply go to the far corner of the yard, sit down and stare out toward the driveway. It was the last place he'd watched his owner leave, and it was the place he expected to see her when she came back to get him. It tore Creed up to watch the big dog do this. Hunter was one of the few dogs here in their kennel that wasn't abandoned by his owner, but there was no way to tell him what had really happened.

But today, instead of going to the corner, Hunter let Grace distract him.

'You've been gone a few days,' Hannah said when she noticed where Creed's eyes were focused. 'He's been playing with Grace and Winnie. Even Scout.'

He saw her swipe at her eyes before she turned back to Dr Avelyn and Jason and changed the subject. 'In seven years, we've never had a problem with bears. You said they'll avoid humans, but what about dogs? Will they attack a dog?'

Dr Avelyn took a long time to respond then she finally said, 'I think it's best we keep them on-leash so we won't find out.'

Creed's cell phone started vibrating in his hand and everyone looked at it as if it were a grenade.

'It's Maggie,' he told them in a calm, casual tone while pretending that his stomach hadn't just taken a nosedive.

12

'Hey, Maggie,' Creed tried to continue the steady calm cadence in his voice when he really wanted to plead with her to tell him every single thing she knew.

'I'm sorry, I don't know much more,' she said. 'But I didn't want to leave you hanging and wondering.'

He listened as she filled him in on the interview she had conducted with Eli Dunn. He understood there were details and information she wouldn't be able to share with him.

'He doesn't seem to remember what happened to the girl in the Polaroid.'

'And you believe him?' *How could he not know*, was what Creed wanted to shout, but again, he tried to keep calm.

'It's possible he might not remember ... exactly.'

'Exactly?' To Creed it sounded like a wiggle word that a criminal may have heard from his attorney. 'And what *exactly* will it take for him to remember?' He caught a glimpse of Hannah's expression and knew his voice was already betraying him.

'Look, this is confidential,' Maggie said, almost in a whisper. Her pause made Creed wonder if she was someplace where she couldn't talk openly. Or was it a ploy to keep him from losing it? Was she worried he couldn't handle the truth?

'Tell me,' he said.

'The Polaroid wasn't the only photograph we found. There were more. A lot more.'

'Okay.'

He tried to remember what else she had told him about the raid. Something to do with human trafficking. Creed had worked a case where a drug cartel had also been trafficking children. This wasn't an unfamiliar topic for him. Maggie knew that, and yet, here she was tiptoeing around the details as if she didn't think he could handle whatever information she had to tell him.

When her silence lasted too long, Creed said, 'I've had sixteen years to imagine what could have happened to Brodie. I'm not sure there's anything you can say that will shock me. Please, Maggie, just tell me. Is it possible this guy knows what happened to her?' He turned his back so he didn't have to look at Hannah's face when he added, 'Is there a chance he knows where she's buried?'

This time Creed waited out Maggie's silence. He thought he heard what might be a door shutting.

'Ryder, I can't tell you that, because I honestly don't know. I'm in the process of trying to see if we can make a deal.'

'A deal?'

'Yes. Dunn knows he's in deep trouble. He's a career criminal. I think he realizes he's not getting off or getting out this time with a slap on the hand and a few years of probation. I need to convince the proper authorities that what he knows is actually worth a deal. Right now, I don't even know what that deal might look like.'

She stopped and Creed heard someone else.

'Hold on,' she told him.

There was a muffled conversation and another sound that could be a door closing.

'You still there?' she asked.

'What kind of deal, Maggie? You think he's just a go-between in a bigger operation?'

'That's possible, but I also think Eli Dunn is directly responsible for some of these victims. This whole raid was a part of a nationwide federal investigation to help shut down human trafficking. I think I can convince them it would go a long ways to work with Dunn instead of just locking him up. Especially if there's a chance we can find a few of his victims.'

Creed swallowed hard before he asked the one question that had been eating at him since Maggie's first phone call. 'Do you think there's any chance at all that Brodie is still alive?'

He expected another long silence, but she surprised him. And this time there was no tiptoeing around his feelings.

'Honestly? No.' But then she must have realized how harsh that sounded, because her voice softened when she added, 'But Ryder, anything's possible. I just don't want you investing too much emotion and hope into this.'

He didn't tell her that it was too late.

13

Omaha, Nebraska

Tommy Pakula checked his watch. He'd showered and shaved down in the locker room, grateful his wife Clare had insisted he keep a change of clothes at work. He wouldn't need to stop at home. Instead, he could drive out to West Omaha for his appointment and still make his daughter's volleyball game. But now in jeans and a polo shirt he felt underdressed even after pulling on his suit jacket.

Ellen Gabriel's call had made it sound urgent that Pakula come today. She was afraid the boy might change his mind if they waited until morning. 'The boy' was the young victim that Eli Dunn had used as a decoy. Pakula had directed the response team to take him to Project Harmony. Their child services experts were trained in working with children of extreme abuse. Not only would they provide a medical examination, but also one of their forensic interviewers would ask the appropriate questions in an appropriate manner, allowing the boy to tell his story. Pakula knew it was the best place, not only for the boy, but for their investigation, too.

He realized he probably should have told O'Dell, but she was preoccupied with throwing together a deal with the Douglas County prosecutor. Actually saying she was preoccupied was a bit mild. Obsessed seemed a more appropriate term. Truthfully, after the way she conducted the interview with Dunn, Pakula didn't really want her along for this one.

He realized that probably wasn't fair. He'd invited O'Dell to this twisted party and now he wasn't sure he trusted how she was handling it. Any time emotions played into a case it was tough to be objective. Discovering that old Polaroid photo seemed to throw a bunch of O'Dell's objectivity out the window.

For all Gabriel's urgency, Pakula found himself waiting in the reception area. He preferred to pace in front of the floor-to-ceiling windows rather than sit in the designated guest chair the receptionist had pointed out. Once in a while she glanced up at him and smiled, and he continued pacing.

The lobby was a beautiful open space with a ceiling that soared and skylights that made it feel like the clouds were part of the structure. Natural light streamed in, even as the sun began to set. Pakula suspected that all this, including the ocean-blue painted walls and the colorful abstract paintings, were part of a strategy to invite and soothe the broken spirits that came through the doors.

He glanced at his watch again and realized that after all his efforts he might still be late for his daughter's game.

Although Pakula had worked with the organization before, he had never been to their facility. Project Harmony worked with abuse victims. Pakula was a veteran homicide detective. Usually the victim was dead by time Pakula was called to the scene. Which was one of the reasons he was surprised when asked to head the local task force on human trafficking and then become a part of the FBI's Operation Cross Country. Some days he wasn't sure what he'd gotten himself into. He tried to view his new position as just an extension of the many investigations he was already used to working. But he was quickly discovering that it was much different.

The deciding factor for Pakula to take the position was actually a homicide six months ago. A drug dealer claimed a prostitute named Ariel – who the drug dealer admittedly pimped – shot herself in the head.

'The bitch,' he told Pakula, 'committed suicide right in front of me.'

The dealer/pimp liked to be called T-Rock. During his interrogation he refused to answer any of Pakula's questions unless he was addressed as T-Rock. That seemed to be his only requirement. Otherwise, he didn't mind sharing his expertise, almost as if he was schooling Pakula. The guy had some real gems like telling Pakula that 'drugs you can only sell once. A good bitch you can sell over and over again.'

It looked like another sad, screwed-up case until Pakula learned that the dead prostitute was only fifteen years old. In that same interrogation, T-Rock had bragged that Ariel's mother had sold the girl to him a couple of years ago when – according to T-Rock – the mother 'let herself get too ugly and skinny to sell herself.' And she still needed to pay for her drug addiction.

T-Rock had told Pakula all this while he shook his head with such exaggeration that his long dreadlocks seemed to come alive. T-Rock liked to emphasize that he couldn't be held responsible for how screwed-up this woman was. But the dealer had gone one step too far when he told Pakula that he'd probably done the poor girl a favor by saving her from her crazy mother.

In his thirty years with the Omaha Police Department, Pakula had seen and heard enough crazy stuff that this case didn't surprise him. He was well aware of human trafficking. Interstate 80 cut across Nebraska in almost a straight line from one end of the state to the other. About 450 miles total. That's a whole lot of traffic. A whole lot of goods, both legal and illegal moving through the state on a daily basis.

Yet, this case felt like a gut punch. This girl, Ariel, reminded Pakula too much of his daughter, Samantha. The oldest of four, Sam was the only one with freckles and thick red hair like her grandmother. Just like Ariel – that long beautiful red hair matted and stained with blood and brain matter – an image Pakula couldn't shake. It didn't help matters that Sam was also fifteen.

'Detective Pakula,' a woman called to him.

He turned away from the windows.

'Ms Gabriel?'

The woman was small, but her voice robust and confident. Her suit looked tailored to fit her, a dark gray that matched her hair. She wore pearls and a gold watch, otherwise there was nothing extravagant, and still, she had an elegance about her.

'Call me Ellen.' She gestured for him to walk with her. 'We usually video record our forensic interviews,' she told him as she guided him along. 'We do that for a couple of reasons. The information can help to corroborate or refute any suspicions or perhaps any existing allegations. The second reason is so that these children don't have to tell their story over and over again.'

'So I'm guessing this boy said something that was—'

'Konnor.'

'What's that?'

'The boy's name is Konnor. He hasn't trusted us with a last

name, yet. He's going through a withdrawal from whatever drugs he was given. We're not sure what those were, but I'm told they might affect his memory. He may appear a bit slow as a result. And actually, he hasn't said much at all. But he has asked to talk to you.'

'To me? I didn't think he even knew my name.'

'He didn't. He asked for the baldheaded cop.' Gabriel blushed just slightly as though she may have insulted him. 'Sorry, that's exactly how he asked about you.'

Pakula smiled. He'd been shaving his head long before it became cool. Besides, it was pretty hard to offend him.

'I'm surprised he knew I was in charge. The scene was a bit chaotic.'

'I don't think he did know you were in charge,' she said. 'When I asked him why he wanted to talk to you, he told me that you gave him your jacket.'

'Really? *That's* why he wants to talk to me?'

She smiled and nodded. 'He said no one had ever done that for him before.'

Pakula shook his head. This new position was definitely different than working homicide or dealing with drug dealers.

14

Pakula hardly recognized the kid.

Konnor wore baggy khakis and a Nebraska Huskers T-shirt. His face was ruddy and clean, his hair fluffy and combed and most importantly, his eyes were clear and bright blue. Gabriel had told Pakula that Konnor said he was twelve. The kid was as tall as Pakula, almost six foot. That was one tall twelve-year-old. But he was thin, skeletal thin.

Ellen Gabriel helped them get settled into a room that looked like someone's living room. There were more windows, a sofa with colorful pillows, two chairs, end tables with lamps, paintings on the walls and even a flat-screen television. But as soon as they sat down – Konnor in one of the chairs, Pakula in the other – Gabriel left them.

On the wall opposite the chairs, Pakula picked out the camera with only a glance. It looked like a round thermostat control. Gabriel had shared Konnor's concerns about being recorded, and told Pakula not to insist. But she also pointed out the remote control she had left on the end table between the two chairs.

'Ms Gabriel tells me you don't want us to record our conversation. Do you still feel that way?'

The boy nodded so aggressively his hair fell into his eyes. He swiped it away and stared at Pakula, waiting for the next question.

'All of us are here to help you, Konnor. Elijah Dunn is in prison. I promise, he can't hurt you anymore.'

'What about the others?'

'There were others that came to the farm?'

Another nod, but this time Konnor looked down at his hands in his lap. Pakula noticed the kid's fingernails were all chewed to the quick.

'Sometimes he took us to them.'

Pakula fought back the acid that churned in his stomach. He blamed too much coffee, but lately, he recognized these cases that involved kids literally made him sick to his stomach.

'Do you remember any of the others?' he asked. 'Or where he took you?'

This time Konnor shook his head and said, 'He made us take pills. They made me sleepy and my eyes got all bleary. But they helped me forget about stuff.'

And Pakula realized Konnor meant that as a good thing. The kid wanted to forget about stuff. Pakula tried to wait out the silence that followed, giving the boy a chance to tell without being prodded. But instead, Konnor continued to stare down at his hands.

'Ms Gabriel told me you asked to talk to me, Konnor. Whatever you want to tell me, I'm listening.'

This time the boy looked up and met Pakula's eyes as if checking to see if there were a catch. It almost looked like he expected Pakula to try tricking him.

'I don't trust cops,' he finally said. 'They're almost never what they say they are. But you gave me your jacket. I figured you're different.'

Pakula wasn't surprised the kid didn't trust cops. None came to save him. Dunn had probably filled the boy's head with reasons to not trust police officers. He wasn't going to argue with Konnor. Nor would try to convince him that he was, indeed, different from the boy's perceived notion. Konnor would either trust him or he wouldn't. At this point, it wouldn't matter what Pakula said. So, he waited.

'There were other kids at the farm before you came.'

Pakula shifted in his chair and stopped himself from leaning forward.

'Do you know what happened to them?'

Another shake of the head. His eyes were back on his hands, this time inspecting them as if looking for a fingernail that wasn't already gnawed down.

'How many others?'

This time he shrugged and it reminded Pakula of a little boy trying to get out of telling something he didn't want to share.

'Boys and girls?'

'Mostly girls.' He found a cuticle on his little finger and started chewing at the edge of it.

'Konnor, I know this isn't easy to talk about, but I really need you to tell me everything you know.' Pakula wanted to reach out and lift the boy's chin so he'd look at him, but he dared not touch him. 'I want to help those other kids, too. Can you help me do that? Can you give me some idea of where I should start looking?'

He finally looked up at Pakula. His finger was bleeding where he'd bit off the cuticle. He was sucking on it now, but stopped.

'He took them someplace.' Konnor shrugged. 'It wasn't that big of a deal. He was always taking one or two of us to a house or a hotel. I was locked in my room. I couldn't see them leave. I didn't know he took all of them.' Then in almost a whisper of a small child sharing a secret, he said, 'I was just relieved he didn't take me.'

His eyes darted to the door and back to Pakula. Just checking, but there was a hint of paranoia. Then Konnor said, 'In the pasture. There's an old barn. Maybe you should check that barn.'

15

'Charlotte, you made a big a mistake this time,' the woman named Iris called down from the top of the staircase in a sing-song that belied her true anger.

All Charlotte could see was Iris' large silhouette looming above her, backlit from the only light. Otherwise, darkness surrounded her. Darkness and the damp scent of concrete and mildew. The basement floor, she realized as her cheek lay against the hard surface. But it was cool and soothing compared to the rest of what her body was feeling. The ache only hinted at the level of pain that would spread like wildfire if she so much as moved.

She tried to look up at Iris again, but her vision blurred, and the bright light behind the woman stung her eyes like lasers. She closed her eyes and stayed still. She knew the woman wouldn't bother coming down the stairs to check on her. And despite Charlotte's earlier bravado, she didn't have the strength to climb up and get pushed down these stairs a second time. In fact, she wasn't sure whether or not she was able to get back up. She may have broken a bone. She was certain she'd blacked out for a minute or two. To move now seemed to only encourage more pain.

'Do you hear me, Charlotte? This was your last chance. Remember what I told you?'

The question was simply reaffirmation. Iris didn't need an

answer. She never did. There wasn't a trace of anger in the woman's voice. Somehow she always managed to keep the same even-tempered cadence that reminded Charlotte of a schoolteacher instructing her students.

Even punishment came in a measured tone with a rhythm and tempo that seemed to only emphasize how ridiculous the infringement was. So when Iris said, 'Oh, what a silly, stupid girl you are,' it sounded like she was singing instead of yelling.

But this was Charlotte's last chance. She knew that even before she made the attempt to escape. Others had made the same mistake. Used up their chances. She had no idea what it meant or where they ended up. She only knew that they disappeared, and she never saw them again.

Wherever they went, whatever happened to them, how could it be any worse than this? In Charlotte's mind, they were the lucky ones.

She had long ago lost track of time. She had no idea how many days or weeks or years had gone by. At some point she had given up trying to distinguish what was real, what was imagined or what was only one of Iris' wicked stories. It was too difficult to hold on to memories when you were so hungry you could only focus on the sound of a door opening and a dinner tray being slid inside your room.

Punishment, no matter how calmly Iris administered it, often came not in body blows or beatings, but rather the absence of one more thing that made Charlotte feel human. Iris would withhold food or water until Charlotte was reduced to a panting, starving animal ready to pounce on a morsel of dry dog food or a half filled bottle of warm water. Punishment came with Iris removing a threadbare blanket during the coldest nights. Or it might simply be Iris unscrewing and taking the only light bulb in the tiny room and not returning it for what felt like too many nights to hang onto an ounce of sanity.

So no more chances? What more could the woman possibly do to her?

Charlotte almost welcomed the prospect of Iris tossing her body along a ditch somewhere. Or perhaps burying her alive in a hole in the ground. Though even that sounded too refreshing. Because just for the briefest of moments she might feel the sun on her skin. She might be able to fill her lungs with fresh air. Even for a few minutes before dirt started raining down on her.

Had she finally gone stark-raving mad that being buried alive actually sounded like a preferred alternative to the life she'd been living? To the hell she'd been living.

It wasn't always all bad. There was a time when she was Iris' favorite. That garnered her car rides in the country. Sometimes trips into town if she agreed to wear the silly ruffled dresses Iris loved. And if she was good, which meant quiet and smiling.

'Remember a nod is as good an answer if anyone asks you a question.' That was Iris, forever instructing, giving commands but making them sound like suggestions.

For a long time after, in the days and weeks and years when she infuriated Iris more than she pleased her, Charlotte would remember those car rides in the country. They became her go-to place in her mind when she needed to escape inside herself. She'd conjure up the blue sky, how big it stretched all the way down to an endless horizon. The rolling meadows of tall grasses that looked like waves of an ocean, only these waves were reddish gold. The horse and cattle and even the birds fascinated her. Once she saw a bald-headed eagle and tried to imagine herself with outstretched wings flying high above the fields. In her dreams, she'd float on the warm breeze, and for a short time she was happy.

She didn't dream anymore. And she hadn't been outside this dungeon for so long, she no longer believed that the outside world even existed. Right now she was too tired to care. She had used all the energy she had conserved for her one last botched attempt to see if there were still meadows and sky and hope.

All she wanted was to close her eyes and sleep, but her mind refused to shut down. Not yet, it seemed to insist. Not just yet, and she could hear Iris talking at the top of the steps. Iris giving instructions.

'Take her out of here.' The woman was telling someone else what to do.

'. . . can't come for her. It might be a week.'

Fragments drifted down the staircase. Another voice, soft and muffled from somewhere behind Iris. It sounded like Aaron – sweet, simple Aaron. They used to play together when they were kids. He was the closest thing Charlotte ever had to a friend. Until Iris made him choose sides. Made him pledge allegiance to her. Poor, sweet, simple Aaron.

'I don't care,' Iris said. 'I want her gone from here. You know what to do with her.'

It was getting more and more difficult for Charlotte to stay awake and listen. She wanted to fold inside herself before the pain started to streak through her body. She wanted to go away and find refuge in sleep.

'. . . the Christmas house.'

It was the last thing Charlotte heard.

Christmas?

Surely, she must have heard that wrong, but it actually made her smile. Had she lost her final grasp on reality? Maybe she'd finally slipped completely off some mental ledge.

16

Florida Panhandle

Creed only now realized how much his head hurt. He fingered the butterfly bandage where Dr Avelyn had debrided the wound on his forehead. There was a deeper cut on his arm from which she removed several small pieces of glass. Creed thought he'd picked all the glass out when he cleaned it the day before. He'd managed to steer Bolo away from a pile of rubble, only to lose his balance and fall into it.

His arm and forehead took the brunt of the fall. He'd cleaned it in haste, trying to get on the road and get Bolo home. He'd plucked pieces out of Bolo's paws and swabbed them with care, but his own wounds, he had simply poured alcohol over then wrapped some gauze around his arm and taped it closed.

That was the problem with disaster sites. Usually Creed's first concern was his dog. He'd been so focused on keeping Bolo safe that he'd neglected his own scrapes.

Butterfly bandages wouldn't work for the gash in his arm. Dr Avelyn ended up suturing the wound. After pinching his skin, she told him he was a bit dehydrated, which probably explained why he'd been so thirsty the last twenty-four hours. She also thought he had a slight temperature, but all she had was a rectal thermometer. Creed said he was willing to take her word. Then she handed him a container of antibiotics to take while mentioning, once again, that he really should have a medical doctor take a look at his arm. Creed trusted her. She'd saved him time after time, but he realized he wasn't being fair to the veterinarian. He had no idea whether or not she could get in trouble for treating him.

Now back in his loft apartment he began unpacking his gear from his last trip. He'd need to do laundry and pack again. He jiggled the pills in the container, and Grace came prancing over. It sounded like the treat container.

'These aren't for you, girl.'

Creed checked the time, popped one of the pills and downed half a bottle of water. Grace was still staring at him. He reached his hand out for her to lick. But then she continued to sniff at his arm. He let Grace wave her nose over the wound that Dr Avelyn had left unwrapped, 'just for the night.' Grace didn't attempt to lick or touch it, but her nose twitched as she investigated. When she was finished she sat down and stared up at him again.

'I'm okay,' Creed said as he scratched behind her ears.

At the same time, he glanced over at Bolo stretched out and asleep on a dog bed at the foot of Creed's bed. Normally, he would have moved the Ridgeback from the clinic back to the kennel, but Creed wanted to keep a close eye on him. Dr Avelyn had cleared Bolo after she finished suturing up Creed. He was fine, though like Creed, a bit dehydrated. She'd instructed Creed to administer another Sub-Q in the morning as a precaution.

On the living-room rug, Rufus was curled up and snoring softly. The Labrador's hearing wasn't as keen as it used to be, even with his left ear folded back. From where Creed stood, he could see the N103 branded on the dog's underflap. That was how the military used to label their K9 dogs, like they were just another piece of equipment.

Creed and Rufus had worked together as a team in Afghanistan. They had developed a special bond so that when they were separated by an explosion – an explosion that sent Creed home but sent Rufus back on duty with another handler – Creed hadn't been able to rest until he brought the big dog home to join him.

All of Creed and Hannah's dogs were special. They'd come to them in different ways. But Grace was definitely the most sensitive to and protective of Creed ever since he'd found her abandoned at the end of his long driveway. She tolerated being away from him, like the past week while he and Bolo were gone. She tolerated it only because she and Rufus could stay with Hannah and Lady – and now Hunter, too – in the big house with Hannah and her two boys.

Grace watched now from her perch on the back of the sofa, keeping a close eye on what Creed packed.

'Don't worry,' he told her. 'You're going with me this time.'

Her ears went back and her tail swiped back and forth, but her eyes darted to the duffle bag.

Creed stepped over to the built-in bookcases that made up one wall of his living room. He searched the shelves until he found the copy of *War of the Worlds* by H.G. Wells. He pulled it out, holding it in his hands with reverence. It was one of his first hardcovers, and it looked almost brand new. His grandmother had given it to him. For a long time, he could open the pages and get a whiff of her lavender perfume. But he hadn't opened the book for years.

He carefully flipped open the cover. Inside his grandmother

had written in blue pen: *To Ryder. Love, Gram.* And then she dated it as she always did. *10-10-01.*

He held the spine in the palm of his hand and let the book fall open to where he'd left the bookmark, almost two-thirds of the way through. Fact was, he'd never finished reading it though it had fascinated him so much he hadn't been able to put it down the whole time he was at his grandmother's. He continued reading it during their road trip back home. The road trip when Brodie disappeared. And Creed never opened the book again. It seemed ridiculous to imagine aliens from Mars invading the world when Brodie's world and Creed's own world had been turned upside down.

Creed plucked the bookmark out. Both he and Brodie had used similar bookmarks for their trip back. He looked at his own, surprised that it hadn't changed much. The Polaroid showed him and his sister posing on his grandmother's sofa.

He could still see Gram and hear her voice. She was fragile and wobbly, but she insisted his mother take the photos – three of them, back-to-back.

'Let me see you smile like you mean it,' she'd say in a silly, happy way that made them laugh.

It was the last time he heard his grandmother laugh.

Creed tucked the Polaroid back inside the book and slipped the book carefully into his duffle bag.

17

Omaha, Nebraska

Maggie dropped her cell phone into her back pocket and tried to tamp down her frustration. She wasn't used to working in places where cell phone reception disappeared with only a few steps. Truth was, she was exhausted and her patience wearing thin.

An hour earlier, she'd returned to her hotel room, showered, pulled on jeans and an old sweatshirt. Her room service tray had barely arrived when Pakula called.

Now here they were again, back at Eli Dunn's farm. Maggie had rushed out without a jacket. The air was chilly and she hugged her arms across her chest. She and Pakula stood outside a weathered grey barn. The double doors swung out and were left open as a CSU team worked inside. Maggie knew the three inside. She'd met them once before, ironically at another farm outside of Sioux City where a serial killer had chosen to make a graveyard for his victims.

Another tech would be bringing portable lights and a generator. The Douglas County Crime Lab's mobile unit had been working the site since the predawn hours. In another hour they'd lose any natural light. The sun was already sinking behind the ridge of trees, creating long shadows.

With all the focus on the farmhouse and the treasure trove of evidence found in the backyard, no one thought to look inside this barn. Actually, only a piece of its roof could be seen from the house. The sagging building sat about a quarter mile from Eli's farmhouse and was partially hidden by cornfields and trees. Grass grew in the middle of the two-lane dirt path that showed very little use. It might have taken days for someone to search for this building or even realize it held any importance. None of them expected to see the RV parked in between the empty horse stalls.

'It's registered to Eleanor Dunn,' Pakula told Maggie. 'Different address than Eli's. Turns out it's a long-term care facility in central Nebraska. That's why it didn't come up on our search.'

'His mother?'

'Most likely.'

'I sure hope we don't find her in the attic or a root cellar,' Maggie said without any intention of humor.

Pakula looked at her and with just a glance she could see a smile at the corner of his mouth. 'My wife keeps telling me I have a wickedly suspicious mind, but I think you might have me beat, O'Dell.'

'Problem is, my suspicions usually prove true.'

She wanted to be inside that RV with the techs, but Pakula had convinced her to let them do their jobs.

'I have to admit, it's definitely clever,' she said. Clever enough that it made her sick to her stomach. RVs inspired images of families on vacation or retired couples cruising across the country. Who would guess a human trafficker would be using it to transport his victims?

'This is a nice one,' Pakula said. 'I'm guessing it's twenty-six or twenty-eight foot long. Two sliders. Lots of storage.'

He pointed to small door panels in several places along the bottom area of the RV. Maggie winced at the size of two of them – large enough for a child to crawl through. She realized the CSU techs would need to process those areas, too.

'Looks too clean,' Pakula continued. 'He probably disinfected it just like the house.'

Earlier, the two of them had walked around the outside of the vehicle. Maggie didn't know enough about RVs but she guessed Pakula was correct. This one wasn't new – maybe a decade old – but it was very well cared for. Despite being surrounded by hay bales and even with dust motes filtering down from the ceiling, the vehicle looked recently washed. The tires were inflated. The windshield, headlights and taillights had no trace of bug spatters. Chances were they'd find nothing inside, but she knew that even the most careful criminals got sloppy. Or better yet, they became too cocky. She could see Eli Dunn being both sloppy and cocky.

'They didn't find anything in the house?' she asked.

Pakula shook his head. 'Just the backyard.'

'But there were definitely others staying at the house?'

'Konnor told me there were others. He didn't see them, but heard them.' Pakula shrugged like it didn't matter. 'Even if we find DNA or fingerprints, they won't mean much. Most of these kids being trafficked aren't on file anywhere.'

She knew he was right. The techs could find blood and they still had no way to verify who it belonged to. And certainly no way to find out where Dunn had taken them.

'Did the boy tell you how many others?' She tried to

restrain her irritation that Pakula had interviewed Konnor without her.

'The director told me he's still coming off the drugs, so he might not remember much for a while. We're still not sure what Dunn was giving him. Konnor said it made his vision bleary and helped him forget.'

She watched Pakula out of the corner of her eyes. His visit with the boy had rattled Pakula though he was doing a good job of pretending otherwise. In Maggie's mind, the boy's faulty memory only provided yet another reason for them to offer a deal of some kind to Dunn. And they needed to do it soon before Dunn changed his mind or before those who had been in his house were carted so far away they might never be found.

Maggie pulled her phone out and checked for messages.

Nothing.

When she hadn't heard back from the local officials she called her boss, Assistant Director Raymond Kunze. Elijah Dunn was being charged with human trafficking. By morning, a murder charge might be added after the remains in his backyard were examined. But technically, the federal offense of human trafficking would give the FBI some leverage. She was counting on it, but it felt like a clock was ticking away.

'They scatter like leaves,' Pakula said.

'I'm sorry, what did you say?'

She noticed his eyes were still focused on the barn. A breeze had picked up. The tall grass waved, and red and gold leaves fluttered from the trees.

'I've been doing this job for less than a year,' Pakula told her, 'but I can tell you this. Whoever else Dunn was holding in his house, they're long gone. That's something one of the veterans on the task force taught me. That's why it's so difficult to stop these guys. You catch one, and there's someone else to pick up and move the victims. In no time, they're in another state, maybe halfway across the country by now. They scatter like leaves in the wind.'

What about the dead left behind? Maggie wanted to ask, but didn't. And already she realized that she believed Creed's sister wasn't one of those that Eli had sold, but rather one of those he had buried.

One of the crime scene techs, a tall brunette named Haney, came out of the barn carrying what looked like a plain cardboard box.

'I think we might have found something,' she told them.

She put the box down on one of the blue tarps that had been laid out for collecting evidence. Then she handed Maggie and Pakula each a pair of latex gloves.

'RVs have all sorts of storage compartments,' she said as she began photographing the box before she opened it. 'We noticed a trace of fresh sawdust in the corner of the closet. Ryan pulled up a corner of the linoleum and found a cutout in the floor. There was a hidden compartment. He obviously didn't want us to find this.'

Maggie and Pakula crouched on each side as Haney carefully eased open the flaps of the cardboard box. In the dim light of the setting sun, it was a challenge to see inside. It looked like a hodgepodge of items. At first glance, it might be easy to mistake them for someone's garage sale leftovers: several books, a few pieces of costume jewelry, a small teddy bear, an old Gameboy and a Hello Kitty purse.

Maggie felt a slight chill. She stood at the same time Haney did. Pakula stayed crouched beside the box shaking his head.

Without saying a word, they all knew they had found Eli Dunn's collection of souvenirs. The trophies he'd kept from each of his victims.

18

When Charlotte opened her eyes again, it was dark. Her vision was blurred and her head hurt, but all of it was familiar. She knew that somewhere on her body she'd find another needle mark where Iris had injected her, yet again. She could barely raise her head, the muscles in her neck screamed with even the slightest movement. She didn't attempt to try her arms or legs. Instead, she used only her eyes to search for any light at the top of the stairs.

That's when she realized she was no longer at the bottom of the stairs.

A tinge of alarm slipped through her body. She could handle the predictable, no matter how painful. Fear was the unknown.

She sniffed the air. It smelled different. No damp, moldy concrete. There was something sweet like peppermint, only faint and dusty. A chemical scent lingered, too. Neither was unpleasant.

Charlotte tilted her head to listen. In the distance she thought she heard a train whistle. That was new. Then closer, a dog was barking, and suddenly her insides cringed. Her body instantly balled up into a fetal position triggered by the memory. Her arms flew up to protect her head and face. In the panic, she no longer noticed the pain in her muscles. Her mind had launched into survival mode, and she could hear the dog's fangs clicking and chomping at her. She could smell its hot breath, inches from her face. In seconds, she would feel those teeth sinking into the flesh of her ankle.

She strained to listen, but all she could hear now were soft whimpers and gasps for breath. It took her several minutes to realize the whimpers and gasps were her own.

She let her arms fall and her right hand jerked down to feel her ankle. There was no blood, but she knew exactly where the scar remained, though she couldn't touch it because a black strap was wrapped tightly over her ankle. Iris' tracking device.

'Now it won't matter whether the dogs can chase you down,' the woman had told her when she snapped the lightweight contraption into place. 'So please don't waste *my* time and *your* energy. Because Charlotte, I'll be able to find you.'

Of course, it didn't stop her from trying again. And failing, again. This time ending up at the bottom of the basement steps. Her last chance. And now Charlotte remembered Iris telling someone she wanted her gone.

But gone to where?

They'd drugged her and moved her. It wasn't the first time. In fact, it had happened so many times, Charlotte had lost track. Just like she'd lost track of so many other things like where she'd come from, who she even was.

Most of the time it was punishment. But Iris had said this was the last mistake. She was finished with her, and Charlotte knew enough about the others before her to know that when Iris was finished with you, you disappeared.

But where? Where had she disappeared to?

THURSDAY, OCTOBER 19

19

Atlanta, Georgia

Olivia James didn't mind working the early morning hours, though some of her staff still groaned and guzzled coffee. Truth was, Olivia rarely slept at night, choosing early afternoon instead. There was something safer about closing her eyes and her mind while the sun was still present. Darkness always brought the nightmares.

She walked into the studio, pleased to see everything set up correctly even as the final touches were being added. It had taken her years to find the right team. Those not up to her standards usually left on their own. Everyone in daytime television knew the business was brutal. Maintaining an Emmy Award-winning show even more so. Those on her staff who stayed were rewarded with appropriate bonuses. Though Olivia admitted she wasn't good at handing down praise or compliments. But why should she? Bottom line, she worked hard, and she expected the people around her to do the same.

Her new assistant, Deena, waved to her from behind the set's kitchen counter where it looked like she was bossing around other staff members into finishing today's setup. It had only been three weeks and already Olivia missed her old assistant. Stacy had been with her since the early days. She was the only person Olivia truly trusted and depended on. But suddenly, the woman was head over heels in love and moving to New York with her new beau. In a desperate attempt, Olivia had offered to double her salary, despite feeling betrayed.

'Olivia, you'll find someone to replace me,' Stacy had told her. 'It's not like you're losing your best friend.'

How was it possible that Stacy didn't realize that she *was* Olivia's best friend? That she was Olivia's *only* friend.

Now she was stuck with Deena, all five foot, five inches and no more than one hundred and ten pounds. Deena had presented an impressive resume along with a confidence that was quickly revealing itself as arrogance.

In the beginning, Olivia had admired that the woman had an uncanny ability to put out fires without a single line of worry on her brow. But now she was discovering that confident, know-it-all Deena could also be a bit cavalier and quick to cut too many corners. She also appeared to be a bit of a bully.

Perhaps the tipping point was last week when the woman had tried to substitute margarine for butter.

'What difference will it make?' she had asked Olivia. 'We'll shoot it from a new angle. The audience will never know.'

'But *I* will know,' Olivia told her, putting an abrupt close to the issue.

Now, Olivia was going through her notes when she heard Deena ordering someone else in her shrill voice.

'Wait! Just a minute, you need to leave.' Deena was telling someone at the back of the studio.

Olivia paid little attention. Despite their best efforts, fans of the show occasionally tried to sneak in and watch them film.

'Sir, you can't have that dog in here. You need to leave.'

This time Olivia looked up. The lights were so bright she could barely see behind the cameras where a tall man and small dog stood. She took off her reading glasses, dropping them on the counter along with her notes, and she came around for a better look.

Deena was standing directly in front of the pair now, pointing to the door. The man was trying to explain to her. He glanced over Deena's shoulder and did a double take when he saw Olivia.

Immediately, she felt her knees wobble and the heat of the stage lights made her dizzy. For a brief moment she thought she must be imaging things. It couldn't be, and yet ... she knew. He'd found something, and he was here to tell her.

'Deena, it's okay.'

'But we can't have dogs in the studio. This is—'

'Ryder, how are you?' Olivia asked as she moved in front of Deena.

'Hi, Mom.'

20

She looked so much smaller ... and older in real life. Creed hadn't seen his mother in almost ten years. Her choice, not Creed's. When he told her he was joining the Marines she said she couldn't bear losing another child. Angry and hurt, she told him if he joined the military that he'd be as good as dead to her. And she was true to her word.

At that time she'd told him that she'd already lost Brodie, her mother (Creed's grandmother), and her ex-husband. But what his mother didn't seem to understand was that Creed had lost all of them, too. Only two weeks after finding his father dead, he'd decided to join the Marines. Actually, he had gone over to talk to his father about the decision only to find his body on the living room sofa with a self-inflicted bullet wound to the temple.

Creed's way of keeping in touch with his mother was watching her on television. Her daytime lifestyle show was on for an hour every morning. He remembered being fascinated the first time he saw her on a TV screen. He'd just woken up in a hospital bed, and there she was. In his hallucinatory state from the pain drugs they'd pumped into him, Creed thought she was there in his room with him.

It was after the explosion. After he'd been airlifted out of Afghanistan, going from hospital to hospital until he was back in the States. A young Afghan boy named Jafar had gained the trust of the Marine unit Creed had been assigned to. One day Jafar blew himself up. Creed was a K9 handler and his dog, Rufus, had detected the explosives underneath the boy's clothing. Rufus alerted to the kid. But it was too late. All Creed could do was yell to warn the others and throw himself on top of his dog.

He didn't remember how many different places they'd taken him. He could hardly remember anything, except that each time he woke up, he'd asked for his dog. He could vividly remember the panic and the anxiety when he couldn't find Rufus. It was the single question he'd asked over and over, again, until someone finally told him the dog was okay. Well enough, in fact, to be assigned for duty to another handler.

Compared to Jason, Creed knew he was lucky, but sometimes he thought he knew what Jason had gone through, because waking up and not having Rufus beside him had felt as if someone had cut off his arm.

His dog was gone from his life, and he was alone. Even his mother wasn't really in his hospital room. She was on TV, telling him how to sort and polish cranberries to make a beautiful holiday wreath.

Now, she was staring at him, looking him over as if seeing him for the first time in her life. She'd escorted him back to her office, leaving the studio despite the young woman trying to follow and throwing questions at her.

She had ushered Creed and Grace into her office then stood in the doorway so the woman couldn't enter.

'Deena, please tell the crew that there'll be a delay.'

'But you know we only have the studio for a set amount of time and you can't—'

'Excuse me, but I can.' And she shut the door.

To Creed, she asked, 'Would you like some coffee? Tea? Or perhaps a soda?'

It had been ten years, and she was playing host. Probably an occupational hazard, considering that's the role she played every day.

'No, thanks,' he told her.

It took him a while to realize her intense gaze into his eyes was no longer disbelief in seeing him. It was curiosity. Still, he was surprised when the whispered question came, 'You know something?'

He knew she meant, *you know something about Brodie,* but she couldn't bring herself to say her name out loud.

He should have been hurt that she didn't ask more about him or that she hadn't even acknowledged Grace who scampered at their feet patiently waiting for attention. But this was simply a microcosm of what their relationship had become; their relationship from the time that Brodie went missing to when Creed joined the Marines.

Every day had become an accounting of news and information, every week a sorting of details and a search for any last tidbit that may have been overlooked. She had dragged Creed from city to city. Someone would report seeing a girl with Brodie's description at a bus station in St Louis, so off to St Louis they went. A waitress at a diner in Memphis was positive she'd served ice cream sundaes to Brodie and another little girl with long stringy hair. Both were accompanied by a strange man. So off to Memphis they went.

Brodie disappeared October 13, 2001. Despite air travel resuming September 14, in the weeks after 9/11, the highways were filled with trucks and vehicles. Everyone was still on high alert, fearful of more Middle Eastern terrorists. A little girl missing from an interstate rest stop didn't garner as much attention as she might have in the weeks before the attacks. Which only seemed to drive Creed's mother to a new level of panic and urgency. No one seemed to be interested in helping her find her lost child.

This woman standing before him, waiting with that familiar glint of desperation in her eyes, reminded Creed of the mother he had come to know. The mother he had to settle for. At the end of the day – at the end of another week, another month, another year – there wasn't anything left for him.

And in just those three words, *you know something*, the television celebrity – the matron of fine living who told viewers and fans how to enhance their daily lives with homemade macaroons and holiday wreaths created with fresh berries – this icon had been reduced to a desperate, helpless woman still clinging to even a scrap of hope.

'I know what you do for a living,' she said when Creed had taken too long to respond. 'I've followed your life.' She pointed at the Jack Russell as if seeing her for the first time, and she smiled. 'This must be your Grace.' She reached her hand down for Grace to sniff then she looked back up at him with a sad weariness. 'Tell me,' she said.

'Someone found the Polaroid photo that Brodie used as a bookmark.'

'A Polaroid photo?'

'A couple of days before, you took three photos of Brodie and me with Gram's camera.'

'Did I?'

'One for Gram. One for me. One for Brodie. We stuck them in the books Gram gave us. We used them as bookmarks because we started reading them at her house.'

He couldn't believe she didn't remember the photos.

The whole trip was so clear to Creed as though it had happened just last week. He and Brodie loved spending time with their grandmother. She had board games she played with them and homemade apple pie. And always she sent them home with a new book, something she'd selected especially for each of them. That fall she hadn't been feeling well. That was the reason his mother stayed with her while Creed and Brodie and their father headed back home. Creed wasn't sure what ailed his grandmother, but he never believed it was the cause of her death a couple of months later, two days before Christmas. In his mind – even his young teenaged mind – he'd always believed his grandmother had died of a broken heart.

'Have you seen this photo?' his mother asked.

He shook his head, surprised with the emotion that suddenly obstructed his throat. Thinking of his grandmother only reminded him of how much loss followed Brodie's disappearance.

'I don't understand,' she said. 'How do you know it's the same photo?' In a matter of seconds she had gone from needing to know everything to questioning what he told her, almost as if she wanted him to be wrong. Almost as if she was ready to dismiss what he had to say, so she could go back to her current life.

He swallowed hard. Too much coffee on the drive up to Atlanta churned in his stomach. It was threatening to push back up. He looked down at Grace who was wagging at him and cocking her head to one side. She was worried about him.

Emotion runs down the leash.

He was starting to regret coming here. But then he remembered why he had.

'It's the same photo,' he said without any other explanation. Then he managed to add in a professional voice, 'I need you to send me the box.'

He knew he didn't need to tell her which box. It was something they carried with them from city to city. It contained Brodie's hairbrush, a couple of baby teeth, several items of unwashed clothing sealed in plastic, a pair of shoes and a few other things that might be used to extract a DNA sample or provide a scent. All were preserved as if prepared for a special time capsule.

'Here's the address,' he said, handing her a business card. 'If you can overnight it, that would help.'

She was quiet now and nodded, a slight bob of her head, her eyes no longer on his. Instead, she watched out the window where the sky was starting to brighten with purple and pink hues of dawn. Creed avoided looking out, afraid he might see the ghosts of regret that she might be seeing. Whatever it was, it had transformed her physical being as well – even her shoulders now seemed to slump and curl inward. He wished he could access his military training and shove away the emotions. Instead, he relied on phrases from some of Hannah's sermons and told himself, *what's done is done*, and *it's time to move forward*.

To his mother, he said, 'And I need to take with me a swab and get a saliva sample.' He handed her the small kit that included everything that was needed: cotton-toothed swabs, cheek scraper and small containers with seals.

'Of course,' she said. She barely glanced at him as she took it, already familiar with what he was asking her to do.

Then without another word, she left through a door at the far corner of her office, into what Creed guessed was her personal bathroom.

And then he waited. He hated waiting. He stood in place, not daring to shift or move or touch anything. He allowed only his eyes to search and examine the décor of the room. Of all the photos on the walls and the desk, none of them were of Brodie or him. They were all from her life as a celebrity with other guest celebrities. It was as if the life with Brodie and him had never existed. She had boxed it all up, and he wondered if she had bothered to keep anything from that period of her life.

He felt a bit lightheaded. Too little sleep and too much coffee. That's all it was, he told himself. And yet, he had never wanted to leave a place as much as he wanted to flee from here, right now, right this second. Instead, he took measured breaths and tried to concentrate on Grace.

He reached his hand down to her and she licked his fingers, but her eyes were still intensely focused on him. He wasn't doing a very good job of keeping calm.

'Not much longer, girl,' he told her.

That's when it occurred to him that not once had his mother attempted to hug him. In fact, she hadn't attempted to touch him. And not once had she asked if Brodie might still be alive.

21

Omaha, Nebraska

With Pakula now on Maggie's side, a possible deal with Eli Dunn was moving through the official channels. Pakula was off talking to the Douglas County prosecutor while Maggie waited. She had expected to have more time with Agent Stevens, but he'd left earlier, headed to Kansas City to assist in another raid. Operation Cross Country was still underway for another two days in other cities. She had hoped Stevens could speed things up. Instead, he had passed it on to her boss. Now, she needed to convince Assistant Director Raymond Kunze.

'You were supposed to be assisting in the profile and the raid,' Kunze told her when they finally connected. 'That's all.'

'It's a little more complicated.'

'Of course it is. It's always more complicated with you, O'Dell. I had you in Nebraska a few years ago for a simple drop-by and you almost got yourself killed.'

Maggie winced and her fingers instinctively rubbed at her temple. She didn't need Kunze to remind her. She still had a scar where the bullet had grazed her head. That 'drop-by' ended up being a government cover-up with threads that led them from the Nebraska Sandhills all the way to Washington, DC. It wasn't the only case that her politically motivated boss had gotten her involved in. She let her silence remind him. However, she should have guessed it wouldn't work. Instead, he seemed content to continue his lecture.

'You know the locals don't like it when you start making deals without them.'

'It's a federal case.'

'No, it is not. Right now Mr Dunn is a possible suspect in the death of whoever may have been buried in his backyard.'

'And human trafficking.'

'From what I understand there was no evidence found of trafficking.'

'What about the boy, Konnor? Not to mention, that Dunn has an entire wall of photographs of other victims.' She couldn't keep the anger from her voice. 'He scrubbed everything down in his house, but there were mattresses on the floor. He was holding that young boy captive.'

'No computer,' Kunze said so casually his words actually stung. 'No individuals other than a stoned teenager who as of this morning still hasn't accused Mr Dunn of a crime.'

Stoned teenager? That's how they saw that poor kid?

Maggie stopped pacing, dropped into a chair. Pakula hadn't gotten much information from the boy named Konnor. Even the cardboard box they'd found inside the RV couldn't be connected to a single victim.

'It's not a crime to scrub clean your property,' Kunze said. 'Knowing what he's done to avoid detection, do you really think this guy will be honest with you?'

Maggie and Pakula had already discussed this. There was a good chance Dunn would send them on a wild goose chase. But what did they have to lose? The bones in Dunn's backyard – which had now been confirmed as human – meant he could possibly be facing a very long prison sentence.

'If we find even one of his victims,' Maggie said, 'it means saving that boy or girl's life.'

'And if you only find dead bodies?'

'We're still able to bring them home to their families.'

Before Maggie had met Ryder Creed she'd never have understood how important that was to a grieving family. Without any evidence to show otherwise, they always hoped and prayed. How could they move on if there was even the slightest belief that their loved one was still alive?

'I've already talked to Stevens and the Douglas County prosecutor,' Kunze told her.

She wasn't surprised that she would be the last on his list. Knowing Kunze, he'd want all the facts, and he'd want them from someone other than her. It was times like this that Maggie still missed Kyle Cunningham. He had been her mentor more than a boss. Cunningham watched his agents' backs. Kunze expected his agents to watch his back.

'It seems Elijah Dunn is anxious,' Kunze told her. 'He actually wants to show where some of the victims are buried, but he wants to go along.'

'What? That's ridiculous.' She hadn't expected this. 'We have his journal. He just needs to decipher it for us.'

'He won't do that. He goes along or there's no deal. In fact, he's not admitting to killing any of these victims. He's claiming he was simply the clean-up man.'

'The *clean-up* man?' She stopped herself from laughing.

When she met with Dunn, she'd looked into the eyes of a killer. No way did she believe he was only the gravedigger.

'If that's true,' she said, 'why not give us the man who did kill them?'

'He says he's already risking his life by offering to show you where the bodies are buried.'

'And what about the victims he was trafficking? We know he moved them somewhere else. Probably in the days before the raid.'

'He claims he knows nothing about that. According to the prosecutor and Dunn's defense attorney, Mr Dunn insists he and the boy were the only ones there. He also insists that the boy was there of his free will.'

'The CSU techs have found traces of others in that house.'

'Think about it, O'Dell. Unless those traces have measurable DNA that can match to someone who a) is missing and b) has had his or her DNA added to CODIS, there's no way to prove who else was in that house, let alone that they weren't there by choice.'

CODIS (Combined DNA Index System) was the FBI's database of DNA collected from crime scenes and criminals. It also included any DNA from missing persons that family members had offered to be in the system. The odds that anything they found inside the house or the RV matched someone declared as missing was a long shot.

Bottom line, Maggie knew Kunze was right.

In the back of her mind, she had to ask herself if she was prepared to go on another scavenger hunt with a killer in tow. The idea brought back memories that were still too fresh of a scavenger hunt gone bad.

Less than two years ago a convict had offered to reveal where his partner had buried bodies in Florida's Blackwater River State Forest. The recovery party had only just begun their search when they were ambushed. Maggie's partner, R.J. Tully, took a bullet and would have been killed if Maggie hadn't handcuffed herself to him. She forced the killing duo to take both she and Tully along when she realized she was the only one they wanted to keep alive.

So many times she wondered how she didn't see that ambush coming. But she would not make the same mistake ever again.

'Agent O'Dell?'

Kunze's voice startled her. She'd forgotten about him.

'The deal doesn't include absolving Dunn of these murders, does it?' She wanted to know.

'No. My understanding is that his cooperation is not an admission that he had anything to do with the deaths. But it'll still be up to the prosecutor to put together a case. The state patrol will take charge in providing—'

'Sir, Dunn is not in the custody of the Nebraska State Patrol. Detective Pakula and I have been—'

'I'm not getting dragged into local politics, O'Dell.'

Of course not, Maggie thought to herself. *You prefer national politics.*

'It's my understanding,' he continued, his voice now taut with impatience, 'that the Douglas County prosecutor is already working out the details with the State Patrol. It's also my understanding that Mr Dunn will not accept any kind of deal unless one particular person is in complete charge of the recovery effort.'

Maggie shook her head and held back her anger. It was out of her hands now. She wasn't sure if she was sorry or relieved.

'Once again, you've managed to wedge yourself in the middle of something you had no business getting involved in,' Kunze told her.

'Excuse me?'

'It appears you made quite the impression on Mr Dunn. He won't make a deal unless you're in charge of this whole fiasco.'

22

By early evening, Maggie was frustrated and impatient with waiting. Pakula had commandeered a small conference room with a long table, comfortable chairs, a computer, coffee-maker and enough room for her to pace.

She was told that her resources would be limited for the recovery team. Everyone agreed that in order to keep it out of the media and prevent a caravan of TV cameras and reporters, they'd need to use only the essential personnel. And most of the essential personnel would be guarding and securing Eli Dunn.

Maggie and Pakula had gone over who and what would be required to pull off the searches. Unfortunately, she needed to trust Pakula to choose a K9 handler and someone to collect evidence. The State Patrol had agreed to process whatever evidence and remains they found. Pakula, however, wouldn't be joining the search and recovery team. He'd stay and work the other side of the case. Both he and Maggie still believed there were trafficking victims who were secretly removed from Dunn's property and carted away to some new location. Pakula would be searching for those victims.

According to Dunn, the initial burial site – but not the only one – was about two hours away. The others stretched over a fifty mile radius. Dunn would only locate them one at a time and had circled the first one on a map.

Maggie stood over that map. She had spread the accordion folds out on the long table. She stared at the area, taking in as much as she could. The closest major road looked to be a two-lane highway labeled Highway 92. Immediately, she noticed that 92 ran parallel with Interstate 80. Maybe twenty-five to thirty miles separated them.

Pakula had explained to her that Nebraska being smack-dab in the middle of the United States meant a high volume of traffic. Interstate 80 was the second longest interstate in the country, stretching from New York to San Francisco.

She moved her index finger along Highway 92 and noticed that it continued to run parallel from Omaha – at the far eastern part of the state – almost all the way to the state's western border, stopping short at Alliance. Somewhere around Halsey and the National Forest, Highway 92 changed to Highway 2, and more miles separated it from the interstate. She'd need to ask Pakula if the highway could be a serious alternative to crossing the state and avoiding the interstate.

Why did Eli Dunn choose to bury the bodies here? Was it possible he took this way with his RV when he was trafficking victims, so that he could stay off the interstate? Maybe her mind was racing too far ahead. There could be another reason Dunn had chosen the area, but it was strange that the circled radius was two hours – about 100 miles – away from his farm. Most killers kept to familiar ground. For a man who may have left bones in his backyard firepit, it seemed off to Maggie that he would travel two hours away to dispose of other victims. Why not just use the cornfields or woods out his back door?

On the other side of the table were the items from the cardboard box that was found in the RV. CSU tech Haney had tagged and admitted into evidence everything they'd found in the RV's secret compartment. Each item was now individually encased in a plastic bag and labeled.

Haney had also left the notebook, the small spiral pad that Maggie believed was Dunn's strange journal. The techs had swabbed the cover and several pages for fingerprints along with any other residue. When Maggie asked about the rust-colored stain on the cover, Haney had said, 'It's not blood residue. We think it's something tomato-based.'

Maggie had smiled at that. Given the opportunity, she imagined the techs would be able to determine whether that tomato-based stain was ketchup or marinara sauce.

A half hour ago, she'd finally convinced Pakula to leave. His daughter had another volleyball game, and she knew he'd missed last night's. As it was, he'd probably already missed the first set. He was still waiting for phone calls, but he could certainly do that from the bleachers.

She checked her cell phone. No messages from Creed. She'd left two for him, each asking to please call though warning him that she had no new information. If she didn't hear from him soon, she'd call Hannah. She hated that she had jumped the gun and told Creed about the photo. They didn't have anything more to connect Eli Dunn to Brodie. Truth was, all she had was a gut instinct that Creed's sister might be one of the victims buried along Dunn's scavenger hunt.

With nowhere to go and nothing to do, Maggie opened the small notebook. The front section was made up of pages and pages of columns. She'd tried to decipher the codes that combined numbers, letters and shapes. The bulk of the notebook was a combination of codes and sketches. Each of these included the universal symbol for map directions.

As for the sketches, they looked like doodles or a child's

simple line drawings complete with stick figures. However, after spending more time examining the sketches, Maggie realized all of them appeared to be landscapes of some sort with trees and grass, roads, fences and even what looked like train tracks. She also noticed that the stick figures were always drawn with arms up and legs out. One drawing put the stick figure at the bottom of a hole.

Another looked to be submerged under the wavy lines of what Maggie suspected was a river or creek.

It seemed obvious that Dunn had recorded where he had buried his victims. And he'd created maps and codes that only he could translate. If he had his way, he'd be their only guide.

She flipped through the pages. So many drawings. So many codes. How many victims were recorded here?

Her cell phone started to ring, and she grabbed it when she recognized Creed's number.

'Hey,' she said. 'I've been waiting for you to call.'

'Sorry, Grace and I were on the road. Have you had dinner yet?'

'No, but I—'

'We brought burgers and fries. Can you come get us?'

'Come get you?'

'We're down in the lobby.'

23

Creed couldn't stop smiling despite having to wait in line. Maggie had dropped to her knees to greet the Jack Russell terrier. She scratched and petted Grace while the little dog wiggled and wagged with her entire hind end until she was twisted into a comma.

'Grace, I missed you,' Maggie said as she hugged the dog.

Usually he didn't encourage his dogs to lick faces, but there was nothing he could do in this case. Maggie had dogs of her own, though Creed had never had the privilege of meeting them. He did know she was connected to them and missed them when was on the road. He also knew that sometimes Dr Benjamin Platt took care of Jake and Harvey while Maggie was gone. For Creed that was proof that Ben and Maggie's relationship was one that Creed shouldn't interrupt.

Finally Maggie stood and gave him an awkward hug. Awkward because his hands were full and his duffle bag bobbed under his arm. And yet, when she pulled away and met his eyes there was still a dose of electricity sparking between them. There was enough intensity for Creed to question, all over again, if perhaps he had already interrupted Ben and Maggie's relationship.

They'd known each other now for almost two years. Every time they found themselves working together it was under too much stress and urgency and never enough time to sort out the feelings both of them obviously harbored. They had saved each other's lives and shared things in confidence. They'd even shared an isolation ward about six months ago. And always, Creed backed off, because Maggie was sort of in a relationship with another guy. Not just a guy – a doctor, a colonel and director of USAMRIID – the United State Medical Research Institute of Infectious Diseases.

The worst part, Creed actually liked and respected Dr Benjamin Platt. So every time, Creed simply reminded himself that he had a strict rule, his own personal doctrine that he didn't sleep with women he worked with.

Maggie's fingers brushed his hair from his forehead when she noticed the butterfly bandage. In that brief moment, he thought *who am I fooling*? He knew he'd throw out that stupid rule in a second if she gave him even the slightest encouragement.

'What happened?' she asked, concern clouded her eyes.

'I got clumsy trying to keep Bolo from getting hurt.'

'Is he all right?'

'He's fine. His paws got scraped up. We were working an explosion site in Texas.'

She was still examining him, though she had taken a step back and was scrutinizing him with her eyes now and not her fingers. But the intensity of her gaze felt like she was still touching him.

In the conference room, he put down the brown paper bags of food then slid the duffle bag off of his shoulder. He'd brought in his gear, knowing it would need to go through the metal detector, but he needed to feed Grace. He'd been driving with few stops. Both of them were starving.

'Do you mind if I prepare Grace's food for her?' he asked, not wanting to unload anything without permission. Evidence bags and maps were spread out on the long conference table. He didn't want to contaminate anything.

'Go ahead.' She slid items to the center, giving him the far end. 'I think there might be some paper plates over here.' She headed to the cabinet against the wall that had a coffeemaker on top.

Creed pulled out a bottle of water and spatula and snapped the lid off of the glass bowl that already had a serving of Grace's food. He poured water over the dehydrated mixture and stirred it. Then he pulled out another bowl and filled it with the rest of the bottled water. He set it down for Grace, but she was too busy watching Maggie.

'I'm afraid I don't know much more than what I already told you,' she said as she brought napkins and paper plates back. She started taking the wrapped burgers and fries out of the grease-stained paper bag.

Creed noticed that her eyes were occupied with unwrapping and arranging. He wasn't sure if she'd be upset that he had decided to come here without an official invitation. Truthfully, he didn't really care. If this was the last place on earth that Brodie had been then he needed to be here. Maybe his mother had influenced his kneejerk reaction with all those times she'd packed them up and drove to wherever Brodie had been last seen.

'Grace and I are here to help,' he told her. He stirred the food some more and checked his watch. To Grace he said, 'Just a few more minutes, girl.'

Then his eyes caught the cover of a book that was encased in one of the plastic bags and his heart skipped a beat.

'Where did you find that?' He pointed.

At first, Maggie appeared guarded until she noticed the look on his face.

'Do you recognize it?'

'Brodie had a copy of *Harriet the Spy* with her when she disappeared.' It had to be a coincidence. 'Is this stuff from the same place where you found the photo?'

'Yes.'

No way this was a coincidence.

'Our grandmother gave us each a book on that trip. We both started reading them.' Creed remembered his own bookmark and turned to his duffle. He dug inside until he found his copy of *War of the Worlds* tucked safely between a couple of his T-shirts. He held it in both hands with as much reverence as though it were a Bible. Then carefully, he tugged the Polaroid out and handed it to Maggie.

'Gram had my mom take three photos. She kept one, and Brodie and I used ours for bookmarks.'

'Creed, there's no way to know whether or not this book was the same one Brodie had. This guy may have had close to a dozen victims. In fact, we don't have anything else that connects him to her.'

'Can you open it?'

By now, Creed's heart banged against his chest. He could see Grace prancing at his feet, but not for her food. She was worried about him, again.

Maggie hesitated but only for a second or two. Then she pulled on a pair of latex gloves. She wrote something on the plastic bag before she broke the seal. Creed's hair at the back of his neck bristled as if someone had opened the door to the conference room and let in a cold draft. He watched her slip the paperback out of the bag slowly and carefully and he caught himself holding his breath.

She held on to it and didn't offer it to him. Instead, she waited for instructions or more of an explanation. He could feel her eyes on him, and he didn't care that there was too much sympathy in them. She didn't believe this was Brodie's book. She was preparing for him to be disappointed. But Creed knew.

'Gram always gave us books,' he told Maggie. 'She picked them out specially for each of us. Somehow she always knew what we'd like. On the inside cover, she'd put the date she gave the book to us. She'd write a simple message.'

He opened the cover of his and showed Maggie the inscription.

To Ryder. Love, Gram
    10-10-01

Gently and slowly, Maggie opened the paperback's cover.
'Oh my God!' she whispered.

The message, written in blue ink, matched the one in Creed's hardcover. He recognized his grandmother's beautiful cursive script.

To Brodie. Love, Gram.
    10-10-01

24

Santa Rosa County, Florida

Jason turned into the circle driveway and rolled down the window before the sheriff's deputy made it to the side of his SUV.

'Sir, you'll need to turn around.'

Jason pulled down the brim of his cap, so the deputy could read the K9 CrimeScents embroidered on the front while he extended his hand with his ID. Creed had told him that people would question him because of his youth.

'Don't get mad,' Creed had told him. 'Let them see your confidence instead.'

And sure enough, the deputy was taking his time, his eyes darting back and forth from the photo on the ID to Jason's face. Then he bent down to search the back of the SUV as if he still didn't believe Jason until he saw Scout in his kennel.

'Black Lab?' he asked.

'Yes, sir,' Jason answered.

'I thought search dogs were always shepherds?'

That was the other thing Creed warned him about. Preconceived notions of what kind of dog should be used would have them asking more questions.

'The military uses a lot of shepherds,' Jason told the deputy. 'We don't discriminate.'

But now he saw the man's eyes dart to his robotic hand on the steering wheel. He looked back at Jason with that look Jason hated – part awe, part wonder. And though no one ever said it, in his head Jason always added words to that look: *What kind of freak are you?*

The deputy handed him the ID and pointed toward the house.

'I'll let Sheriff Norwich know you're here.'

Jason drove slowly the rest of the way, pulling in behind the two sheriff's department vehicles. The two-story house was set back from the road on about an acre surrounded by huge live oaks, magnolias and long-leaf pines. Large camellia bushes were full of deep crimson blooms. With the window still down he could smell the fresh pine straw. He recognized the pecan shells used on the paths in the landscape. Across the street were similar well-manicured yards with modest homes. A nice middle-class neighborhood. But behind all of them was a thick forest that would be dark in a few hours.

He looked in the rearview mirror and saw Scout checking out the surroundings, his nose twitching in the direction of the open window.

'Creed and Hannah say you and me are ready for this,' Jason told the dog. Scout cocked his head but only for a second or two before his nose started testing the air again.

A thirteen-year-old girl was missing since last night. The mother thought the girl had walked to a friend's house. She only discovered earlier this afternoon that the girl wasn't with the friend. In fact, she'd never arrived, and the friend claimed she never expected her. There had been no plans for an overnight stay.

Hannah had told him the basics, most of which he made

her repeat so he could write it all down. This would be his first search all by himself . . . not all by himself. With Scout. But only the two of them. They'd never done an entire search without Creed.

The girl's mother . . . What was her name?

Jason grabbed the notebook from his shirt pocket and flipped pages to find it. He was awful with names. Woodson. Shelly. The daughter's name was Raelyn. He flipped more pages. He didn't remember Hannah telling him the father's name.

'You the guy with the dog?'

Jason jerked to attention. Another deputy had wandered over. Jason dropped the notebook into his pocket and opened the door.

'Jason Seaver,' he told the man but he didn't offer his hand. Instead, he walked around to the back of the SUV and opened the tailgate.

Scout was excited. Too excited. Jason slipped his fingers into the crate, and the dog came over to get scratched under the chin. He'd already put Scout's vest on. Now, he needed to put on his own gear, except that the deputy had followed him. Everybody wanted to see the dog. Creed said there were types of people when it came to K9 searches. Those who believed it was magic, and those who thought it was simply luck.

'Deputy, I need to prepare my dog.'

'Oh sure. I'll get out of your way.' He backed up a few steps. 'I thought search dogs were usually German shepherds.'

'Not this guy,' Jason said, and this time he let the deputy see his robotic hand as he worked open the duffle bag. It didn't take long, and he heard the crunching footsteps leaving.

He went over a mental list, double-checking the items in

his daypack. He weaved his new cell phone holster onto his belt on one side and clipped on a new canister of bear spray on the other side. The daypack went onto his back after he made sure he had Scout's collapsible water bowl and bottles of water. He tied the kerchief around his neck. The kerchief had been soaked with Hannah's organic concoction of bug repellant. Scout's vest had some sprayed on it, too. Last, he pulled Scout's rope toy out of the duffle and transferred it to the daypack, letting the dog see it.

Now, before he opened the crate, he made Scout sit and waited for the dog's eyes to stop looking for the toy and meet Jason's.

'Scout, this is it. Time to get to work.'

Then to himself, Jason muttered, 'I hope I don't screw this up.'

25

Sheriff Norwich came out the front door as Jason and Scout approached the house.

'Come on up,' she told them.

There were four steps to the landing of a roofed portico. The first thing Jason noticed about the sheriff was that she was older than he expected. The second thing was that she had kind eyes, a warm brown that showed concern.

'I'm Jason Seaver. This is Scout.'

'I'm Fran Norwich,' she said and offered her hand.

Jason watched the sheriff's eyes when he reached out with his prosthetic hand. The black metal looked like something out of a Transformer movie. Material resembling skin would come in the next stage, or so Jason was promised. They needed to make sure they had the sensors in the correct places first.

To her credit, the sheriff didn't flinch. Instead, she surprised Jason by giving the hand a regular shake and looking Jason straight in the eyes when she said, 'Thank you for your service.'

That line always created an annoying lump in Jason's throat along with a bitter taste when he bit back the emotion. He was relieved when the sheriff bent down to greet Scout, offering the dog her hand to sniff.

Norwich was Jason's height, but she was wider with a

stocky, solid build. She wore her gray hair in a chin-length bob that she pushed back behind her ears. Her uniform shirt and trousers were pressed and crisp.

The sheriff turned around and stood in the doorway as she asked someone inside, 'The K9 unit is here. They're gonna need to come in. Is that all right?'

Jason knew what the sheriff was really asking. When it seemed to take too long for a response, Jason told Norwich, 'If it's a problem, we can have a couple of the girl's items brought out to him.'

The sheriff glanced over her shoulder and shook her head. 'No, that's okay, Jason. I've already explained to Mrs Woodson that this works better if you can start in Raelyn's room.'

And yet, Norwich didn't move, still waiting for an answer with one hand on her hip, the other holding open the door. Jason felt like he and Scott were caught in the middle of a standoff.

Finally, the sheriff opened the door wider and gestured for them to follow her into the house.

Mrs Woodson stood behind the kitchen counter watching them as though she were watching a movie. She was a tall woman with shoulder-length blond hair. Jason guessed she was in her late thirties, maybe early forties. She grasped a mug of coffee. He could smell a freshly brewed pot, but Jason thought her eyes – though red-rimmed – looked more like she might be high or drunk. He realized that wasn't fair. The woman was probably just in shock.

As soon as Scout came into her line of vision, that's where her eyes stayed. Jason tried to figure out if Mrs Woodson was afraid of dogs or simply didn't like having one in her house.

The place looked spotless. It was modestly decorated, but even Jason could pick out some expensive touches like the Oriental rug in the living room, a couple of abstract paintings and a large crystal vase on the side table.

'Mrs Woodson, this is Jason Seaver and Scout.'

The home's open floor plan allowed Jason to stay in the foyer close to the staircase. He was hoping he could take Scout up to the girl's room and not have to make polite chit-chat. Still, he waited for permission.

'Remember what I told you,' Norwich said as she stood in the living room between the foyer and kitchen counter. 'I've used K9 teams before. They can find more in an hour than a team of my deputies can find in six to eight hours. I know this is difficult, but do you want to take Jason and Scout up to Raelyn's room? Or would you rather tell me where it is and I can take him up.'

'Why does he need to be in her room? I already told you she wasn't here last night.' She pointed out the kitchen window. 'She might still be out in the woods. We need to check out there.' And now Jason could hear the panic in her voice.

Norwich shifted her patience from one foot to the other, but Jason answered.

'That's exactly where we plan on looking,' he said. 'But we need to start by letting Scout get familiar with your daughter's scent. I promise we won't disturb anything.'

When she still didn't move, he continued, 'Sometimes one item will work, but the best way is for Scout to be surrounded by her things.'

She stared at them for a long time before she left her spot, and when she did, she grasped the countertop and backs of the bar stools as though she needed them to keep her balance.

Jason caught Norwich's eyes, and in them he saw that the sheriff also knew Mrs Woodson had been sipping more than just coffee. Now, Jason understood why Norwich had been over-explaining and talking to her as though she were hard of hearing.

Jason followed the woman at a distance, keeping Scout on a short, tight leash. She climbed the stairs slowly and grasped the handrail with every step. At the end of a long hallway, she stopped outside the door. She went in and positioned herself against a wooden dresser. Jason would have preferred to do this without her scrutiny, but he didn't dare ask her to leave.

He found himself filling in the silence with information that he hoped made him sound like an expert and not just a nervous newbie.

'All of us have our own unique individual scent,' he said as he led Scout to the girl's bed. 'It sounds weird, but little bits and pieces of us leave our bodies every minute. I like to think of Pig Pen from the Charlie Brown comics.' He glanced back at her with a smile, but her eyes were on Scout again. 'The bits and pieces are called skin rafts, but they're not just made up of skin. Actually they're a mixture of skin cells, the shampoo we use or other hygiene products along with sweat and hormones.'

He bent down alongside Scout and held the bedspread up for Scout to sniff. In between the sheets would be plenty of rafts, uniquely Raelyn's scent, perfectly trapped and secured by the bedspread. As Jason did this, he said to the dog, 'Scout, this is Raelyn.'

In his excitement, Scout nosed the fabric, snorting and sniffing so loudly, Jason avoided looking at Mrs Woodson. Instead, he pulled the sheets back far enough for Scout to get a deep whiff and also smell the girl's pillow. He continued his monologue.

'These skin rafts are what Scout can smell. And he can distinguish between people.'

He started to smooth the bedspread back in place when he noticed a stain on the corner of the pillowcase. Was it a rust-colored stain or had the printed flowers simply bled into each other?

'She may have just run off,' the woman said from behind him. 'That girl never listened to me.'

He looked up and could see her in the mirror on the opposite wall. She was clinging to the dresser like she needed it to keep her balance. Her face looked swollen from crying, but there was something hard and unforgiving in her eyes.

He didn't know what to say. This wasn't part of the job. Families of the victims could muck things up. He needed the basic information but none of the emotional drama. It just messed with a handler's head and ended up running down the leash.

He turned to her as she started to teeter. Jason caught her elbow before she stumbled. He steadied her until she retrieved her balance then he offered to help her down the stairs.

'I'm fine, ' she told him. 'Are we done here?' she asked with a pained look on her face.

She obviously wasn't going to leave him alone in the room no matter how uncomfortable she became. *Not a problem.* Jason didn't want to waste time. As it was, he and Scout only had a few hours of daylight. In Raelyn's open closet, he found a well-worn pair of sneakers. He grabbed one and held it up.

'Do you mind if I take this for Scout?'

'You're going to let him chew on my daughter's shoe?'

'No, absolutely not at all.' He shook his head, wondering if the woman had heard a word he'd said. 'It has Raelyn's scent. I'll use it as a trigger for Scout.'

'Of course, I'm sorry.' She wiped her nose with a tissue. 'It's just so painful to be around her things, imagining what she might be going through right now.'

It wasn't until she turned to lead them out the door that Jason noticed Scout sitting in the middle of the room with his head cocked to one side, watching Mrs Woodson.

Too late.

The dog was already sensing the drama. Jason could only hope it wouldn't be a continuing distraction.

26

Charlotte had no idea how long she had been asleep. Or passed out. It was harder and harder to know the difference. Her stomach told her it was too long. She'd gotten into the habit of eating as little as possible, because food was where Iris usually hid the drugs that played with Charlotte's mind. But hunger pangs threatened to send her stomach into spasm. One lick of her chapped lips and she realized how dry her throat was. Suddenly, she wanted water more than she wanted food.

When Charlotte finally opened her eyes this time, she was surprised to find that she was no longer surrounded by pitch black. The room had a yellow tint. Two lines of sunlight came in from somewhere, and she watched dust motes travel the stream. This was a rare luxury. She hadn't seen sunlight in weeks, maybe a month by her internal clock.

Her body still hurt, and she didn't dare test it, afraid she might find a broken bone. It had happened before.

Stupid girl, she could hear Iris' voice as though the woman were standing in the corner. *You went and broke your arm, didn't you?*

That was years ago. Charlotte was only a girl. She remembered how fierce the pain was. Of course Iris wouldn't take her to a doctor. The woman set Charlotte's arm herself.

Now Charlotte squeezed her eyes shut tight and shook her head. She didn't want to remember. She couldn't afford to remember. The memories only made her feel weak and helpless.

Without lifting her head she turned to look from side to side. She wanted to see her new surroundings, her new prison. She suspected this place would be temporary until Iris had her carted away to wherever the others had been taken.

This was definitely not the basement.

Charlotte didn't recognize the room, and she thought she knew every single room and closet in the Big House. The wallpaper was peeling, a long swatch flapped free. Iris would never allow that.

So this wasn't the Big House.

A glint of silver caught her eyes close to the ceiling. A strand of glittery tinsel with bright green and red balls was strung up along the archway between the two rooms.

Two rooms?

Her pulse started racing, and she strained to listen.

Was there anyone else here? Were they watching her?

She considered calling out, but instead, she swallowed hard only to find that it hurt to swallow. That's when she remembered Iris' beefy fingers clamped around her throat. Charlotte ran her own fingers over the bruised area to make certain nothing was protruding and there were no gaping wounds.

Satisfied that her neck was okay, she turned her head with much effort and some pain, to investigate in the other direction. Her entire body jerked when she saw the man sitting in the corner. He didn't move or respond to her. He just sat there.

She blinked and tried to refocus. Then she wanted to laugh.

Sitting in a rocking chair was a life-sized Santa, dressed in a red suit, complete with belt and boots. His glassy eyes looked very real underneath the Santa hat and full beard.

The Christmas house.

Iris had told someone to take her to the Christmas house.

In Charlotte's fevered delusion, she thought it was some strange metaphor for something sinister. But now she realized Iris' words were literal. She glanced at the tinsel and glass balls. There were more over the boarded windows.

Windows!

But boarded up from the outside. Still, slivers of light streamed in.

She could glimpse the top of a Christmas tree with more glass balls and tinsel and a star on top.

It must have been decorated years ago because Charlotte could see the dust and spider webs. Whoever lived here, whoever had decorated this house, was long gone.

27

Omaha, Nebraska

'Grace and I are going with you,' Creed said after Maggie explained what she had planned.

'That's not a good idea.'

'Finding Brodie is one of the reasons I started a K9 business.'

'This is different.'

'It's not different. Every time I search for a missing girl or a young woman or whenever we've recovered remains, I've always been thinking about Brodie. That it could be her.'

'Ryder, I know—'

'No, you don't know.' He wiped a hand over his jaw as if checking for remnants of the cheeseburger, but he really wanted to rub the emotion from his face. It was too late, and he could feel his pulse already racing.

'People don't understand when I say this,' he tried to choose the right words. 'It probably sounds heartless, but it would be better to find her remains than to find nothing. Not knowing whether she's alive or dead, that's the toughest part. Hanging onto a thread of hope when you have no idea whether there's anything to hope for. Everyone tells you to move on. Find closure. But there is no closure without finding her. If she's dead, so be it. I just want to bring her home. Then I'll know there's nothing more I can do for her.'

When he looked over at Maggie he caught her wiping at her eyes. The tough-as-nails agent didn't easily show her emotion. But he didn't say any of this to play to her emotions.

'My mother agreed to send me some of Brodie's personal items. I brought a DNA swab from her.'

'Sounds like you came prepared.'

'It'd be a relief if this was the end of the line.'

'Ryder, I know you're a professional. You wouldn't purposely risk a search and recovery. You think you've handled this in the past because you're always thinking the next victim you find might be Brodie. But this is different. It's very likely one of these bodies *is* Brodie. You have no idea how that will affect you. And how much it might affect the entire search effort.'

He looked away and shook his head. He couldn't believe she didn't get it.

'So you're simply worried that I might screw up your expedition,' he said.

'That's not fair.'

He could hear the hurt in her voice, but he didn't glance back. Instead, he stayed by the window and looked down at the street below.

'You know having a family member along isn't a good idea,' she continued. 'You know that probably better than anyone. You shouldn't have come here presuming that you could insert yourself into this investigation.'

He stared out the window, giving her his back. He didn't dare look down at Grace. He could feel her eyes on him as she stood at his feet. He was beyond exhausted, and maybe Maggie was right. Maybe it was wrong for him to think he could drive all this way and automatically be included.

Creed and Hannah had taken on hundreds of cases over the

last seven years. In many of those, Creed had put the missing and the lost ahead of himself – and in some instances – ahead of his dogs. The explosion site he'd just worked was a prime example. He'd pushed Bolo at the risk of cutting the dog's pads. He'd pushed himself to exhaustion. And he'd done so because as long as there might be just one person alive in the rubble, he couldn't leave. At least not, until another dog and handler team arrived to replace them.

He turned slowly around then waited for Maggie to meet his eyes, though he could see she wasn't comfortable doing so.

'Last spring you asked me for a favor. I agreed even when I realized my dogs might be at risk of catching a deadly virus. I've never been the type to call in favors, but if that's what it takes then I will. I'm asking you as a favor, Maggie. I want to be a part of this search. I *need* to be a part of it. Don't deny me the opportunity to bring my sister home.'

He felt his heart banging in his chest, but he held her eyes. She could send him home. She might even deny him access to any and all information. It wouldn't be the first time someone he cared about and respected would betray him. He'd lived with the simple fact that his own mother would rather pretend he didn't exist than deal with losing him. If this cost him his friendship with Maggie then perhaps there was no friendship to begin with.

She was the first to break eye contact, rubbing her hands over her face in a gesture of pure exasperation. Then suddenly, she began stacking items back in their place, folding the map and slipping it into a portfolio. She resealed Brodie's book and used a Sharpie to mark the evidence label. She picked up their empty food wrappers, stuffing them into the greasy paper bag and tossing it into the trash.

Then finally, she looked back at him, now glancing down at Grace as well.

'Okay,' she said. 'But if it gets to be too much for you, you need to be straight with me. You need to tell me. That's the deal breaker.'

'Absolutely,' he said with a nod, all the while realizing that she still didn't understand. It had nothing to do with how difficult it was for him. This wasn't about him. But rather than argue, he accepted her terms.

'So where are you and Grace staying?'

'I guess I hadn't thought that far in advance.'

She pulled her cell phone out of her pocket and started scrolling for a number.

'I'm down in the Old Market at the Embassy Suites. I'm pretty sure they allow service dogs. Their suites have refrigerators, a wet bar, and microwaves.'

Before he could remind her that he and Grace had slept on a cot or even a sleeping bag on the floor at disaster sites, she was on the line making sure they had a room for him and Grace, including extra bottles of water.

Maggie O'Dell was definitely an enigma. He wondered, and not for the first time, if he'd ever figure the woman out.

28

Santa Rosa County, Florida

Jason was told the trail Raelyn used to go to her friend's house started in back of the Woodsons' property, but he and Scout barely stepped into the backyard when Scout started chasing his tail. The dog had been cooped up too long. He was bored.

'Scout,' Jason tried to keep the embarrassment out of his voice. Sheriff Norwich and Mrs Woodson were only ten feet behind them.

He gave a tug at the leash and tapped his left fist against his chest. Scout stopped in mid spin and his eyes flew to Jason's fist, now watching to see if the hand went anywhere near his rope toy. But instead of the toy, Jason pulled out the teenager's worn sneaker and offered it for Scout to sniff.

'Raelyn,' Jason said while the dog dipped his twitching nose into the shoe. When Jason didn't take it away, Scout shoved his nose even deeper into the toe area.

Jason knew he could call the scent just about anything as long as he communicated to Scout it was what he wanted him to find. Creed had them use the word 'fish' for drugs. It made it easier calling out, 'go find fish,' in a busy airport than alerting drug dealers by using the word 'drugs.' But Creed had also taught Jason it was best to call the scent of a missing person by the person's name. Especially a child. That way if there was even the slightest chance that Raelyn was within earshot, but was lost or injured, she might hear Jason calling her name whenever he asked Scout to find her.

'Raelyn. Find Raelyn,' he told Scout as he showed the dog the shoe.

This time, Scout started out with his nose poking the air. Jason kept him restrained. After the bear incident he wasn't letting the dog go off leash into the forest. But instead of running to the tree line and the trampled area where the trail began, Scout headed for a small shed at the corner of the yard. The dog stopped and bobbed his head then double-backed to a tree. Jason accommodated him, keeping pace. He was spending too much time sniffing the base of the tree, and Jason worried his dog was more interested in another dog's piss than he was in Raelyn.

'Scout,' he reminded him. 'Find Raelyn.'

The dog gave what sounded to Jason like a resentful snort. Then he peed on the tree and continued on to the shed. His nose was twitching, his breathing growing more rapid. He barreled to the shed door, stopped and pawed at it.

'What's in here?' Jason asked glancing over his shoulder and disappointed to see just how close Mrs Woodson and Norwich were following.

'Nothing really,' Mrs Woodson told him, her arms crossed over her chest as though she was chilled. Even with the sun dipping toward the horizon, the air was still warm and clammy.

'Raelyn ever come out here?' Jason was watching Scout. The dog was tugging at the end of the leash. He looked back at Jason then tapped his paw against the door like he didn't think Jason was paying attention.

'I guess I've caught her out here, sneaking a smoke.'

'Mind if I take a look?'

'There's nothing there. My ex-husband used this old shed for his tools and the mower. Oh, and there's an old deep freezer with packages of fish. That man loved to fish but he didn't like eating it much.'

Jason twirled the nylon leash around his wrist, cinching Scout close to his side as he opened the door.

Immediately, he heard the hum of the freezer, an old beat-up chest that took up one side of the shed. There was a padlock on the latch. In front of the freezer was a rusted-out mower and a wheelbarrow with dirt still in it. On the wooden bench along the other side was mostly discarded fishing equipment.

'I've been meaning to get rid of that old thing,' Mrs Woodson said, meaning the freezer, but Jason thought it sounded like she might still be talking about the ex-husband. 'I made him put a lock on it. We have little kids in this neighborhood.'

'I need you both to move back at least twenty feet,' Jason told the pair. He didn't want them distracting Scout. When he didn't hear any retreating steps behind him, he shot a look at Norwich.

'We need to give the dog some room to work,' the sheriff told Mrs Woodson.

Jason still waited a minute then let out some of Scout's leash, letting the dog bound into the shed. It was a small area with a low ceiling and unfinished beamed walls. Scout's nails clicked on the concrete floor. His nose was going crazy, surfing over the wheelbarrow and under the old mower. He pawed at the side of the freezer.

'Come on. There's nothing here.'

Jason pulled on Scout's leash. When the dog didn't budge, Jason reached down and grabbed the handle on Scout's harness and gave a tug. Scout was still sniffing, but now he eye-rolled back to see if Jason had his rope toy for him.

'Come on,' Jason told him, leading him out the door.

They hadn't even started, and Jason was already regretting using those stupid treats for rewards. He should have listened to Creed the first time, and he could hear his mentor clearly.

If you use food as a reward, don't be surprised when your dog alerts to spoiled scraps or discarded food containers along the trail.

Or even a chest freezer filled with frozen fish.

29

The breeze ruffled Jason's hair. It was coming towards them. A lucky break. Those scent rafts he was trying to tell Mrs Woodson about would be riding on the air currents. He imagined them as millions of fluffy dandelion seeds. The light wind would bring them to Scout's nose. The heavier rafts would have already fallen to the ground, catching on the shrubs and settling into the pine needles. The temperature started to cool and that was good, too. Cool air falls like water flowing downhill. It'd bring the scent closer to Scout.

All the conditions were in their favor and yet, twenty minutes into the search they hadn't found anything but a few cigarette butts. Scout wasn't interested in any of those. Instead, the dog shifted from side to side, impatiently waiting for Jason to bag them.

As soon as he was finished, Scout darted off again, hot-dogging in between the trees and straining at the end of the leash. Jason could barely keep up with him. Finally, he slowed to a more manageable trot. He was still throwing his head one way then another. His nose poked the air then dipped down into the shrubs.

Jason checked his watch. Scenting dogs would breathe 140 to 200 times a minute compared to thirty times a minute when the dog was on a regular walk. And all that sniffing wasn't just breathing. The dog would take in air and send it in different directions, filtering and separating to identify the variety of scents.

'Time to take a break, Scout.'

The dog was still yanking to go forward until he saw the water bottle Jason pulled from the daypack. Jason weaved the handle of the leash up over his boot and wrapped the nylon tightly around his ankle. He didn't trust his prosthetic hand to hold on to the dog while he used his other hand to get Scout's collapsible bowl out of the pack.

While Scout lapped water, Jason let his eyes skim over the surrounding woods. Only now, did he notice that his jaw had been clamped tight and all his nerves seemed to be dancing on high alert. Shadows were growing longer and he found himself searching each of them for another bear. He hadn't thought about it until now, but what if Raelyn had run into a bear on this trail? Creed said they rarely attacked people, but rarely certainly didn't mean never.

He cast aside the thought. If anything like that had happened, Scout would have bee-lined to the attack site. As it was, the dog seemed to be having a tough time getting a bead on anything that could be remotely Raelyn's scent. Which was strange if the girl had been on this path in the last day or even two days.

Inside the forest, the last of the sunlight squeezed between the tree trunks, coming in at a slant. Jason estimated they had another thirty minutes. He pulled out Raelyn's shoe, again, and watched Scout's reaction. The dog sat down and kept his eyes on the sneaker. For a brief moment, Jason's stomach did a flip when he thought Scout was looking at the shoe like he expected Jason to toss it for a game of fetch.

'Scout, find Raelyn,' he told the dog in a steady, calm voice despite tamping down the acid creeping up from his stomach.

Scout got to his feet, but he wasn't in a hurry. In fact, he stayed put and his paws shuffled like he was marching in place while he looked around. There were no head jerks. No pokes or ducks. His movements looked measured and thoughtful. None of his usual jackass motions. Then he tilted his head and did his signature eye-roll to look back and up at Jason. His nose twitched, but with less enthusiasm. It was as if the dog was trying to tell him there was nothing here.

Jason scanned the surrounding woods, again, searching to see if the ground foliage had been disturbed or the lower hanging twigs broken. If Raelyn ventured off the trail, her scent cone would be a much larger swatch. And if she left the trail early on, they may have passed over and out of the targeted area.

Now, he was second-guessing himself. Was it possible he'd guided Scout down the trail and missed the dog trying to steer him into the woods? Ideally, he'd let the dog off the leash, but he couldn't risk it. No way did he want to even think about Scout coming up on a bear again.

He looked down at Scout and the dog was watching him, waiting for more instructions. The working relationship of dog and handler was complicated to Jason. They were expected to be a team, yet the dog's nose worked independently. For the dog, it was one big game of fetch that they played together, but it was up to the handler to make sure they were communicating and staying on track. Jason had learned that a dog could be trained to find just about any scent, but the handler needed to queue the dog with hand signals, choice words and even different harnesses or leashes.

But Jason was also aware that a handler could easily get

in the way by showing too much interest in something that wasn't important. No matter how well trained the dog was, he still wanted to please his handler.

Jason held up the shoe, but now he turned around to face the trail where they'd just come from.

'Scout, find Raelyn.'

This time, Scout head-butted Jason's thigh and his eyes darted to the daypack.

Jason bit back a curse and the acid found its way up into his throat. He'd screwed up big time. Not only had he muscled his dog away from the scent cone, but now, his bored partner wanted his rope toy.

30

Florida Panhandle

Olivia tapped the GPS screen in her Lexus' dashboard. She had a pain in her neck from straining to see the map and watch the road. For five hours, the automated voice had guided her, telling her to take the next right then the next left, but after leaving the interstate the roads continued to grow narrower and less traveled. The latest instruction had landed her on a gravel road. Every ping against the car's underside made her wince. There were no shoulders, so she kept the vehicle in the middle, staying away from the deep gashed ditches on both sides.

She could still hear Deena lecturing her. When in the world had she started to allow a twenty something-year-old to tell her what she could or couldn't do? Deena's rants had only provoked Olivia to go forward with her plan, despite all the signs telling her what a bad idea it was.

She told her crew that she'd be taking the next several days off. Truth was, she hadn't taken a day off in forever, and they always filmed well in advance. Right now, they were a week out. Worse case scenario, they could run a few repeats. The world would not come crashing down without a new episode of *Life in Style with Olivia James*.

She glanced at the box sitting on the passenger seat. It had accompanied her like a silent guest guarding its precious secrets. She used to know every single item inside. Once upon a time, she had wrapped each carefully into plastic bags that remained sealed despite how many times she had taken them out of the box and let her fingers absorb the memories. This box was all she had left of her little girl. Protecting it, treasuring it, had become an obsession.

She absolutely couldn't bear to wrap it up and put it in the mail. What if it didn't make it to the destination? What if it got lost? What if she never saw it ever again? And yet, she had promised Ryder.

So here she was in the Panhandle of Florida. She was within the last miles of delivering the box herself to the address on the business card he had left with her. The sun had set and the car's headlights were showing her an unfamiliar backwoods landscape that made her more uncomfortable than she expected. She wasn't used to driving outside of the city. No streetlights. Very few signs. If not for the GPS system, she would have been lost miles ago.

'*Turn right*,' the voice startled Olivia. '*And you have reached your destination.*'

How was that possible?

She stopped at the end of a long driveway. From this vantage point, Olivia couldn't imagine what was on the other side of these woods. Through the trees she could barely see the roof of a building.

News articles hinted at the scope of the facility Ryder had created. They said his business was 'a multi-million dollar operation' that included 'a fifty-acre training campus'. But none of the reporters had been allowed on the property, and there were no photographs. She wasn't surprised that Ryder went to such lengths to protect his privacy, especially after a childhood that had ended up in the public's eye through most of his teenaged years.

In the days and weeks right after Brodie disappeared, Olivia wouldn't let Ryder out of her sight, and she didn't dare leave him with his father. After dragging him out of school one too many times, she figured out what she needed to do to home-school him. There were some nights that relearning algebra, in order to teach her son, was one of the few things that kept her from completely losing her mind. But in her efforts to pro-tect him, she had kept him from other important things – like having friends.

Seeing him that morning made her realize that her son had become an incredible young man. And he had done it without her help or influence for over almost a decade. How could she have allowed that much time to go by? Somehow she had managed to lose a daughter and throw away a son.

Now, Olivia was curious to learn what kind of life Ryder had constructed for himself. Slowly, she started down the winding driveway. Her entire body perched forward on the edge of the seat, so that the steering wheel – with her fingers clenching tightly around it – was practically against her chest.

In the dim light of dusk, the stretch of road seemed to last forever before she finally saw lights in the windows of a lovely old colonial-style house. Other buildings began revealing themselves as she drove up to the front door. Her legs threat-ened to not hold her as she made her way out of the vehicle and around to the passenger door. She gathered the box into her arms as though it were a sleeping toddler. Before she got to the front door, it opened. In the doorway stood a tall black woman with shoulder-length hair, bright intelligent eyes and a lovely Rubenesque figure.

'May I help you?' she asked.

'You must be Hannah.'

'That's right.'

'I'm sorry,' Olivia said. 'I know you have no idea who I am.'

That's when the woman's eyes grew wide with recognition as she said, 'Oh, I know who you are. You're Olivia James.'

'That's right.'

'I just have no idea why you're here.'

'Ryder wanted Brodie's things.' Olivia lifted the box to show the woman. 'I couldn't bear to put this in the mail, so I decided to deliver it myself.'

Hannah looked at her then the box and back at Olivia as she tried to process the information. That's when it occurred to Olivia that Ryder hadn't told his business partner. The realization and the weight of it felt like a slap in the face. What in the world had she expected? Of course he hadn't told her.

'I'm Ryder's mother,' Olivia finally said.

31

Omaha, Nebraska

'So this is the guy?' Creed examined the photo Maggie handed him.

He'd just unloaded his gear in the hotel suite when Maggie showed up at his door with coffee for him and a Diet Pepsi for herself. Her room was on the same floor but on the other side of the atrium.

Creed was dead tired, but he was the one who insisted on hearing anything and everything she was willing to share. To Creed's surprise, she had brought along her messenger bag. So while Grace lounged on the king-size bed and was checking out the view from the third-story window, Creed and Maggie sat at the table.

'Understand that Elijah Dunn might not know anything about Brodie,' Maggie told him.

'Then how did he end up with the Polaroid *and* her book?'

'I'm new to this trafficking stuff. The only reason I'm here is because they needed a profile to narrow down their search efforts. Dunn hadn't been someone they were seriously looking at until recently. They think he might simply be a link to a much bigger network.'

'But the photo and the book were found in his house.'

'On his property. But his farmhouse could be a temporary holding station.'

'Holding station?'

She wouldn't meet his eyes. She busied her hands taking items out of her messenger bag, setting them on the table and sorting through them like she was looking for something in particular.

'Do you remember two summers ago,' Creed said, 'when Hannah and I rescued that young girl who was being used as a drug mule?'

The girl named Amanda had sought out Creed and Grace at the Atlanta Airport, begging him, pleading with him to help her.

'And the cartel ordered hits on both of you,' Maggie reminded him.

Creed winced from the memory of Hannah in that hospital bed, tubes and machines keeping her alive. It was bad enough that Creed had stolen away Amanda, but he'd also screwed the cartel out of another delivery.

Choque Azul, the Colombian cartel, had been working to establish a new route up through the Gulf of Mexico. They used commercial fishing boats, stashing bags of cocaine under boatloads of mahi-mahi. Creed and Grace interrupted a delivery, but it wasn't drugs that Grace had sniffed out. There were young children hidden under the floorboards. Some of them were runaways, but others had been snatched from truck stops and rest areas.

'Those kids Grace found were being trafficked from the States to Colombia,' Creed said. 'That's my only experience with human trafficking. But you forget that I'm a Marine. I spent several eventful years in Afghanistan. And I've seen hundreds of different ways that human beings treat other human beings. Grace and I have found and seen things that nobody should see. But you already know that.'

'Of course.'

'Then why are you still handling me with kid gloves?'

'Okay, you're right. I'm sorry.' She held up her hands in surrender.

She took a sip from the Diet Pepsi then continued. 'One of the things that piqued our interest was how many miles Eli Dunn travels, oftentimes across country. The guy doesn't appear to have any gainful employment, and we don't believe he's dealing drugs. Or if he is, he hasn't been caught and none were recovered on his property. But we also didn't find anyone at Dunn's house except for a teenage boy. He used him as a decoy. Sent him running out the front door while Dunn tried to escape out the back.'

'So there wasn't anyone else? What does that mean?'

'He knew we were coming. And he knew far enough in advance that he could transfer any others he was keeping there. The boy told Pakula there were others.'

'Can he identify them?'

She shook her head. 'Sounds like they were kept separate. All the rooms in Dunn's house had deadbolts that locked from the outside. The entire place looked like he tried to scrub it down.'

'So they didn't find any evidence of other victims?'

'Even if they do, it'll be difficult to match. Most missing persons aren't in CODIS.'

Creed reached over to his duffle bag and unzipped an inside pocket. He took out the small sterile package and laid it in the middle of the table.

'My mother's DNA swabs.' He moved the package closer to

Maggie, but held on to it. 'Is there any way . . .' It was a lot to ask after pushing her to allow him on the recovery team.

Maggie laid her hand over his. 'Of course,' she told him. 'The techs will be glad to have anything to test against what they've found.' She kept her hand over his. 'There's something else.' She was watching him now, measuring his reaction. 'The CSU team found some bones in a backyard firepit. It'll be a while before we get the results back, but there's a good chance they're human remains.'

He nodded.

'Where did you find the photo?'

'Inside what must have been his makeshift office. He had a wall of photographs.'

She'd paused and stared down at the table. When she looked back up at him and continued, her voice was barely above a whisper, 'There were so many of them they over-lapped each other.'

'Victims he's helped traffick?'

'I think so. Some that he claims he helped bury.'

'Helped? He's clever,' Creed said.

Maggie's phone started to ring, and she pulled her hand away from his to grab the phone.

'It's Detective Pakula,' she told him. 'He's heading the local task force. He's also putting together the search and recovery team.'

She answered without standing or leaving for privacy, so Creed stayed put, too.

'Tell me what you know.'

Creed watched her nod. She grabbed one of her notepads and jotted something down.

'How long before we can get a certified diver?' she asked.

'I'm a certified diver,' Creed interrupted.

'Hold on a minute,' she told Pakula.

Her eyes met Creed's, and in an instant he saw the concern and hesitation before she neatly blinked it away. He thought she was about to tell him 'no'.

Instead, she said, 'One of the bodies is in a lake. It's the first site Dunn's identified. That's where we want to start tomorrow, but they can't get a diver until the next day.'

'Grace and I have done water searches. We'll need a boat if it's a big lake.'

To Pakula, she asked, 'How big is the lake?' She held the phone away and told Creed, 'It's over 600 acres.'

'Definitely need a boat then,' he told her. 'I have gear in my Jeep, but I'd need a tank.'

She was staring at him. He didn't think he could hear Pakula's voice, so she wasn't just listening, she was thinking, debating, comtemplating. Finally she said to the detective, 'Remember the K9 team I told you about? He and his dog have done water searches, and he's a certified diver. We'll need a tank for him and a boat.'

Creed could hear the man's voice but couldn't make out his words. Pakula had asked her something, and she met Creed's eyes. Again, he saw the hesitation then she looked away and asked Pakula, 'What about Lucy? Will they let us use her?'

In the middle of the table, Creed's cell phone started ringing. He glanced at it and saw that it was Jason. He picked up the phone and stepped into the bedroom area, so he wouldn't be talking over Maggie. Grace was stretched out and pretending to be asleep, but one eye peeked at him.

'Hey Jason.'

'I think I screwed up really bad.'

32

'Slow down,' Creed told him. The kid sounded panicked. 'What do you mean, you screwed up?'

'A girl went missing from one of those nice residential areas off Garcon Point. She took a trail from her house to a friend's on the other side of the forest. That was yesterday. The mother only found out this afternoon that the girl didn't make it to the friend's house. Sounds like the friend wasn't even expecting her.'

'How long's the trail?' Creed asked.

'Do you know the area? Probably about five miles south of Mary Kitchens Road. On the map it's called Yellow River Marsh Preserve State Park.'

'Okay, yeah, I know the area. That's a big swatch of land to cover.'

'It's a helluva a big swatch. She must of left the trail at some point. Scout seemed to have a scent when we started and now ... nothing. I've taken him back to start over, and he's just looking at me like I'm crazy. I don't know what to do.'

'First off, calm down. Where are you?'

'We're in the middle of the son of bitchin' forest, and it's getting dark.'

'You need to head back.'

'But the little girl—'

'You know I don't like having dogs out after dark,' Creed

told him, doing Jason a favor and taking the decision away from him.

'What if she's hurt?'

'Scout would have found her.'

'How can you be so sure of that?'

Creed hated hearing the uncertainty in Jason's voice, because he knew it wasn't Scout that Jason had lost faith in. It was himself.

'Look, it's not unusual for a dog to come up empty. Same thing with false alerts. It happens. It happens a lot more than handlers are willing to admit. But from my personal experience, a good portion of those incidents are because a handler didn't read their dog correctly.'

'That's what I'm telling you. I screwed up. Maybe I didn't give him enough time in her room. I took one of her shoes, and he seemed to really get it. But then, nothing.'

'Scout is one of the most honest dogs in our kennel,' Creed said. 'He hasn't had any of the life experiences that our rescues have had. He's never had to fight or scrap for food. He's never lived out on the streets and gone hungry. I think he's being honest about his alert. You need to trust your dog.'

'How can I trust him if I screwed up?'

'Jason, you're not listening. If Scout didn't find anything on that trail, it could be because the girl didn't take the trail.'

He waited out Jason's silence, listened to the deep breaths without interrupting.

'You really think she's not here?' he finally asked.

'If you want to start the search fresh again, you need to wait for first sunlight tomorrow. Take Scout home. You both need to get some rest.'

'Okay.'

'Sometimes we don't find them,' Creed said. It was one of the hardest lessons he had learned early on. 'You can't let it defeat you. And you can't let it defeat your dog. Go on home.'

'Okay.'

'Jason, one other thing.'

'Yeah?'

'Play with Scout for a bit.'

'You sure? He didn't find anything.'

'Don't let him have his rope toy reward, but find another way to play with him.'

'Okay.'

Creed barely told Jason goodbye and another call came in. He glanced at the caller ID. It was Hannah. He thought she might be worried about Jason.

'Hey, Hannah.'

'Don't hey me. Why didn't you tell me your mother is Olivia James?'

It wasn't at all what he expected.

'I didn't think it was important,' he told her. 'How did you find out?'

'She's here.'

'What do you mean?'

'She didn't feel comfortable sending Brodie's things so she brought them down herself.'

'I had no idea she'd do something like that. Tell her she doesn't need to send them. We'll use her DNA sample for now. Hannah, I'm really sorry she showed up like that.'

'Don't be sorry. I already told her she's not leaving until I get her gumbo recipe.'

Creed shook his head and smiled. He was still smiling when

he hung up and went back into the other room. The smile slid off as soon as he saw the grimace on Maggie's face.

'What's wrong?'

She held up a notecard pinched carefully between her thumb and index finger. The envelope it had come from sat in the middle of the table.

'When I was packing up my things I remembered this. The front desk handed it to me when we came in earlier. I didn't give it too much thought.'

'What is it?'

She placed it on the table and rummaged through her messenger bag until she pulled out a package of latex gloves. Creed came around behind her chair while she snapped the gloves on.

The small notecard actually had *thank you* foil-stamped on the front. It looked like one of those that came in a package of twelve. Maggie opened it, still careful where she touched the corners.

The lettering was bold and the use of a marker made it stand out even more. There was no punctuation. Only two lines. Six words total.

RELEASE DUNN
OR BURN IN HELL

'Who would have guessed,' Maggie said, much too casual, 'that Eli Dunn would have a fan base.'

33

It was getting dark again, but the good news was that Charlotte was starting to feel more clearheaded. The drugs were wearing off. But that also meant the pain throughout her body would have no buffer. She rolled over onto her side and realized she had wet herself.

Iris would be so angry.

But Iris wasn't here.

Then Charlotte wanted to laugh. If she wet herself maybe she wasn't as dehydrated as she thought she was.

Her vision was clear, too, despite the dim light inside. She'd been left in the dark so often her eyes seemed to adjust to the least amount of light. She used her hands to push off the floor and sit up. She waited for the spinning sensation. She prepared herself for the rooms to start twirling.

But they didn't move.

She sat still and listened. She tucked a tangle of long hair behind her ear and cocked her head to the side. She expected a response to her movement.

Was anyone in the house watching her?

Charlotte had spent too many years listening in the pitch dark to not hear anything, no matter how quiet. Without the dulling effect of the drugs, she'd be able to hear someone breathing.

Her eyes darted to the Santa mannequin in the rocking

chair. She could see a tiny glint from the glasses on his nose. She could see the outline of the two rooms and an open doorway to another part of the house.

And then she heard it.

A faint scratching. It sounded like it was coming from the room beyond the doorway.

She squinted, trying to see into the shadows.

Movement!

A skitter across the floor, like nails trying to gain traction.

But Charlotte didn't flinch. Her pulse began to race. She wasn't used to the flutter of blood rushing in her ears. Usually the drugs dulled her body's response. Still, she didn't jerk away. She had learned to keep her body motionless, her breathing calm and steady. A lesson she had learned years ago. If Iris couldn't hear or see her in the dark, she'd have to switch on a light.

Darkness was one of Iris' cruelest punishments until Charlotte learned to cope without light. In the beginning, Iris had taken away books and magazines, because she knew Charlotte loved to read. But then Iris kept finding her with discarded empty boxes of detergent, labels from paint cans or an old furnace manual. When she realized Charlotte would read anything she could get her hands on, that's when Iris began leaving her in the dark.

Learning how to deal with darkness, however, wasn't the most difficult part of that lesson. Fending off the creatures that thrived in dark, damp places was worse. Charlotte had learned how to keep her body completely still while a rat sniffed her flesh trying to decide whether Charlotte was prey worthy of a bite.

Another scratch-scratch. It was coming from the room

beyond the doorway. Was it possible whoever it was – or whatever it was – hadn't heard or smelled Charlotte?

Impossible.

Charlotte knew she smelled bad. It was only a matter of time before the intruder got bored in that room and ventured out to this area.

Her eyes darted around without moving her head. She searched for something to use to defend herself. The best weapon was something that extended her arm and fit comfortably in her small hand. Heavy, but not so heavy that she couldn't swing it. There was a lamp on one of the dusty side tables. Spider webs laced over the shade, but the base looked like it might be metal.

Now that Charlotte's mind wasn't obstructed by drugs, she needed to make the rest of her body work before she could crawl to her feet. Bare feet. She couldn't remember the last time she wore shoes. She had found an old pair of socks once and coveted them, stashing and hiding them until Iris discovered them.

Charlotte pressed her hands together, intertwined and flexed her fingers, all the while keeping quiet. Satisfied when she didn't feel any pain in her hands, she ran them over her feet. The right ankle hurt but it wasn't swollen. There was a cut on the bottom of the foot. She felt a bruise on her hip. The right side must have taken the brunt of her fall down the basement stairs.

Her oversized T-shirt smelled bad but it didn't appear to be torn. Otherwise, all she wore were underpants, but those were now urine soaked. None of that mattered. She hated that her hair was long, tangled and dirty more than she cared what she was wearing. She'd give anything for pants and long sleeves to cover her wounds and give them a chance to heal, protecting them from scraping open again and again.

Both her knees were skinned raw. She didn't need to check her elbows. They were always scraped and scabbed in a perpetual cycle that never healed. That's why she tried so hard to protect her feet. On hands and knees, or worse, on elbows and knees, was a slow way to travel. When her feet were in good shape she was quick. She could outmaneuver Iris and run so fast, the woman couldn't catch her.

Until the day Iris sent the dogs after her.

She shook her head. She didn't want to remember the fangs clamped around her ankle and yet, once again, her fingers shot to the area and wrapped around it as if to protect it. That was the ankle that hurt. It was the ankle Iris had strapped the tracker onto. The skin had barely healed from the dog bite, and Iris pulled the strap tight, locking it in place. She told Charlotte she would never be out of her sight no matter how fast or how far she tried to run.

Now Charlotte felt a sinking feeling. The tracker was still on her ankle. She could see the tiny green light. Why hadn't Iris removed the tracker?

Her eyes scanned the shadows, up and down. She strained to listen. The sound had quieted. She tested her feet while holding onto the side table. It surprised her how strong she felt. Still, she gripped the edge of the table.

A crash came from the other room.

Something had fallen or was thrown, and this time Charlotte jerked to attention. She reached for the lamp and ripped off the shade in one swipe. She tiptoed toward the sound, acutely aware of too many distractions, too many sensations overwhelming her senses. There was carpeting beneath her feet. Moonlight streamed through the boarded windows. Her hair stuck to her forehead and snaked around the back of her sweaty neck.

As she drew closer to the doorway she saw something run across the floor in the next room. She heard claws on a hard surface floor and felt her stomach clench. Still, she tiptoed forward, holding the lamp as a weapon and peeking around the doorframe until she could see inside the room.

Moonlight washed across the countertops of the kitchen. It was coming in a small window high above the sink. Too high to look out but not boarded up. Two brown paper bags were pushed over on their sides. Boxes and packages, apples and bananas spilled out of them onto the counters. There was a stack of water bottles next to the bags. Several had been toppled over.

Charlotte's mouth watered at the sight in front of her. It took every ounce of control to stop herself from running and ripping the cap from a water bottle. Even her stomach threatened to spasm, again. But she stood stock-still, expecting to see someone watching from the shadows. Her eyes darted to every corner, scanning the appliances, the table and chairs. Certainly, whoever left this bounty of food would be waiting to see if they had tricked her. Why bring it and scatter it all over if not to tempt and tease her?

But while her eyes examined all the places she expected someone to hide, she had forgotten about the floor. That's when she felt the fur rub against the back of her legs. Her breath caught in her throat, making her gasp out loud before she could control it. Without moving anything but her head and eyes, she glanced down just in time to see the kitten turn and rub the length of her small body against the front of Charlotte's legs.

34

Omaha, Nebraska

Maggie left Creed and Grace. She had sealed the note and envelope appropriately to hand off to the Douglas County Crime Lab. She stopped back at the hotel's reception desk, but the clerk who gave her the notecard hadn't been on duty when it arrived. That clerk would be back in the morning.

Maggie had had her share of ominous notes delivered in a variety of fashions. This was tame by comparison. But it was always an interesting development when something struck a nerve and propelled someone to threaten law enforcement officers. In her mind, she was already conjuring up a profile for Eli Dunn's vengeful messenger.

Now, back in her own suite, she stood against the door and released a long sigh.

Be careful what you wish for, was something her friend, Dr Gwen Patterson said often. It certainly applied in the case of Eli Dunn. She had wanted to push the man into making a deal and telling his secrets. What good were those secrets if he took every last one with him to prison? But of course, things never played out quite as planned.

She checked her voice messages and scrolled through her texts. Everything seemed to be ready for tomorrow morning.

Pieces were in place, but something nagged at her. Something didn't feel right.

It was Creed and Grace.

She was feeling overly protective. But that wasn't all she was feeling. From the minute he walked into the conference room back at police headquarters it was as if all her nerve ends had been turned on. There was undeniable electricity between them that always took her off guard. Those indigo blue eyes against his tanned skin, that carefully manicured bristled jaw, the subtle smile that started in his eyes then hitched up the corner of his mouth. There was a quiet confidence like he simply didn't care what others thought of him. He had an unsettling affect on her, and yet, he was one of the few people she trusted to not hurt her. Beneath his handsome, rugged exterior was a heart of a rescuer.

It was late. An hour later on the East Coast, and she scrolled until she found her friend's number. She hesitated with her finger over the CALL button then tapped it anyway.

Gwen answered on the third ring.

'Sorry to call so late,' she said in place of a greeting.

'Not a problem. R.J. and I were just having a glass of brandy.'

'Brandy?'

Maggie tried to imagine R.J. Tully sipping brandy. He was her sometimes partner and Gwen's significant other. In Maggie's small repertoire of trusted friends, Tully came very close to the top. Together they'd worked some of the most difficult cases of their careers. Once upon a time she'd rescued him on that scavenger hunt in Blackwater River State Park. He was brave, principled and honest, but Maggie had witnessed the man eat a stale honey bun from a hotel vending machine.

Tully also considered pork rinds an appropriate serving of protein. So she was having a difficult time imagining him sipping brandy.

'We're celebrating,' Gwen told her. 'I'm one year cancer free.'

'Oh, Gwen, that's fantastic!' Watching her friend battle breast cancer had been one of the scariest things Maggie had experienced.

'What's going on?' Gwen asked, cutting to the chase, not because she wanted to get back to her celebration, but because the woman had a keen sense of detecting when something was wrong. There was fifteen years between the two women and sometimes Gwen's maternal instincts toward Maggie came to the surface.

Gwen was the one who convinced Maggie to tell Creed about the Polaroid.

'Remember you said I needed to let Creed know and make his own decision?'

'Sure.'

'I did.'

'Good. I really believe he deserves to know.'

'He's here. He and Grace showed up, and he wants to be a part of the search and recovery for the victims.'

'And you're thinking he's too close to the subject matter to do that?'

'Of course I'm thinking that. Wouldn't you be?'

'From what you told me about Ryder Creed, he's been doing exactly this for the last . . . what? Seven years?'

'This is different.'

'Why?'

'Because there's a good chance Brodie is one of these victims.'

'But, Maggie,' Gwen said in her calm and steady voice. 'He believes she could be one of the victims. That's exactly why he's there.'

Maggie let the silence hang between them no matter how uncomfortable. She had been pacing, and now she sat down on the sofa.

'Maggie,' Gwen said softly. 'Could the problem be that you're realizing that you care about him much more than you thought?'

'Ben and I—'

'No, don't use Ben to weigh your feelings for Ryder. You've spent your career learning to compartmentalize your emotions. Separate the feelings you have for both of these men. How you feel about one should have nothing to do with your feelings for the other.'

More silence.

Maggie leaned back, but the sofa cushions were stiff and unyielding.

'I hate it when you make so much sense,' she finally told Gwen.

'It's probably the brandy. Now tell me everything else that's going on.'

But before she could start filling Gwen in, she had another call.

'I have to take this other call,' she told her friend and they exchanged quick goodbyes.

'Lucy,' Maggie said, clicking over. 'Please tell me you're able to join me on this scavenger hunt.'

Maggie had met the retired medical examiner on one of her previous trips to Nebraska. At the time, the county sheriff had prefaced Maggie's introduction to Lucy Coy by calling her 'that crazy old Indian woman' who practiced 'black magic.' But Maggie's first impression of Lucy included absolutely nothing that would come close to including the words 'old' or 'crazy'.

In fact, Maggie remembered the first time she saw the woman coming down a rain-soaked ridge in the middle of a forest. She was reminded of a dancer, toe-stepping in hiking boots and making her descent look graceful and elegant with an unassuming confidence.

Since then the two women had kept in touch with brief phone calls and texts. Lucy lived outside of North Platte, Nebraska, in the shadows of the National Forest. Her beautiful acreage was a secluded retreat where she took in and cared for abandoned dogs. One of those dogs – who looked more like wolf than dog – had rescued Maggie. Now, she couldn't imagine Jake not being a part of her life. But despite their history, Maggie knew what she was asking of Lucy was significant. The retired medical examiner just happened to be in Lincoln, some fifty miles away, teaching forensic investigation to state troopers. She wasn't just asking the woman to interrupt her schedule, she was asking Lucy to accompany her on what could be a difficult search and recovery.

But of course, Lucy Coy wouldn't look at it that way at all. Her answer only reminded Maggie of the calm and steady guidance the woman would bring along.

'Of course I'll join you, but I believe the term "scavenger hunt" needs to be replaced. Perhaps we should consider it a spirit walk.'

FRIDAY, OCTOBER 20

35

Florida Panhandle

When Jason got back, a car with Georgia plates was parked in front of the house. He didn't want to interrupt if Hannah had company, so he went directly to his trailer. He slept better than he expected. Scout was asleep as soon as his head hit the pillow. The dog had already gotten into the habit of sprawling on his side of the bed, rolling onto his back, feet in the air and sometimes pedaling in his sleep.

It had only been about two months since Jason and the dog had moved from the floor in the spare bedroom to the queen-sized bed in the master. The trailer was luxurious compared to what he was used to, and somehow he felt more comfortable in his sleeping bag on the floor of the empty bedroom. Scout was happy to sleep curled up alongside him no matter where they were.

The night Jason moved from the floor to the bed was the first time he believed he might be finished fighting the demons left over from Afghanistan. Explosions still visited his nightmares, but those were becoming less frequent. It actually helped to be woken by a tongue-bath, and there were times Scout had nudged and licked Jason awake in the middle of the night.

He wondered what the dog thought when he watched his

partner thrash around in his sleep. The undeniable evidence surrounded him when he opened his eyes to blankets bunched up, sheets pulled off the mattress and once, even a lamp knocked to the floor. But every single time he woke up, Jason saw that big nose, bright eyes and felt the long tongue licking his face.

These days Jason got up smiling and laughing instead of stashing pills and planning on what order to take them by their shape and size and ability to take him away from this world as quickly and painlessly as possible.

This morning he had a text from Hannah to stop by for breakfast. He knew she'd want to hear how yesterday's search had gone. He felt better about things after talking to Creed, but this morning he couldn't wait to get back to the Woodsons' and start again.

Sheriff Norwich had reassured him that their search efforts went beyond Jason and Scout's help. She had deputies knocking on doors. An Amber Alert had been issued. Neighbors were keeping an eye out for anything suspicious. And Jason had overheard the deputies talking about a truck driver boyfriend of Mrs Woodson's. But still, Jason felt the weight of his failure.

His failure, not Scout's.

He'd convinced himself that he must have missed something in the dog's communication. The more he thought about it, the more certain he was.

As soon as Jason opened the back door to the kitchen he smelled bacon and coffee. His mouth watered and his stomach groaned. Hunter, Rufus and Lady accosted him before he could take two steps inside. Lady tried to herd the two bigger dogs out of the way. Jason kneeled to greet them all, and that's when he realized there was someone else alongside Hannah.

'Good morning,' Hannah said then gestured to the other woman. 'Olivia, this is Jason Seaver. He's one of our handlers. Jason, this is Olivia James. She's Ryder's mother.'

Jason brushed his hands – both of them – on his jeans making sure there were no remnants of dog hair or saliva before offering his black metal fingers over the counter to her.

She glanced at the hand then into his eyes, but she didn't hesitate for a second before shaking it.

'Hello, Jason. You must be one of my son's Marine friends.'

'Army Rangers,' he politely corrected her. 'It's a pleasure to meet you, Mrs James.'

She grimaced and said, 'Call me Olivia.'

'Jason just returned about two years ago,' Hannah explained. 'He's becoming a fine protégé of Ryder's.'

Jason felt Hunter head-butt his thigh, and he was grateful for the opportunity to give the dog attention instead of letting the women see his embarrassment. There was nothing *fine* about the way he handled yesterday's search.

'What can I do to help?' he asked.

'Not a thing,' Hannah told him. 'Get yourself a cup of coffee. We're almost ready. Olivia is treating us to cinnamon pancakes with a blueberry sauce that is yummy enough to eat by the spoonful.'

Jason had been so concerned about keeping his failure under wraps that he hadn't noticed how happy Hannah seemed to be about sharing her kitchen with Creed's mother.

There was something familiar about Olivia. Maybe he'd seen a photo somewhere in Creed's loft apartment, although he couldn't remember Creed ever mentioning his mother. They'd talked about Creed's father. Jason knew the man had committed suicide, and Creed was the one who'd found him. But he couldn't think of a single mention about his mother. Which made Jason curious.

He poured coffee while nonchalantly accessing the woman. He guessed she was in her fifties. Probably about 5'5', not exactly slender but a woman who definitely took care of herself. She certainly had a presence. Jason recognized that her slacks and sweater were most likely designer labels. Her watch and bracelet looked expensive. She wore her hair short and styled. Her fingernails were manicured. This early in the morning and her makeup looked freshly applied, though a bit too much. She looked like she could have stepped off the cover of a magazine, and it was at that moment, he realized that's exactly where he had seen her before – on the cover of a magazine.

'How'd the search go?' Hannah asked. 'Were you and Scout able to find that girl?'

Jason saw Olivia turn around, her eyes interested. 'I heard there was an Amber Alert when I was driving here.'

'Raelyn Woodson,' Hannah said. 'A thirteen-year-old. She was supposed to have walked over to a friend's house and never arrived.'

Both women were staring at him now, waiting for the details.

'We checked the forest, but we didn't find anything. Creed told me to stop searching after dark. I figured Scout and I'll go back and start fresh.'

Hannah simply nodded as she handed him a loaded plate, but Olivia's eyes stayed on him even as she sat down, and Hannah placed a plate in front of her.

'Would it help if I go with you?'

Jason almost dropped his fork. He looked over at Hannah as if he needed an interpreter to translate a foreign language.

Before either he or Hannah could answer, Olivia said, 'Maybe that sounds crazy.'

Jason took that as an all-clear signal and dug into his food, but then Olivia continued, 'I know what it's like. Perhaps I could at least be there to talk to the mother.'

'That's very generous of you, Olivia,' Hannah told her.

Jason remained quiet, continuing to slice and shovel in his pancakes. This was something Hannah would need to handle. So he was totally floored when Hannah said to the woman, 'I'll check with Sheriff Norwich.'

36

Charlotte thought she had paced herself, and still, she ended up vomiting all the food she had eaten. Her stomach hurt, the spasms coming in waves and bending her in two. She'd been without food for too long and now her stomach was treating it like a foreign substance. And yet, she was excited to discover a door off the kitchen that led to a small bathroom. A toilet to throw up into and running water to wash herself was such a treat she almost didn't care about the pain. She'd spent the night curled up on the cool linoleum floor.

The kitten had been beside her, rubbing against her as long as Charlotte was opening cans and packages and sharing food. Now, that it was well fed, the cat had wandered away. But Charlotte felt comforted knowing there was another living, breathing creature inside this old house, a creature that had no interest in hurting her.

Still weak, she forced herself to walk back into the kitchen. She sipped water while gathering the contents spilled across the countertops. She wanted to assess her good fortune while she stacked everything neatly. Even last night, she had scrutinized each food package, expecting to see whether someone had tampered with it. There had to be a catch. A trick. Why offer all this food if they hadn't inserted or injected the drugs that kept her under control?

That was how Iris explained the need for the drugs.

According to Iris, Charlotte 'behaved badly'. She lashed out, tried to escape. She had stolen and hidden items. She didn't make good decisions. Of course, she couldn't be trusted any longer. She needed the drugs 'to make her nice' and better behaved. They would help bring her 'under control'.

Whatever the drugs were, they made Charlotte numb and her mind fuzzy. Sometimes even sounds were muffled. It felt as if she were constantly trying to wake up, never quite certain if she was conscious or simply dreaming. Nothing was a dream as much as it was a nightmare. Usually she ended up sleeping. And most of the time she welcomed the sleep.

She started pulling out the few items left in the brown paper bag, and that's when she saw the magazine. Her eyes darted around the room even checking the window above the sink that was too high for her to see out and anyone to see in.

Was this a trick? She suspected this house was a temporary holding place for her before Iris sent her away for good. Charlotte had no idea how much time she had before that happened, but she was certain that it would happen. Someone would come for her. Whoever had left the food. And the magazine. And the kitten.

The kitten – where was it? Suddenly, she needed to find it.

A sense of dread of swept over her. What if her stomach had rejected the food because it was poisoned? She'd thrown it up, but what about the kitten? Could Iris be that cruel? Would she give Charlotte something to pet, to feed and to love only to watch it die a horrible, terrible, painful death.

Yes, Iris could be that cruel.

'Kitten,' she called out as she stumbled from the kitchen.

Skinny streams of sunshine danced across the walls and floor. The two open rooms hadn't changed since she'd left

them. Charlotte peeked behind the Christmas tree and
between the wall and the sofa. She looked under furniture and
moved the plastic reindeer to search the shadows in the corner.
She knocked over a stack of old magazines and pieces of paper
fluttered to the floor. Panic began to set in, and she ignored
the mess. The door to the only bedroom was still closed.
Charlotte had discovered it last night. She'd peeked inside, and
for a brief moment, was tempted to crawl beneath the covers.

Now, she hurried to the front door and pulled at the knob.
It didn't move. There was a back door in the kitchen. She hurried to check it.

Her pulse raced and her heart felt heavy, a sensation like
none she had experienced before. All she could imagine was
that the poor little kitten had crawled into a small crevice and
died.

She felt the tears dripping down her face before she realized
she was crying. That's when she collapsed to her knees and
curled up into a ball, the only way she knew how to deal with
anything that was painful in a way she knew couldn't heal.
She heard herself whimpering and didn't attempt to silence it
like she had in the past.

Then whiskers brushed against her arm, and a paw swatted
at a tangle of her hair.

Nebraska

Maggie was trying to listen to Lucy Coy tell her about this area. On a picnic table close to the boat ramp, they had spread out a contour map of the lake. Maggie had downloaded and printed it earlier that morning when she could no longer toss and turn in her perfectly comfortable hotel room bed.

Creed and Grace had parked close to the boat ramp. His Jeep Grand Cherokee's tailgate was open while he prepared. Grace didn't leave his side though she wagged at Maggie every time she noticed Maggie look her way. And Maggie was having a difficult time not looking that way, especially when Creed started taking off his clothes.

'The word Wahoo,' Lucy was saying, 'comes from the Dakotas. Wa nhu meaning arrow wood. But there's also a shrub that grows in these parts that's called the wahoo. I'll point it out to you if I see it. It's quite lovely. The leaves are finely serrated and elliptical. The seeds are a beautiful scarlet. But none of it is as fascinating as Mr Creed's fine sculptured body.'

It took Maggie a moment to notice that Lucy had stopped talking and to realize what she'd said. It took but a second to know she'd been busted, and immediately, she felt the flush spread from her neck to her face.

'I take it your doctor is out of the picture?' Lucy asked before Maggie could respond. Lucy was referring to Dr Benjamin Platt, who Maggie had been dating on and off again.

'Ryder and I are just friends,' Maggie said.

Lucy raised an eyebrow, a single gesture that spoke volumes.

Though the forensic expert was retired, Maggie had no idea how old the woman was. Her face showed few distinctive lines other than laugh lines at the corners of her mouth. Otherwise, her skin was smooth and taunt over high cheekbones. Her dark eyes had the power of looking so intensely, so deeply that Maggie was convinced those eyes could see into the depths of her soul.

This morning, Lucy wore hiking boots, blue jeans and a white buttoned shirt that she left untucked with the tails sticking out from underneath her jacket. There were featherlike wisps of silver in her dark hair that was cut short and stuck up in places. On anyone else it would have looked messy. On Lucy it looked stylish.

Like Maggie's friend, Dr Gwen Patterson, it was tough for Maggie to get anything by Lucy Coy. Both women were perceptive to the point of clairvoyant, so it was pointless for Maggie to now pretend that Creed's body hadn't mesmerized her as he stripped down to the tight neoprene shorts before getting into his dive suit.

'The two of you have a history.' Lucy said. It wasn't a question.

'We've worked together on three or four cases. Remember I told you about the scorpion pit I fell into?' Maggie tried to make it sound casual, but just mentioning the incident brought back the memory of their stings.

'Yes, but you failed to mention that the former Marine dog handler was hot.'

Now Maggie saw that Lucy was enjoying the view, too. When she noticed Maggie staring at her, Lucy said, 'I'm old. I'm not dead.'

And of course, it was at that moment that Creed glanced back to see what had gotten Grace's attention. As if on cue, both women waved. Creed waved back. Then Lucy and Maggie immediately gathered themselves around the map again.

'How old was his sister when she disappeared?' Lucy asked.

'She was eleven. Ryder was fourteen.'

Maggie glanced up to see another Sheriff department's vehicle now parked alongside Sheriff Timmons' pickup. Both vehicles were blocking the main entrance to the recreational area. Timmons was the Butler County sheriff that would be a part of their search and recovery team. He'd beaten them out here to oversee the delivery of the boat and the dive tank. Maggie vaguely remembered him from the dozens of officers who were involved in the raid of Eli Dunn's farm. Operation Cross County utilized law enforcement from across the entire state.

According to Pakula, Timmons was a forty-year veteran who had volunteered for the human trafficking task force early on. He didn't look like a sheriff. He wore jeans, shiny new cowboy boots, a flannel shirt and a ball cap with an embroidered sheriff department's emblem. Tall and lean, the only indication of his age was the gray at his temples and the crinkles at his eyes. He had a slow, easy gait and a handsome face that made him look friendly instead of threatening. The one memory Maggie had of him from the night of the raid was when he came into Dunn's house with an armload of bottled water to offer to those inside.

Timmon's jurisdiction, Butler County, was next door to this area. From examining the map Maggie knew that his territory would fall within the fifty-mile radius where Eli Dunn claimed he'd helped bury several bodies. Hopefully, having him along would allow them access to any farmland they needed to trespass on.

When they arrived, the sheriff stood in the middle of the main entrance. He had greeted Maggie and Lucy, letting them pass, and waited for Creed and Grace to enter the recreational area. Then he backed his pickup across the road to block further access. His deputies were parked at the other access roads.

The state troopers escorting Eli Dunn were thirty minutes behind them, a strategy to avoid looking like a caravan. The county prosecutor wanted them to be careful of drawing too much attention, not only because of the media, but in case Dunn's associates were watching. After Maggie alerted them about the note she'd received, they all realized that despite their efforts, someone could, in fact, be watching.

Lake Wannahoo stretched along two major thoroughfares, one that led to the city of Wahoo, located to its south, and another route that curved around the city. Maggie couldn't help noticing that there were more trees in the middle of the lake than along the shore. Although they were some distance away, there was nothing to block anyone driving down either of those two highways from seeing their activity. Fortunately, that worked both ways, because there was no place for a car to pull aside and watch without being observed.

Sheriff Timmons had seen to it that no one else was on the

lake or using any of the campsites. It was a gorgeous day in October, and Maggie wondered how many hikers, boaters and campers Timmons and the local law enforcement officials had to evacuate.

Now, in his dive suit and Grace in her LifeVest, the pair made their way down to the picnic table.

'Pretty day for a dive,' Creed said.

'Have you ever been in a Nebraska lake in October?' Lucy asked him.

'No ma'am, I can't say that I have.'

'It'll likely be ice cold.'

'How deep are we looking at?' he asked, coming in close to get a glimpse of the map.

'Anywhere from eight feet to thirty-two,' Maggie told him. 'Will you need to dive from the boat?'

'Depends where Grace tells me. I'm glad they gave us a smaller boat. Sides are lower. Ideally, I'd like her to be level with the water.'

Grace was prancing around Lucy's legs until Lucy scratched under the dog's vest.

Maggie wanted to question whether Grace would be able to smell a dead body on the bottom of a lake at thirty-five feet down below the surface. She tried to visualize how deep that was – almost four stories. And with cold water, decomposition would be slower.

Maggie stood with her hand to her forehead, blocking the sun as she looked out at the glimmering surface. Six hundred-plus acres. Hopefully Eli Dunn's memory and simplistic diagrams would narrow the perimeter.

She'd left Eli's notebook safely back in her hotel room, but she had made copies of the pages. Now she pulled them out and smoothed the folds. There was one in particular she suspected could be this burial site.

Creed came in beside her, so close her shoulder brushed his arm. She ran her finger over the scribble that looked like a first grader's version of water.

'I couldn't figure out why the surface would be this far up a tree, but now I understand.'

In the middle of the lake, scattered tops of trees stuck out, making the area look more like a disastrous flood than a reservoir.

'They left the trees to provide a natural habitat,' Lucy said. 'But I imagine those trunks and roots could also provide a place for a body to get tangled up.'

'Is that a wheel?' Creed asked, pointing to the circle in the line drawing.

'Could be.' Maggie hadn't been able to decipher this one, but it was one of the few that included anything that looked like water.

'He hasn't shared any details?' Lucy asked.

'Only the location. Dunn refused to say anything more until he gets here.' Maggie glanced up just as the State Patrol SUV slowed down on the highway. 'And speak of the devil.'

38

Creed stood back and watched. He tried to imagine this skinny weasel of a man enticing children to climb into his vehicle. And he tried to think of him as any other perp, quashing his personal feelings. He was slump-shouldered with a flop of dark hair over his forehead and curling over his collar. They allowed him to wear his street clothes because the county prosecutor didn't want an orange jumpsuit to attract the attention of bypassers. The prosecutor was banking on them being too far away for anyone to notice the shackles around Dunn's ankles and wrists. But Creed wondered how they expected to explain the two state troopers in full uniform, one on each side of Dunn, each grasping an elbow as if they expected the man to bolt.

Sheriff Timmons joined them, and Lucy Coy greeted the troopers by name then introduced them to the sheriff, Creed and Maggie. Gregory was big, square-shouldered, with a square jaw and a notch in the bridge of his nose that made him look like an ex-boxer. Vegaz had a shorter, more compact body.

'Both of these young men were in my forensic workshop last week.'

Lucy offered it as an explanation of how she knew them, but it made Creed take a closer look at the two men. He wanted to ask if it was an advanced forensics workshop. Surely, they wouldn't have rookie patrolmen escorting a prisoner.

Maggie didn't seem to notice, or perhaps care. She was anxious to get started, and Creed could see that she had been studying Eli Dunn from the moment the man stumbled out of the back of the SUV. The fascination appeared to go both ways, because Dunn hadn't taken his eyes off Maggie, except to shoot a worried look at Grace every once in awhile.

It wasn't just a guarded or cautious glance or even a look of interest. It was more like he didn't trust the dog. Dunn was wary of Grace. Maybe he was even afraid of her. It probably didn't help matters that Grace hadn't stopped growling at him since he arrived.

Emotion runs down the leash.

Creed tightened his grip on Grace's leash, but he didn't ask her to quiet down. Instead, he let her voice his own opinion of the man.

In no time and with very little prompting, Dunn was pointing and gesturing to places on the lake, especially close to the submerged trees. He seemed anxious to share what he knew, though he kept prefacing certain points by saying none of this meant he had a thing to do with the death.

'Keep in mind, I was simply the undertaker,' he said with a grin that didn't belong with that sentence.

'How long ago?' Maggie wanted to know.

'Oh, this one's pretty fresh,' Dunn said as if he were a waiter talking about the fish specials for the day. 'Let's see.' He stared off, trying to remember. 'Maybe the first or second week of February.' Then he looked to Maggie. 'You got that notebook? The date would be in there. It's upside down and printed backwards.' He smiled at her, again, like he had revealed a secret and expected a reward. 'But don't go thinking all of them are like that.'

He wanted to make sure they knew he hadn't disclosed his entire coding system. Maybe the guy wasn't as stupid as he appeared to be.

'You anchored her down.' Maggie said it as fact, not a question.

'Oh, she's not coming up anytime soon.'

Not even fifteen minutes had gone by, and Creed wanted to punch that grin off Eli Dunn's face.

'No way you'd ever find her without me,' he added.

'I think Mr Creed's dog would eventually find her,' Maggie told him, and Creed was surprised that she sounded like she was goading the man.

'That scrawny mutt,' Dunn said, and he looked down at Grace trying not to show his discomfort, but Creed had already seen it.

This time, Grace bared her teeth at Dunn. Creed could see the man's eyes flash, but it wasn't fear. It was anger. Creed caught a glimpse of Dunn's fingers balling into fists.

'Come on, Grace,' he told the dog then to Maggie, he said, 'We'll meet you at the boat.'

He'd had enough of this guy. He needed to focus and calm down his dog. But he'd need to calm himself down, first.

39

'Lucy said this lake hasn't been here long,' Maggie told Creed. 'I'm hoping that means less debris for you.'

Creed had placed Grace on the seat next to him while Maggie guided the boat toward the trees. The trolling motor hummed quietly enough that she could hear the water lapping against the sides of the boat.

'It's over an old creek bed, right?' he asked.

'I think so.'

'Sediment can churn up pretty easily. Too bad Sheriff Timmons didn't get us a boat with sonar.'

Maggie glanced around the interior of the boat. She hadn't even thought to ask, and now she wondered if they should have waited. Why was she in such a hurry?

But she knew exactly why. Because at any moment she expected Eli Dunn to wise up and shut up. It was surprising that his appointed public defender hadn't already gotten him to shut up.

Here on the water, she realized how immense an undertaking this was, even with Dunn pointing out the location. Bodies could move with the current. Even bodies anchored down. Once tissues and organs started breaking down, gases of decomposition could churn a dead body into a floater. But that obviously hadn't happened in the last eight months.

That was another thing. Maggie didn't like the smirk on

Dunn's face or how cocksure he was that he'd secured the body. Right now, she wasn't sure if part of his game was sending them on a wild goose chase. What if there wasn't even a body?

She guided the boat along, making a wide circle around the section Dunn had pinpointed. They'd been on the water for several minutes when Creed gestured to her.

'Slow down a little,' he said. 'Stop before we get close to the trees.'

'Are you worried I'll run into them?' She was trying to lighten the mood, but Creed's first concern was always his dogs, and once he started a search there was no joking around.

'The current is moving toward us. That means the scent will be moving toward us. I want to give Grace a chance to find the scent cone.'

He kept his hand on Grace's back. Grace had moved to the edge of the boat. It looked like she wanted to put her front paws up on the side, but Creed was restraining her. Already her nose moved from side to side, testing the air. Her ears flapped in the breeze.

'Eight months in the water. Does that make it easier or more difficult for Grace?' Maggie asked.

Grace looked back at the sound of her name, and Maggie wanted to kick herself. There was a reason Creed liked to be alone with his dogs when he did searches. But he didn't admonish her. Instead, he slid over and dipped his fingertips into the water while he kept a firm grip of Grace's vest with his other hand.

'From what Lucy said, I'm guessing this water stays cold most of the year. There might not be much decomp.' He scooped up water in the palm of his hand and held it for Grace to sniff.

'Maybe we should wait for a boat with sonar,' Maggie told him, trying not to expose all of the second-guessing she was doing.

'Don't worry about it. We're already here.'

But when she looked up, she caught him studying her.

'What are you thinking?' he asked.

'Nothing, really.'

'You think he's screwing with us?' As he asked the question his eyes slipped past her to the shore.

He was facing the boat ramp, and could see the group watching them. Maggie refused to glance back and give Dunn the benefit of knowing she was having doubts.

'It's crossed my mind,' she said. 'He's already lying about not having anything to do with their deaths.'

'You don't believe he's just the undertaker?' he asked, using Dunn's self-proclaimed role.

'Not in a million years.'

'Guess we'll find out soon enough.' He gestured toward Grace. Her whiskers were twitching, and she was snorting in quick breaths.

40

Creed clicked on the dive torch he had strapped to his right forearm as he glanced at his dive watch. Not even ten feet down, and it was like swimming through a murky green fog. He could make out the shapes of the tree trunks, a fascinating underwater forest. Skeletal arms with crooked fingers reached out to him. He stayed far enough away to avoid getting tangled in the spider webs of discarded fishing line he could see snagged on leafless branches.

He focused on the trees, shooting the beam of light in that direction. It made sense that Eli Dunn would want to use the trunks as an anchor system. But Creed couldn't see any ropes or bungee cords. No sign of any large object caught or wedged in between the trees.

He adjusted his mouthpiece. He'd tested all his gear when he'd first gotten into the water, but now it felt like there was drag in the line. Probably nothing. He checked his dive watch again.

He pushed farther away from the trees and started to dive deeper still sweeping his light down and across the tree line. Creed was so focused on the algae-covered branches and anything else that might be attached or strung around them, that when he noticed the object in his peripheral vision, it made him jerk around.

To his left, almost behind him, was a shadowy hulk. At first glance, Creed thought it was a sunken boat. Then he saw what looked like a bumper. His torch caught a glint off a side window. Buried in the sludge was a tire. The vehicle itself was covered in a blanket of green. Slowly, he swiped the stream of light over the crusted surface.

He double-checked his coordinates. He was still directly below the boat. He calculated in his mind the distance from the shoreline.

It was too far. No way a vehicle could have driven into the lake and ended up this far away from the shore. Even if it was driving at a high speed and catapulted off the boat ramp. Maybe it could have floated out a bit before sinking.

Okay, that was possible.

The front window on the driver side was gone or maybe it had been open when the car started to sink. Someone trying to escape.

Breathing was becoming more and more difficult. He tried to check his hoses. No kinks. The pressure gauge didn't register anything unusual and yet, he felt like he was struggling to pull in a regular breath. He found the knob on his regulator and made an adjustment, but it didn't seem to make a difference.

Still, he decided to search the inside of the car. He prepared himself before he took a look.

He shot the light inside but couldn't see a body. Seatbelts dangled. Sediment had settled over the seats and dashboard. He couldn't estimate how long this vehicle had been down here. Maybe it was even here when they flooded the area and made it into a reservoir.

But then Creed remembered the drawing in Eli Dunn's

notebook. They'd commented that it looked like the stick figure was anchored down with a circular object. A circle that could be the steering wheel or tire of a car.

Creed sucked hard, and his fingers grabbed at the regulator's adjustment knob. He turned it all the way open and back a quarter so the spring would be at its least compressed point. There was no change in the airflow. He needed to head back to the surface soon. His tank registered enough air, but he was struggling. It was becoming harder and harder to breathe. There was one more thing he needed to check.

Creed pulled himself close to the driver's door and made sure no broken metal would bump him or his gear. He reached his right hand inside, letting the light of the torch guide his gloved fingers. With the torch strapped to his forearm he could point with his hand and there was light. He began tapping the dashboard, feeling for buttons or a lever. Finally he hit something and heard a muffled pop.

Creed made his way to the back of the vehicle. The lever had released the trunk. He slipped his fingers under the lip, but it still wouldn't open. Closer to the middle, he could feel the latch holding, and his fingers worked it loose.

It took some effort to lift the trunk against the water pressure and the unyielding hinges. He shoved it open but his hands held on to the lid, so the torch beam shot upward. Before he could bring his arm and the light down, a large object came floating out of the trunk. It hit him square in the chest.

His arms swung to push it away but the movement also sent his only light whipping around. Yet, the object kept pushing against him. With one hand he grabbed hold of what looked like black plastic. With his other arm he steadied the torch.

The next thing Creed saw was the bloated face of a woman who could be his sister.

41

Maggie held on to Grace's vest, gripping the security handle just like Creed had instructed. Both she and Grace stared at the surface where they'd last seen him before he went underwater. Neither of them dared look away.

It felt like he was down there a long time. Too long.

When she finally saw bubbles coming to the surface she breathed a sigh of relief. But then she noticed Grace's ears pinned back to the sides of her head. The dog was trembling. And Maggie felt her insides clench. She tightened her grip on Grace and leaned farther over the edge.

The object that bobbed to the surface was not Creed. It looked like a bloated garbage bag. But then she saw the tentacles of long hair and the bone-white patches of skin.

'It's okay, Grace,' she reassured the dog who was now squirming trying to get a better look over the side of the boat. But Grace wasn't interested in what had floated to the surface. The dog was still looking for her owner.

Maggie found a grappling hook tucked under the bench and gently tossed it, snagging the plastic and keeping it from floating away. She tied it down all the while scanning the surface of the lake.

'Where is he, Grace?'

With every second Maggie's pulse accelerated.

Why hadn't he surfaced yet? Something was wrong.

'Come on, Ryder. Where the hell are you?'

Grace was getting more and more anxious, too. She showed no interest in the body floating next to their boat even though it was the scent she had been asked to find. Instead, she was shifting her front paws, tap-tap-tapping impatiently. Her eyes searched the water, and the more unsettled Grace became, the more panicked Maggie grew.

Her cell phone rang, and she jumped. Still hanging on to Grace, Maggie pulled the phone out, only to silence it, but then saw it was Lucy.

'What's going on?' Lucy wanted to know.

'Something's wrong!'

'Is he hurt? I thought I saw someone surface.'

Maggie twisted in her seat to look back at the shore.

'Get Dunn the hell away from here,' she told Lucy. 'He doesn't get to see this.'

She waited and watched as Lucy approached the troopers, gesturing and talking to them. Immediately, the men turned Eli Dunn around and marched him back to the SUV.

Suddenly, she felt Grace nudging her arm. The dog tucked and pushed so forcefully, she shoved Maggie's phone hand away from her face. Grace was panting now. Maggie shut off the phone and dropped it into her pocket. She hugged Grace close to her chest and rested her chin on the dog's head.

Maggie contemplated jumping in. Would she be able to even see him? Why the hell didn't they have a backup plan?

Her heart pounded so hard against her ribcage it hurt to breathe. Grace wiggled free and darted to the other side of the boat. Maggie lunged for her, and the boat rocked enough to flip her stomach. There was a splash, and she half expected to find that Grace had fallen over the side. But instead, the little dog stood on her hind legs with her paws leaning on the edge. Her tail whipped back and forth.

That's when Creed came crashing to the surface, gulping for air.

42

Hunting for the kitten made Charlotte realize she had a whole house to explore. At least, until they came to take her away.

She found women's clothing in the bedroom closet and dresser. Whoever lived in this house must have left so suddenly she hadn't been able to take anything with her. There was a whole drawer of underwear. She opened another and found it filled with socks. She sat down on the bed and simply stared.

The pants were too short and the waistband too big, but she found a belt. It felt strange to have sleeves wrapped around her arms, but the material was soft. And the socks were such a luxury. She tried on a pair of shoes, but found them too painful to wear. She padded across the floor going from one room to the next.

It was a small house. The two rooms in the center were connected with a large archway, so they really appeared to be one big room. Other than the bedroom, there was the kitchen, a small pantry and the bathroom. Compared to the cramped spaces or the damp basement Charlotte was used to, this was a mansion.

In some ways, it was overwhelming. She felt uneasy not being able to keep an eye on both the front door and the back at the same time. But there was something comforting in having the kitten now following her everywhere. Charlotte wanted to believe it was bonding with her, but she suspected it was simply hungry again.

She was careful about what she ate this time, choosing a banana and peanut butter. She opened a can of tuna for the kitten.

'I need to call you something other than Kitten,' she said out loud. The cat didn't bother to look up from its can.

It was a female and was mostly dark gray with white mixed in, but from the tip of her chin and all the way across her belly, she was pure white. So was the tip of her tail. It looked like she had dipped it in paint.

Charlotte paced the rooms again. She wanted to say she was investigating but it felt more like she was on patrol. She wandered through the Christmas decorations when she saw the stack of magazines she had knocked over in her frenzy to find the kitten. She gathered them up carefully, brushing the dust off and taking in the covers. She flipped through some of the pages, eager to read, though all the dust made her eyes water. That's when she noticed several pieces of paper that had fallen to the floor.

When she saw the handwriting, Charlotte thought she had stumbled upon a personal letter of the woman who'd lived here. The woman who had decorated her entire house for Christmas and had to leave suddenly. She was anxious to see what the woman might have to say.

But the first sentence told Charlotte this wasn't a letter the woman had received or had written. Instead, she knew immediately the letter was meant for her. Not just her, but any of Iris' captives.

It wasn't the first note Charlotte had found. She had seen other messages from those who had come before her. Behind the basement hot water heater there had been one scratched out on the wall that read, *Never give up. B.C.*

In the upstairs closet in the Big House, a piece of wallpaper had been peeled back, deep in a corner where Iris would never look. It read, *I will not be destroyed. K.U.*

Before Iris had taken away the furnace manual, Charlotte had found the note written on one of its back pages. It was longer, but Charlotte had memorized every word. *Don't let her trick you. She can take our names, but don't let her take away who you are. C.T*

And now, this letter that Charlotte held in her hands. It was another warning. It began:

Don't trust Aaron. He's not sweet or innocent. If you made it to the Christmas house, you only have a few days left. Please believe what I have to say.

43

Charlotte wondered if it was another trick. The other messages only included initials. This was signed by Kristel. And why in the world would this person tell her not to trust Aaron? She couldn't possibly think of Aaron as dangerous. He had never tried to hurt her. In fact, she was pretty sure he was the one who brought her here and left all the food. He may have even left the kitten to keep her company.

When they were kids – before Charlotte made Iris so angry that the woman started leaving her in locked rooms, then closets, then the basement – Charlotte and Aaron played together. He was a big, chubby boy, younger than her. He was always gentle and polite and so quiet that for a long time she wasn't sure whether or not he could speak.

Iris called him 'stupid' and 'slow', and Charlotte felt sorry for him, because she could see how much it hurt his feelings. He'd do anything for Iris even though she treated him so badly.

Recently, she hadn't seen Aaron very often. Only when she needed to be moved. A few times in her drug-induced stupor, she'd open her eyes and find him carrying her or lifting her from where she had fallen, or had been pushed by Iris. He cradled her in his big arms, and Charlotte actually felt safe. He smelled of the outdoors, hay and grass and fresh air. But he always did what Iris asked.

Now, that she thought about it, why had he never helped her escape?

Once Charlotte had managed to make it out the back door, out of the front yard and past the barn. But Iris sent the dog after her. Charlotte grabbed at her ankle. The GPS strap prevented her from rubbing it. She knew there was a scar.

Aaron had rescued her. He told the dog to sit. The dog released her ankle and sat down. She remembered how grateful she was when he picked her up, and how disappointed when he carried her back to the house, back to Iris. At the time, she didn't blame him for not helping her escape. In a way, she thought he was as much a prisoner as she was.

She looked down at the letter. The brand new magazine in the grocery bag had told Charlotte what the current year was. The date at the top of this letter was from four years ago.

Don't trust Aaron. He's not sweet or innocent. If you made it to the Christmas house, you only have a few days left. Please believe what I have to say.

He will leave you food and water. Don't be grateful. He's doing it just to fatten you up. I heard him talking to someone outside the house. Another man. Aaron called him Eli.

Damn boarded windows! I couldn't see either of them, but I heard them.

The other man was telling Aaron what he was going to do with me. How much men would pay for me. Pay to do things to me. Bad things. Awful things.

I found a pair of scissors in one of the drawers. They're long and sharp. I want to kill myself, but if I don't have the courage, I'll leave them for you. They'll

be under the bathroom sink. I'll tape them to the back
wall, behind the pipes.

   Save yourself!
   Kristel

44

Santa Rosa County, Florida

Jason was relieved that Mrs Woodson offered Olivia coffee and even more relieved the two women stayed behind in the kitchen while he and Scout went back upstairs.

Sheriff Norwich told Jason that she had moved her deputies from the neighborhood on to other searches. One of which was Mrs Woodson's new boyfriend. Yet at the same time, she told Jason she'd welcome any information he and Scout might find.

Jason was tempted to ask more questions. If the boyfriend was involved, did he take the girl from the house? Or from the trail? Creed said that sometimes it was better to know less, or there was the temptation to conduct the search to match the narrative.

He wanted Scout to have another chance to get acquainted with Raelyn's scent. There was a chance that Mrs Woodson's presence the previous day had been too much of a distraction.

'We'll start fresh,' Jason told Scout as they entered the girl's room.

Immediately, Jason knew something was different. When he realized what it was he felt a chill slide down his back. The bed had been stripped down. Bed sheets were gone. Pillowcases gone. Even the bedspread.

'Son of a bitch,' he muttered then regretted it immediately when he felt Scout shift beside him. 'It's okay, boy.'

He needed to keep his shock and exasperation out of his voice. Except it wouldn't matter. Scout would be able to smell Jason's anxiety no matter what tone he used.

He checked the closet where he'd found the sneakers yesterday. He remembered there had been a clothesbasket with a few items tossed inside. The entire basket was gone.

Okay, so she tidied up. Probably needed to keep herself busy. Maybe she didn't like that he'd had Scout sniff all over the bedding. He still had the worn sneaker, and its companion was right here. He picked it up and offered it to Scout.

'Raelyn. Scout, this is Raelyn.'

Scout stuck his nose down into the shoe exactly like he had done the day before.

Jason kneeled beside him then decided to check under the bed. Maybe he'd score a dirty sock. Nothing under the bed but something had dropped in between the nightstand and the bed's frame. It was wedged so tightly he'd never have noticed it from above. Jason repositioned himself so he could squeeze his hand into the space and grab it.

He pulled out the object and sat back on his heels staring at it.

What teenage girl would leave behind her cell phone?

He glanced back at Scout and found the dog with the sneaker in his mouth. When he saw Jason, he started twirling.

'Okay, okay,' he told Scout. 'We'll get going.'

He slid the phone into his back pocket. He'd need to get it to Sheriff Norwich.

Back on the trail again, Scout seemed to be following a scent. Jason practically had to drag the dog to the head of the trail and away from the shed with the freezer full of fish. He was convinced that's where he went wrong the previous day. He shouldn't have let Scout even get a whiff of the frozen fish. Instead, he'd keep him focused.

For the first forty minutes, Scout swung his huge muzzle back and forth. He snorted and inhaled the air around him like he had definitely caught Raelyn's scent. This time, Jason allowed the dog to lead the way even when he took them off the trail and into the thicket. Scout weaved around and jumped over the prickly shrubs that grabbed at Jason's pantlegs and threatened to trip him.

Off the trail and inside the forest, Spanish moss hung low and kudzu grew thick, choking out the sunlight. The air was humid, so thick with moisture that Jason worried Scout would get overheated fast. He'd made the dog take a water break after twenty minutes. He'd need to stop him again, soon, but he was working a scent, nose poking the air.

Suddenly, Scout stopped and stood still while he waved his muzzle back and forth. He adjusted his body to follow his nose, but then stood still, again. He took a few steps forward, turned and headed back in the direction they'd just come from. Jason didn't correct or question him. Instead, he simply tried to keep up.

Scout loped then began thrashing through the low brush, hopping over fallen branches and zig-zagging between pine trees. Once when Jason tripped and almost fell, the dog turned around and wagged his head at Jason like he was trying to be patient.

Old leaves and pine needles crunched beneath their feet. Jason had to duck under a few low branches that almost snatched his ball cap. Sweat dripped down his face and his

T-shirt clung to him like a second skin. Still, he was glad he wore the long-sleeved button shirt even if its tails flapped behind him. He could feel the sleeves protecting his arm from what otherwise might be deep gouges as he and Scout propelled forward.

Finally, Scout slowed down and pulled Jason toward a clearing. He could see a rooftop and the musty smell of the forest grew less pungent. They came around a hedge and as soon as Jason realized where they were, he felt like the air had been knocked out of his lungs.

They were back on the Woodsons' property coming around from the other direction. The rooftop belonged to the shed, and now Scout was leading him to that damned freezer full of fish. He eye-rolled back to look at Jason, his tongue hanging out the side of his mouth. He sat down in front of the door and raised his paw. Then he stared at Jason's daypack, waiting for his reward.

45

Nebraska

Maggie was relieved when Lucy took charge and insisted they call it a day. She could see Creed was exhausted, but he'd never admit it. He'd been so quiet, too quiet.

'I don't recognize her,' he'd said to Maggie.

It wasn't until Creed said it a second time that she realized he actually expected to be able to identify the body.

'She has blue eyes,' he told Maggie. 'Brodie's eyes were brown.'

They stood on the shore and watched Sheriff Timmons and Trooper Vegaz bringing the body out of the water. Creed's eyes stayed on the men even while he tossed Grace her pink elephant. She caught it in mid-air. The toy was her reward for alerting, and the little dog pranced with it in her mouth, biting down and making it squeak-squeak-squeal. Her joy and excitement contradicted the somber mood. She brought it back and dropped it at Creed's feet, ready for him to toss it again.

This time when he picked it up and flung it, he said to Maggie, 'Grace thinks death is a squishy pink elephant.'

Maggie noticed his sad smile.

Lucy had called the Douglas County Crime Lab's mobile unit, and when it arrived, she met the CSU techs while Maggie left Creed and Grace to talk to Trooper Gregory. Trooper Vegaz had already returned to the SUV. They'd kept Eli Dunn secured in the back of the vehicle parked far enough away, but Maggie could see him twisting and straining to try to see the action.

'Take him back,' Maggie told Gregory.

'He's insisting he talk to you first,' Gregory said. 'But honestly, I think he just wants to brag about how he drove that car out on the ice and left it.'

'How could he just leave it and no one notice?'

'I actually remember someone talking about it. There was a sign in the window for a local car dealership. I think everyone who saw it thought it was a stupid advertising gimmick.'

'Is it legal to park a car on the ice?'

Gregory shrugged. 'People ice-fish.'

'But you said there was an advertising sign?'

'With a bogus phone number,' Sheriff Timmons said, coming up from behind them. 'The car dealership didn't exist. By the time any of us knew that, the weather decided to warm up.'

'So you saw it?' Maggie asked.

'Sure I saw it. I drive this stretch all the time when I'm going to and from Omaha. My county's next door to Saunders. Me and the missus live just on the outskirts of David City.'

'You didn't think it was odd enough to investigate?'

'I just told you, I checked it out.'

Maggie heard the hint of his irritation though he kept it from his face.

'It was a bogus dealership and phone number,' he told her. 'No license plates from what we could see. Once the ice started to melt, none of us were gonna risk our necks or our resources to try and retrieve it. You have any idea how much it costs to bring a vehicle up thirty feet from the bottom of a lake?'

There was a silence as the three of them watched Lucy with the two CSU techs. Not fifty feet away, Creed was still tossing the elephant for Grace. Maggie could hear the jubilant squeaks.

'How the hell would anyone think there was a body in the trunk?' Sheriff Timmons finally said, shaking his head as he started to walk to his own vehicle.

'What should I tell Dunn?' Gregory asked Maggie, and the sheriff spun around.

'What do you mean, what do you tell Dunn?' Timmons wanted to know.

'He's insisting he talk to Agent O'Dell before we take him back.'

'That son of a bitch needs to shut up and rot in hell,' Sheriff Timmons hissed. Then as if he realized he'd let his anger slip too far, he added, 'I'll see y'all tomorrow.' And he left.

Gregory was waiting for Maggie's answer. Truth was, she was sick of Dunn, too.

'Tell him I'll talk to him when he gives me the location of the next body.' And she started walking away but turned and called out, 'No stops on the way back, okay?'

'Of course not.'

'No, I mean it. Not for gas. Not for coffee. Take him directly back. Don't trust him for a second.'

She waited for Gregory to realize how serious she was. He nodded then headed back to the State Patrol's SUV.

Maggie tried to relax her shoulders, tried to flex her fingers and stretch the muscles in her back. The tension was tight in her neck. That panic of thinking Creed was hurt, was still too close to the surface. But her own anger surprised her.

Eli Dunn could have told them about the car before the dive. He had plenty of time to brag. Why hadn't he done so from the beginning?

But she knew the answer, and she hated the answer.

Dunn was already playing games.

46

Omaha, Nebraska

Tommy Pakula sat across the table from the pimp-slash-drug dealer who liked to be called T-Rock. Six months ago Pakula had interrogated the man after one of his prostitutes shot herself. According to T-Rock, the fifteen-year-old committed suicide in front of him.

'That bitch put the gun to her head, and damn, if she didn't go and pull the trigger.'

That was what he had told Pakula at the time. And no, T-Rock had no idea where the girl named Ariel – the girl with the beautiful long red hair who reminded Pakula of his daughter – had gotten the gun. The serial number had been sandblasted away so professionally the forensic team couldn't raise it.

T-Rock had been released. They'd probably never have enough evidence to charge him with the girl's death. But when Pakula noticed the man was back inside – of course he was back, this time on drug charges – he wondered if, by chance, T-Rock might know something, anything about Elijah Dunn.

'I'm checking out this guy,' Pakula told T-Rock as casually as if he were asking about a regular acquaintance. 'I'm wondering if you might know him.'

'Know him? You mean like off-the-record know him?'

Pakula held back a smile. This guy was good. He'd forgotten how sharp and smooth the man could be, all at the same time.

'Maybe you've traded with him or bought from him,' Pakula said. 'You know, during one of the busy times – big sporting event or the State Fair when you needed a few more girls.'

'Hey, I don't *need* to buy from anyone.' He pretended to look insulted, pouting his lips. 'The girls *flock* to T-Rock.'

'Okay, maybe you just know him. Heard of him. His name's Elijah Dunn.'

T-Rock crinkled his nose as if the sound of the man's name smelled bad.

'I don't know any dude by that name.'

Pakula pulled out a photo – Dunn's mug shot – and slid it across the table.

It took only a glance.

'Oh, that dude.'

'So you do know him?'

'I know *of* him. He's one crazy son of a bitch. But wait a minute. You can't play that game. What do I get if I tell you what I know?'

Pakula hesitated and T-Rock watched him with a look that seemed to be reading Pakula's mind. He started shaking his head, the dreadlocks swinging from side to side.

'Dude, you know I didn't kill that bitch.'

'Calling her a bitch doesn't help your situation.'

T-Rock pushed Dunn's photo across the table and sat back.

'I'll see what I can do,' Pakula told him.

'See what you can do? That's your best offer?'

'You've heard about me.'

'Yeah, I heard about you.' His lips pursed and he stared hard into Pakula's eyes. 'I heard you're one tough son of a bitch. That's what I've heard.'

'But I keep my word.'

Now T-Rock leaned forward, studying him, tilting his head as though he was looking for a trick. Finally, his big shoulders relaxed.

'What do you want to know?'

'Has Dunn ever approached you to sell girls or boys?'

'Whoa!' He brought up his chin and shook his head again. 'I don't deal in boys. That's not natural. Screws a boy up for life.'

Pakula took a deep breath, pushed down the bile making its way up from his stomach. There was nothing that made him want to run his fist into a wall more than a scumbag like this pretending he had a sliver of morals. Ruin a boy's life? What about all the young girls' lives? Pimping and selling fifteen year old girls was natural?

He needed to calm himself. He kept his fists under the table and out of sight. Another deep breath. *Focus.*

'Just tell me about this guy. Whatever you know.'

'From what I remember, he started out all vanilla. I don't mean just white girls, but they all looked alike. It was creepy. Like he was trying to clone or repeat the same girl over and over. Same hair color and long, parted down the middle. All of their faces looked alike. They were the same weight and height and age. I didn't want any of that weird crap.'

'So he was trying to sell them?'

'Oh, he always tried, after they got a little older. He wanted the ten, eleven and twelve-year-olds. By fourteen or fifteen, he was getting rid of them, like they aged out.' T-Rock rolled his eyes. 'That's when they're just getting experienced. If you know what I mean. I know some guys like to keep their merchandise fresh. Low mileage, right? But this guy? It was strange. It was like he wanted to keep replacing that same ten or eleven-year-old.'

Pakula pulled the Polaroid out of the pocket inside his jacket. He slid it to the middle of the table.

'Did he ever try to sell you this girl?'

'Dude, that's one badass photo. You don't have anything better?'

Pakula unfolded the computerized copy and placed it beside the photo.

'She is definitely his type. But no, I can't say that I've seen her at any age.'

'You ever hear of him using an RV? Picking up kids at inter-state rest stops?'

'No, but that's pretty damned smart.'

Pakula hated that T-Rock looked like he had just given him a great idea.

'Anyone hear him say where he keeps those girls?'

'Of course not. Dudes don't share that kind of info.' Then he smiled at Pakula, but he sat back, signaling he was finished. Still, he couldn't seem to help himself, and he added, 'Can't do that or before you know it, FBI's knocking on the front door of your nice farmhouse.'

Pakula bit back his curse. T-Rock knew a lot more than he was telling. *Honor among thieves.* They'd cover for each other no matter how much they disgusted each other. They were all a bunch of bastards.

47

Florida Panhandle

Jason had kept quiet the entire twenty-minute trip from the Woodsons', and for some reason, Olivia was quiet, too. It was as if both of them were surprised by and disappointed in their failed attempts. Or at least, that's what Jason thought.

He pulled in front of Hannah's expecting to let Olivia out and drive on to his trailer, but when he stopped, Olivia looked over at him and said, 'Can you come in for some coffee?'

'I really need to—'

'Just for a few minutes.'

He stared at her, trying to figure out if she was going to complain about him in front of Hannah. What else could it be? After all, she'd had more than 'a few minutes' to talk to him during the drive back. As intimidating as the woman could be, he saw Creed's eyes every time he looked into her face. So he simply nodded, parked and went around back to get Scout. He could hear Rufus, Lady and Hunter in the fenced yard behind the house, so he took Scout and let him in with the others before he followed Olivia into Hannah's kitchen.

As if it were her own house, Olivia went directly to the counter where the coffee pot was. She knew which cupboard to open to get two mugs.

'Do you use cream or sugar?' she asked as she poured.

'Sugar, no cream.'

She gestured for him to sit and took the chair across from him. By now, Jason's foot was tapping under the table, and his teeth were clenched. She set a mug in front of him. He took a gulp of the coffee, not even flinching when it scorched his throat.

'Do you know Mrs Woodson very well?' Olivia asked.

'I only just met her yesterday.'

'She's lying about her daughter.'

'Wait a minute, what?' It wasn't at all what Jason expected her to say.

'Dealing with media and publishing people over the years, I've developed what I like to call my bullshit-meter. In the hour and a half that I spent with that woman she was registering off the charts.'

'I'm not sure I understand what you mean? You don't think Raelyn is missing?'

'Oh, I don't doubt that poor girl's missing, but her mother is lying about something.'

'Why do you think she's lying?'

She sipped her coffee, but her eyes never left his. They were the same blue as Creed's, not a fleck of green or hazel, but true blue. All Jason knew was they were difficult eyes to lie to. He knew that from personal experience.

'She vacillated back and forth,' Olivia told him. 'She'd say Raelyn disappeared. That someone must have taken her. Fifteen minutes later she told me the girl had run off before, and she'd probably run away this time.'

'Sheriff Norwich said they were questioning Mrs Woodson's boyfriend.'

'Where's Mr Woodson?'

Jason shrugged. 'She said they're divorced. She didn't tell you about her ex-husband?'

'No, she didn't. That's odd. Why aren't they questioning the father?'

'I don't know.' He glanced at his watch. He didn't want to spend his afternoon gossiping about Mr and Mrs Woodson. He already felt bad enough that he had screwed up a second time with Scout. 'We don't ask those kinds of questions,' he said, when it looked like she was waiting for an explanation. 'It's better if we know less, so we don't influence our dog with preconceived notions of what might have happened.'

'That's smart.' She nodded then stared off over his shoulder, out the window.

'Maybe that's what I was doing,' she said. 'Maybe I expected her to act differently because of my own experience with losing my daughter. It's such a horrible thing to happen to a mother.'

He didn't mean to be rude, but he also didn't want to talk about it anymore. He scooted his chair away from the table, hoping to find an excuse to leave when he felt the weight in the back pocket of his jeans. He'd forgotten about the cell phone he'd found in Raelyn's room.

'What is it?' Olivia must have seen the realization on his face.

Jason pulled the phone out and set it on the table between them.

'I found it between the nightstand and the bed in Raelyn's room.'

'What teenage girl goes anywhere without her phone?'

It was the same question Jason had asked himself.

'Maybe she lost it. It was stashed pretty far back. I'm sure Sheriff Norwich will want to review her calls and messages. I better go call her.'

He stood up and took his coffee mug to the sink to rinse. The coffee was making his stomach churn. He didn't really like coffee, but it seemed impolite to say no when someone invited him in for a cup. Especially since it was hardly ever about the coffee.

He glanced back at Olivia. She hadn't moved and was still staring out the window. He slipped out, leaving her to her thoughts.

48

'Olivia? Are you all right?'

She had no idea how long Hannah had been standing there staring at her. Olivia's hands were wrapped around the ceramic mug, but it looked like she hadn't taken more than a sip. The mug was no longer hot. It was lukewarm at best. Her mind had gone not just miles away but to years past. Disappointingly, she could conjure up those weeks – the sights, the smells, the panic – with very little effort.

Hannah sat down across the table from her. Her brow furrowed and her dark eyes narrowed with concern. Genuine concern. Why hadn't Olivia been able to see any of that in Mrs Woodson's eyes?

'You look like you've seen a ghost,' Hannah told her in a gentle voice.

This was a woman with a big personality but an undeniable sense of compassion. She filled the room with warmth. It was comforting just being in her presence. Comforting and safe. And for Olivia James, who had spent years not needing anyone to make her feel safe, or needing anyone to confide in, she suddenly found herself wanting to unleash it all.

'You must think I'm an awful mother,' Olivia finally said.

'Why in the world would you say that?'

'You never realize what you're capable of doing until something awful happens,' Olivia said, ignoring Hannah's question. Ever since she'd left the Woodsons' she was feeling a deep sense of darkness and a surprising bit of regret.

'When Brodie disappeared I blamed her father. I was so angry with him. He should have never let her go alone to the bathroom at that busy rest stop. All because he wanted to listen to his precious football game.'

She stared out the window, but she could feel Hannah's eyes on her.

'I blamed Ryder, too,' Olivia continued. Sitting with Mrs Woodson had managed to bring it all back to her – all of it crashing down around her, despite years of trying to bundle up those emotions and stow them carefully away. 'I was so upset that he hadn't watched out for his little sister.' She shook her head. 'But he was just a boy. His father deserved the blame. Not Ryder.'

She looked at Hannah and asked, 'He hasn't told you about any of it, has he?'

Hannah shook her head, but said nothing. This was a woman who knew how to listen.

'I dragged him from city to city,' Olivia told her. 'Pulled him out of school. Any tidbit, any morsel of information, and I'd pack us up. Sometimes I'd drive all night. When Ryder was old enough, he'd help drive. Each and every time I hoped and prayed that we'd find her. That she was still alive, just waiting for us to rescue her.'

She went quiet as she watched the branches swaying in the breeze. The sky couldn't be bluer if it tried.

'But God wasn't listening to me. I gave up on God the day I had to give up on finding my little girl,' Olivia said it in such a whisper she wondered if Hannah could even hear her. She felt the woman's hand reach across the table then take hers. 'But I should have never given up on Ryder.'

'Why did you?'

She met Hannah's eyes now and saw there was no judgment, only the question.

'My emotions were still so raw. It truly felt like I had deep gashes that wouldn't heal. I'd patch them up only to have them rip apart and bleed some more.' She shook her head, wanting to clear away the images. 'Then his father committed suicide. Did you know about that?'

'Yes. Rye told me he was the one who found him.'

Olivia nodded, and her eyes darted back out the window.

'It hadn't been a week or two after that, and all of a sudden, he told me he was joining the Marines. I thought he was angry with me about his father. I thought maybe it was his way of lashing out at me. I told him I refused to lose another child.'

She glanced back at Hannah, her vision blurred, and only then did she realize she was crying. She swiped at her eyes. 'I told him I would never speak to him again, if he joined the military.' She attempted a laugh that sounded shrill and fake and more like a cry for help. 'I was nothing if I wasn't true to my word.'

Hannah continued to hold her hand, and now, she squeezed it.

'I'm the reason Ryder hasn't had a mother for almost ten years.'

'You can fix that,' Hannah told her.

'You really believe that?'

'I know Rye. He has a big heart. I'm sure there's room for you.'

Olivia smiled and took back her hand, gently, so she could wipe away the tears. She took a deep breath and gathered herself. Then she asked, 'Are you and Ryder . . . you know, are you two a couple?'

Suddenly, Olivia could see Hannah sit up straight and her eyes flashed with an uncharacteristic spark, a hint of defiance, that Olivia hadn't seen before.

'Would that be a problem for you if we were?'

Yes, Olivia was right. She had struck a nerve. The last thing she wanted to do was offend this woman who had been so kind to her.

Olivia shrugged and tried to make light by saying, 'It's really none of my business. I was only thinking you might be a bit older than him.'

Hannah stared at her then suddenly she did something that surprised Olivia. She burst into a melody of laughter. This time, Hannah wiped tears from her eyes and her chest was still heaving when she said, 'I thought for sure you were going to say because I'm black.'

Olivia smiled and shook her head. 'Of course, that's not what I meant all. I just want him to be happy.'

'Ryder and I are family,' Hannah explained. 'We depend on each other. We support each other. I suppose in some ways I'm a big sister to him.'

'Believe it or not, I've tried to keep track of him as much as possible. He was in the news quite a bit a year ago. *USA Today* and even on *Good Morning, America*.'

Hannah nodded. 'And he hated it!'

'Does he have a woman in his life?'

'Oh, he has several.' And Hannah laughed, again. 'In fact, I've had to ask him to stop letting them spend the night at his place. I can't have my boys asking why there's a woman they don't know leaving Ryder's apartment in the morning when they're getting ready for school.'

'But no one special?'

'I don't think he lets anyone get that close,' Hannah said, now serious. 'Don't get me wrong. He's good to them. Your son is charming and sensitive and most likely, a gentleman. I've never heard any complaints, if you know what I mean. His closest relationships are with women, but I know he has a strict rule about not letting himself get involved with women he works with. You know who makes him happiest?'

Olivia perked up to listen.

'The dogs.' Hannah raised her hand as if she believed Olivia would pass judgment. 'I know that might sound strange, but he loves each and every one of our dogs. When we built his apartment over the kennel, he pretended it was because he wanted to be close, so he could protect what he always calls our most important assets. Like he really believes those dogs are business assets. Too many times to count, I've found him down in the kennel curled up and sleeping with the dogs.

'The fact is, that man feels happiest and the most comfortable when he's in the company of dogs. And I doubt there's a woman who'll be able to change that.'

49

Nebraska

Earlier at the lake, Creed had loaded the dive tank into the back of his Jeep without anyone noticing. When he came to the surface gasping for air he let Maggie believe it was the shock of finding the body. She was already concerned about having him be a part of this search team. He didn't want to give her another reason to tell him to go home.

So he wrapped the tank in an old blanket and placed it into a separate duffle bag. He was convinced someone had tampered with it, but he wasn't sure he'd be able to prove it. In all the dives he had made as a civilian and as a Marine, he'd never had a problem with a tank. Maybe it had malfunctioned simply because of poor maintenance, but he wanted someone to take a look at it. Someone other than Sheriff Timmons who had arranged for the boat and the tank to be delivered to the lake.

He kept thinking about the note Maggie had gotten the night before. If someone wanted Eli Dunn set free would they go so far as to tamper with the search equipment? And if so, how would that be possible?

For Creed, it was easier to concentrate on a possible conspiracy to sidetrack the recovery effort than it was to keep remembering that woman's startled face. He wished he could scrub that image from his mind. He could still feel the body bumping up against him. The plastic garbage bag, the confines of the car trunk and the cold lake had preserved her from the regular rigors of decomposition. She certainly didn't look like had died eight months ago.

And she didn't look like Brodie. Blue eyes, not brown.

He wasn't sure why that was such a relief. Isn't that why he was here? Because he believed he'd find her amongst the dead and finally have some sense of closure?

He'd seen it happen for other families whose missing loved ones he'd helped find. A body, even if it was reduced to bones, brought an odd sense of peace. It allowed hope to be tucked away, instead of the rollercoaster ride of emotions when hope was the only thing you had left to cling to.

And yet, as soon as he realized this woman couldn't be Brodie, Creed had felt an enormous sense of relief. So much so, that he couldn't imagine what he would feel if and when he found her remains.

Now back at the Embassy Suites, Creed prepared Grace's food and fed her. Then he put on her soft harness with the label: WORKING DOG. DO NOT PET. Grace knew this wasn't a working harness. As a multi-task dog, Creed had her trained to know the difference. Grace could distinguish what he wanted her to search for by the type of vest, harness or leash he put on her as well as the word or phrase he used.

But it wasn't always that simple. Because she was trained for so many different scents, she couldn't ignore one even if Creed had asked her specifically to find another. So Grace alerted to drugs if they were anywhere in the vicinity even if Creed hadn't asked her to 'find fish.' 'Fish' was his search word for drugs.

Recently, he'd started doing searches at nursing care facilities. The dogs were able to sniff out C. diff, a particularly nasty bacteria that could be fatal by the time any symptoms began to show up. To keep residents calm and not suspicious, Creed instructed his dogs to 'find soup.' He used a special vest for explosives and for human remains. But it was still tricky with multi-task dogs like Grace. Every once in while, she alerted to something or someone Creed hadn't asked her to search out.

But this vest told her to relax. She was off duty, and the dog pranced and wagged despite staying close to his heel. They made their way down the hall into the elevator and to the restaurant below. At the hostess stand, Creed prepared for an argument. Some places didn't want dogs outside of the rooms, but the woman simply smiled at him and said, 'They're waiting for you.' She grabbed a menu and gestured for Creed and Grace to follow.

There were only a few diners but every single one turned to get a glance at the dog. Grace, however, was more fascinated by the rock waterfall, the tropical plants and the stream that flowed through the atrium. Obviously, the indoor vegetation provided interesting scents.

Maggie and Lucy had drinks in front of them. The women sat across the table from each other. Maggie scooted over on the booth's bench to make room for Creed next to her while Lucy scooted in the other direction to greet Grace.

'Is it just the three of us?' Creed asked.

'Detective Pakula's a few minutes late,' Maggie told him. 'He said we should go ahead and order.'

'I'll get your waitress,' the hostess said as she placed the menu in front of Creed. 'Can I get you something to drink from the bar? Perhaps a bowl of water for your partner?'

He glanced at the women's drinks in front of them. Maggie had a beer, Lucy a glass of wine.

'I'll take you up on that bowl of water. And a beer for me.'

'Would you like me to tell you what beers we have?'

He pointed to Maggie's glass. 'I'll have what she's having.'

When the hostess left, Maggie said, 'I was telling Lucy about your facility. She rescues dogs, too.'

Creed raised an eyebrow and met the woman's eyes. 'Why am I not surprised by that?'

It was the first time he'd seen the woman smile. Everyone kept saying Lucy Coy was retired, but Creed had a hard time figuring out how old she was. Her eyes were soulful, her skin radiant, and she had the poise and confidence of woman who was content with herself and her life.

'I take care of mine,' Lucy said. 'But I don't have the skills to train them.'

'If you're ever interested in learning, you could come down sometime.'

'Ryder and Hannah have a long waiting list for dogs and for training handlers,' Maggie said. 'Last spring they signed a contract with DHS to provide virus-sniffing dogs for the airports.'

'Impressive.' Lucy sipped her wine and the smile turned thoughtful. 'I may take you up on that offer.'

A waitress named Rita interrupted to take their orders. She'd turned to leave when a man called out to her. Creed would have guessed he was a cop even if the guy had been in a crowd.

'Hold on minute,' the man said as he slipped into the booth next to Lucy.

He wore a sports jacket over a black T-shirt and jeans. He scraped his hand over his shaved head and waved off the menu she offered.

'You still have that eight-ounce filet?'

'You want steak fries with that?'

'Of course I want steak fries, but you better give me whatever vegetables you have instead.'

She'd barely left the table and the man stretched out his hand to Creed.

'Tommy Pakula. Call me Tommy. Call me Pakula. Whichever you like.'

'Ryder Creed. And this is Grace.'

'Grace, the wonder dog,' Pakula said as he offered his hand to Grace, keeping the fingers low so she could sniff without putting her head back. It was a gesture of someone who knew how to approach dogs.

'Have you found out anything?' Maggie asked.

'It's good to see you, too, O'Dell.' Pakula's tone was that of a colleague comfortable enough to exchange barbs. He laced his fingers together and placed them on the table. 'I called in a favor. She'll be moved to the top of the list tomorrow morning. But the CSU techs found something interesting when they were transferring her.'

Pakula glanced around to see if anyone was in earshot. Creed knew the detective purposely avoided referring to the victim by using the words body or corpse for anyone close enough to listen.

'She had a gadget on her ankle.' Pakula pulled his cell phone out. He swiped the screen a couple of times then handed the phone to Lucy first, who passed it to Maggie and Creed.

'Looks like a tracking device.' Creed recognized the small

black contraption with a nylon strap. 'I use a similar one with my dogs. They're small enough to wear on their collars. I usually drop one into the pocket of their vests. I can locate a dog if she gets hurt or lost.'

Pakula was nodding. 'We're checking to see if this one has a memory card or an internal data storage. Anything that we might be able to download.'

'Wait a minute,' Maggie said. 'Are you saying there's a chance we might be able to track where this woman was before she ended up at the bottom of the lake?'

Pakula raised an eyebrow at her and did a quick glance around. Then he looked to Creed, waiting for him to answer.

'It's been in the water for almost a year,' Creed said. 'Mine are water resistant, but I'd say it's a long shot as to whether or not the data storage is still available.'

'Any guess how she died?' Lucy asked keeping her voice low.

'I'm leaving that to your buddy Fox to tell us tomorrow.'

'Harold Fox?'

Pakula nodded.

'He's very thorough.' Lucy seemed pleased with his selection to do the autopsy. To Maggie and Creed, she said, 'He was one of my favorite students.'

'I'm trying to keep our team on this small and tightlipped,' Pakula told them. 'I only want people I can trust. I'm still trying to find out who else was in that house and where they went. Dunn had to have someone helping him. I think they're holding them somewhere else.'

'How well do you know and trust the people you have on the team right now?' Creed asked.

Rita brought their food, and Creed could feel all eyes on

him as they waited while she distributed the platters around the table. As soon as she was gone, Pakula put his elbow on the table and leaned forward, 'What the hell do you mean by that?'

'My dive tank malfunctioned while I was underwater.'

'Wait a minute,' Maggie said. 'Why didn't you tell me?' In the next instant he could see the memory register with her. 'That's why you came up gasping.'

'I couldn't breathe no matter how much I adjusted the regulator. No kinks in the lines. I checked for leakage in the hoses but didn't find anything.'

'What are the chances of a tank just malfunctioning?' Maggie asked, but Creed could already see she didn't believe that's what had happened.

'I'd say the chances are pretty slim,' Pakula said, his eyes on Creed. 'You think someone tampered with it.' A statement, not a question.

'Yes.'

'Son of a bitch,' Pakula muttered and swiped his hand over his jaw. 'You still have it?'

'In the back of my Jeep.'

'I'll have our lab guys check it.'

Then as if he remembered something else, he dug a folded piece of paper from the inside pocket of his sports jacket. Without unfolding it, he handed it over the table to Creed. 'Take a look at this.'

'What is it?' Lucy asked.

Creed opened the paper. Inside was a colored drawing of a woman's portrait. It was a computer rendering. She was attractive with an angular face, high cheekbones, brown eyes, long brown hair parted in the middle. There was something very familiar about the woman, as if he'd met her somewhere.

'I had one of our techs zoom in on that Polaroid then run it through an age-progression software.'

Creed blinked and took a closer look. That's why she seemed familiar. So, this was what Brodie would have looked like as a young woman.

SATURDAY, OCTOBER 21

50

Nebraska

Creed followed Maggie's directions. She rode with him and Grace this morning. Lucy had volunteered to personally deliver the DNA swabs of Creed's mother to Harold Fox. She'd meet them later.

Creed followed Highway 92 again, and when they passed by Lake Wannahoo he noticed Grace's nose in the air. An hour and a half later, they hadn't seen much traffic, and the distance between farms continued to grow as they saw fewer and fewer houses.

Maggie had been to Nebraska before, so she was familiar with the landscape, but she faced the passenger window, staring out as if it captivated her attention. Creed knew her silence had nothing to do with the rolling meadows and cornfields. She'd been uncharacteristically quiet all morning, outside of giving him an occasional direction. Something was bothering her. Whatever it was, he'd leave her to decide if and when she talked to him about it. He was content to deal with his own thoughts, and he actually welcomed the silence.

It didn't seem real to him that this was where Brodie had come to die. Of all the places he and his mother had traveled to follow up on tips, rumors or sightings, none had been in Nebraska. Detective Pakula talked last night about how

Interstate 80 was a major thoroughfare for human traffickers. It was possible that this state was simply a stopping place along her torturous journey. He had spent too many years trying to imagine what she was going through. Whether she was scared or hungry. Now, he wasn't sure what difference it made to know what she had gone through, to find out how many more years she had lived or even how she had died.

The two-lane blacktop was a straight ribbon that rolled over and between meadows. To either side, Creed could see creeks and ravines cutting through some of the steeper areas. Pastures of tall grass were dotted with black cattle – sometimes reddish brown – roaming along the hills and valleys. Some of the cornfields were terraced, tall edges cut into the earth. Others grew in rows that circled and weaved along the hills at impossibly steep angles. Huge pivot-irrigation systems stood idle, their work finished for the season. The light brown cornstalks had very little green left, almost ready for harvest.

Small ponds were filled with geese. Hawks glided overhead in a blue cloudless sky. Creed had noticed one perched on a fence post watching the grass-line ditch.

As they moved farther west, the landscape began to flatten. Windmills and grain siloes were the tallest structures for miles. Giant cottonwoods and straggly cedar trees lined the highway, but Creed was struck by how well he could see the horizon, since most of the trees were cluttered around farmsteads.

He didn't quite understand why Eli Dunn couldn't or wouldn't just give them directions. All the man had done the previous day was point to a section of the lake. He didn't even tell them about the sunken car. In the dark green fog of the lake with churned-up sediment, it would have helped for Creed to know that minor bit of information. Instead, Grace had pinpointed the dive area more definitively than Dunn.

'You should have told me about the tank,' Maggie said without glancing at him. Her eyes stayed on the view out her side window.

Her voice startled Creed. He'd almost forgotten she was there.

So there it was. The reason for her silence.

He wasn't good at detecting others' moods and emotions. That was Hannah's expertise. But there was definitely a hint of anger in Maggie's tone. No, it wasn't anger. What was it?

'I didn't want you to take me off the case,' he told her. It was as simple as that.

More silence. More miles.

'Up ahead,' Maggie finally said. 'There should be train tracks that cross the highway. There'll be a sign to our left for Brainard. We want to take a right turn just before the tracks.'

'Before or after the sign?'

'Before.'

It didn't take long, and he could see the tracks and the sign. The turn to the right, however, was not so easy to find. If he hadn't been told it was there, he could easily have driven past without even noticing. The narrow gravel road was flanked by cornfields on each side. So much for seeing the horizon.

Maggie was double-checking her notes. Creed noticed that she'd brought Eli Dunn's small notebook, but she wasn't referring to it at all for any of the instructions.

'Not quite a mile then a left turn,' she said. 'This next one's a dirt two-track into a pasture. There's a large dead tree just before the turn.'

'None of these details are in his notebook?'

'They might be, but I can't seem to break his code. I've even sent copies to our expert at Quantico.'

'Are you sure there really is a code?'

'We've thought about that.'

Creed waited for more, but that was all she offered. Her mood had not lightened.

The dead tree could be seen from a mile away. It was huge with scraggly branches jutting out in all directions. It looked like the slain skeleton of a monstrous creature, bony arms and legs flailing, reaching toward the sky even after it was sliced in half by a mighty bolt of lightning. Creed couldn't help thinking the tree was an appropriate marker for a graveyard.

Before he took the turn he saw the State Patrol SUV and the Butler County Sheriff Department pickup. The pasture road was a rutted two-track with grass in the middle. It ran so close to a stand of cedar trees that Creed had to go wide and off the narrow track to avoid the branches swiping at the side of his Jeep.

He glanced at Maggie. She didn't look pleased that the troopers had beaten them here. She was unbuckling her seatbelt and practically opening the door before Creed had come to a full stop. She marched through the tall grass, leaving Creed and Grace behind without a word.

Creed went about his business, preparing the gear he and Grace would need. A land search was definitely easier than a water search. But there was a lot of territory to cover. He avoided glancing over, though he was curious what Eli Dunn had in store for them today. He wanted to tell Maggie to send the man back. All Grace needed was the general vicinity. He didn't trust the guy. And more importantly, he didn't trust himself around Eli Dunn. Because all he had to do was look into the eyes of that bastard and Creed wanted to choke the life out of him.

Grace waited patiently in back of the Jeep, watching out the open tailgate, and suddenly she saw something that made her wag. Creed turned to see Lucy Coy's vehicle bouncing its way over the path. He scratched Grace under her chin and smiled.

Maggie had told him that some law enforcement officers said Lucy Coy had mystical powers because of her Indian heritage. There was no denying that the woman brought a calm reverence to these scenes. Creed could already feel the throbbing in his head slowing down. If today was the day he found Brodie's remains, he was grateful that Lucy Coy was here.

51

Florida Panhandle

Jason had agreed to meet with Sheriff Norwich at the Waffle House on Avalon Boulevard. Over eggs, grits and bacon and, of course a plate-sized waffle, he handed off Raelyn Woodson's cell phone.

She clicked it on, saw that it was locked then placed the phone beside her coffee cup.

'You didn't mention this at all to Mrs Woodson?'

He shook his head and forked another bite.

'There's something else,' he said. 'I took Scout back to the girl's bedroom yesterday. Thought I'd let him get a fresh scent of everything. The bed was stripped down. Laundry basket in the closet was gone.'

He didn't want to make a big deal out of it. Maybe the sheriff had even told Mrs Woodson that she could clean the room. If Jason had done a better job the day before, it wouldn't have mattered at all. But from the look on Norwich's face, he knew immediately that no such permission was given.

She slid her plate aside – scrambled eggs and bacon, only a bite or two taken – and planted her elbows on the table. He caught himself wondering if it would be rude to ask if he could take what she left for Scout.

'Confidentially, we're looking at the boyfriend,' she told Jason.

'Not the father?' Normally, he wouldn't ask, but Olivia had made him curious.

'Father's deployed in Afghanistan.'

Jason nodded and shoveled in another bite.

'But the boyfriend is new. Couple of the neighbors said Raelyn didn't like him. Which is really not unusual. Kids are going to side with their fathers.'

'Does the boyfriend have an alibi?'

Sheriff Norwich picked up her coffee cup and held it up for the waitress who was making the rounds. She waited until the woman left the table. Took a sip, put the cup down then planted her elbows again and leaned in.

'He's a long-haul truck driver. It hasn't been easy getting a hold of him. Or rather, it's been easy for him to put off being available. Truth is, I've nothing to connect him to her disappearance, but I'd sure feel better knowing she's not somewhere in his truck.'

Jason wasn't sure why she was telling him all this. All he wanted to do was bring her the girl's phone.

'Fact that you found her cell phone makes me believe she didn't run off on her own. The longer she's gone, the more her mother wants to believe the girl's run away. I guess she's done it before. Not long after the divorce.'

She sat back and sipped her coffee. Her eyes were watching the other customers. Without looking at Jason, she said, 'I sure wish your dog would have found something.'

And his stomach clenched, mid-bite. He continued eating only because he didn't want the sheriff to see that it mattered. She wasn't passing judgment. Just stating a fact. Jason was the only one passing judgment on himself.

Last night, he'd texted Creed. Told him that a second search had come up empty. He was too embarrassed to tell him that Scout had taken him up and down a bunch of trails only to bring him back to the shed with the freezer.

Those stupid training treats.

Creed's reply was short:

TRUST YOUR DOG.

So if there was nothing there, there was nothing there. Plain and simple. His dog couldn't say it any simpler. He thought about the bed sheets and how Mrs Woodson had watched him pull the covers back and let Scout sniff in between them. He wondered if she had been disgusted with the dog nosing through her daughter's bedding. But what if he'd missed something else?

'Do you have a few minutes this morning to stop by the Woodsons' with me?' he asked the sheriff.

She'd been watching the other customers, but her eyes darted to Jason's. She didn't ask him why. She simply said, 'Sure.'

52

Nebraska

'Look!'

Maggie's eyes followed where Lucy Coy pointed to a bird with a black head and throat, long black tail and white belly. The contrast of black and white was as bold as the bird that didn't appear threatened by them as it watched from the fence post not five feet away.

'It's a magpie,' Lucy told her.

'Seriously? I've never seen one before.'

Maggie had shared with Lucy that her father used to call her his magpie. And of course, the woman remembered. Maggie missed her father less and less these days. As more time passed, his presence felt like a dream rather than a reality. A firefighter, he was killed in the line of duty when Maggie was twelve. Her mother took up the nickname, but when she called Maggie 'Magpie' it wasn't said as a term of endearment as much as a sneer.

It wasn't until much later that she learned why her mother harbored such disdain for the man who Maggie had adored. To her mother's credit, she didn't tell her daughter until she was an adult: the secret of her father's infidelity and that she had a half-brother.

'They're quite remarkable birds,' Lucy told her. 'They can

mimic other birds, a dog, even a human voice. In some Native American legends, the magpie is a loyal friend who warns them of danger. The Cheyenne consider the magpie a sacred messenger of the Creator.'

'So what does it mean seeing it here?'

'If you believe Indian legends, it could be warning us about something.' Then Lucy shrugged. 'They feed on road kill as well as the insects that hang around cattle. Actually, it's not that unusual to see them in Nebraska pastures.'

Maggie was pretty sure she didn't believe in legends and myths anyway. But it was a reminder that something had been nagging at her all morning. She couldn't figure out why Eli Dunn had gone through the trouble of dumping dead bodies this far away from his own farm.

She was a profiler. She made her living putting together the pieces of why criminals acted the way they did. If she could discover their patterns and habits, she could predict their motives – and sometimes she could predict their next move.

With her hands on her hips she turned slowly, full circle as she scanned the surroundings. A line of large evergreens, side by side with very little room in between, ran almost the entire length of the dirt path into the pasture. On the other side of the trees was a cornfield. She'd noticed there were plenty of dirt roads into pastures and cornfields for miles. Why had Dunn chosen this one?

The majority of killers dumped the bodies of their victims less than a hundred feet from a main road. But Dunn had left Highway 92 and traveled several narrow gravel roads before he chose this dirt path into a grassy pasture. Was it the huge dead tree that attracted him? It was certainly a landmark that wasn't going to be moved any time soon.

She felt Lucy staring at her.

'You're wondering why he chose this place?' she asked.

'The CSU team found what they believe are human remains in a firepit in his backyard. His own farm is surrounded by cornfields and pastures and woods. Why take them two hours away to dispose of their bodies when he has all those isolated areas all around him?'

Before Lucy could answer, Maggie continued, 'And the body in the lake. He didn't just weight her down and toss her in. He may have stolen a car, put her in the trunk and drove the car out onto the ice leaving a sign that made it look like the whole thing was an advertising gimmick.'

Her eyes darted to the State Patrol SUV though Dunn was still in the backseat, and she could only see the back of his head.

'I don't get it,' she finally admitted.

'I think he has a connection to this area.'

'So you agree he didn't just drive these backroads looking around for some random place?'

'I've looked into his eyes,' Lucy said, 'and I see a man who constantly wants to impress and brag about what he's done. He wants us to know how smart he is, and that he's gotten away with things he believes a man less cunning would have been punished for.'

'When I showed him the photo of Brodie Creed, I asked him if she was in his precious notebook,' Maggie said, still taking in the quiet and isolation. 'He told me it depends if she's one of the ones that got sold or one of the ones that got buried.' She stopped to meet Lucy's eyes. 'What do you suppose it depends on? How did he chose which ones to sell and which ones to bury? Wouldn't it just be easier to sell them?'

'That's your territory,' Lucy told her. 'I'm trained to look at the body and the evidence. Trying to delve into the minds of madmen can be a dangerous endeavor.'

She pointed to something back behind Maggie and said, 'Looks like Mr Creed and Grace are ready.'

53

Creed waited for Troopers Gregory and Vegaz to lead Eli Dunn back to the SUV after performing his hocus-pocus. Creed thought it was a ridiculous waste of time. He couldn't believe that Maggie even allowed the man such a privilege. From what he understood, it was the price they had to pay in order for Dunn to narrow the search to this pasture.

When asked exactly where the body was buried, the man shrugged and lifted his arms in an over-exaggerated gesture suggesting he couldn't possibly tell them more while his wrists and ankles were shackled. Without a K9 team, maybe that little ploy would have worked. Maybe that was why Dunn stared at Grace with such venom while he grinned at the rest of them.

Creed waited until Dunn was back in the vehicle before he let Grace off her leash, but he could still feel the man's eyes on the dog. Grace didn't seem to notice or care. She had her vest on for recovery, and she was ready to get to work. In some places the grass and the wildflowers were taller than the dog, making her hop and zigzag through. Creed kept an eye on her while he followed and looked for craters of dirt or body burns.

His eyes skimmed over the brown and red grasses, watching for any drastic changes. Bodies were rarely under mounds. Instead, the earth tended to dip and sink when decomposition reduced it to less than the bulk that was originally buried.

Sometimes the soil turned acidic from the decomp. That's what was referred to as a body burn. Either way, there was often a change in the plants that grew up over the area. Weeds might not be quite as tall as the surrounding weeds.

Grace worked from side to side, parting the waves of grass, her nose up and sniffing. Every once in a while she'd skid to a halt from a dead run. She'd poke the air and sometimes backtrack before moving on.

Creed didn't know how long ago Eli Dunn had buried a body here. He didn't want to know. Maybe it was long enough that the plants had grown back and nature had resumed its normal course. No matter when it happened there was a chance wild animals had disturbed the grave. Maybe a coyote or raccoon had even pillaged and dragged off some of the remains. In that case, the scent cone would be wider.

They had been at it for over twenty minutes. Creed was about to call Grace for a water break when he noticed the change. Her head lifted higher to gather more samples. She was moving at a steady lope instead of racing from side to side. He let her continue, checking his watch. He didn't want to push her. Though the day was cool, the rapid breathing could exhaust a dog more quickly. She disappeared into taller grass, and all Creed could see was her tail poking up.

Suddenly, he saw the tail stop. Then he watched it curl.

Grace had found something.

Creed pulled two fluorescent orange flags from his daypack and pushed them into the ground to mark the spots, because Grace wasn't finished. He stopped her long enough for a drink of water and to run his hands over her body and paws. He'd noticed some sandburs along the dirt path earlier and knew Grace wouldn't complain even if one were stabbing in between her pads. After another thirty-five minutes she stopped on her own. This time her head turned back to find him. Then she stared into his eyes.

They were in the middle of the pasture, over a hundred feet away from where they had started. He planted another fluorescent flag before he tugged Grace's pink elephant out of his pack. She had to be tired, but she still danced on her hind legs when she saw her toy.

'Good girl, Grace! Good work.' He squeaked it then tossed it for her to catch. 'Don't go far.'

Only now did he notice that the sky had darkened with clouds. He had been watching Grace so intensely he hadn't paid attention to the thunderheads on the horizon, rolling toward them.

He saw Maggie start approaching with Sheriff Timmons at her side. Creed put his hand up, his palm out to stop them. He grabbed his cell phone out of his pocket and decided to text her instead of calling, so Timmons wouldn't overhear.

Just you.

He watched her fish her phone out and casually turn away so Timmons couldn't see the screen. Within seconds she was telling the sheriff something. He looked up and stared at Creed. It was too far away to see the man's face under the brim of his ball cap, but Creed could still feel Timmon's scowl.

As he waited for Maggie he inspected the ground. The grass was shorter here, some of it yellow. In places it was flattened as if something had been resting on top, long enough to yellow the grass. He stopped so he wouldn't trample what could be evidence. He swiped a hand over his bristled jaw while his eyes continued to scan and search. Then he saw the spot Grace had alerted to. The ground had been churned up, recently enough that nothing had started growing on top of the carefully patted-down mound. He could see chunks of dirt discarded in the grass, no longer necessary to fill the hole, because something else was buried here that hadn't left room.

'What is it?' Maggie asked, now coming up beside him.

'When did you say you arrested Dunn?'

He glanced at her when she didn't answer. She had to think about it. For the first time, Creed saw her exhaustion. She ran her fingers through her hair while the other hand stayed on her hip.

'Tuesday night. Actually after midnight, so Wednesday morning.'

'Looks like something may have been moved. And this ground has been dug up recently.'

She stared at the mound of dirt. She started to look back over her shoulder, but stopped herself.

'Maybe the landowner moved something?' But Creed didn't think she sounded convinced and before he could respond, she continued, 'He could have done it the day before we arrested him. We know he moved the other captives from his house.'

'I guess that's possible. But why even bring us here?'

Grace came prancing over to show Maggie her elephant as she squeaked it in her mouth. Creed didn't send her away, and he was glad Maggie didn't either.

'Hey, Grace. What a good girl you are,' Maggie told the dog as she held out her hand for the toy.

Grace dropped it carefully into Maggie's palm. Creed could see it was sticky with dog drool, but Maggie didn't flinch.

Instead, she tossed it gently into the air making an easy catch for Grace. Then she slipped out her phone and kept her body carefully in between the grave and their search party while she took several photos.

The rumble of thunder made them both look up. The dark clouds were now swirling overhead.

'Lucy mentioned she has a couple of tarps,' Maggie told him, as she was texting a message. Before she finished, Creed saw Lucy pulling up the tailgate of her SUV.

The breeze that came with the thunderheads was cooler than the day had been. Creed felt a chill where sweat had plastered his T-shirt to his back. He was grateful for the button-down shirt he wore unbuttoned, untucked and with the sleeves rolled up. The shirttail whipped around him now from a warning gust.

In no time, they had the gravesite covered, the corners of the tarp weighted down. They stretched a second over the other two sites where Grace had alerted. Drops of cold rain started to fall just as they got back to their vehicles. Maggie had told Lucy, Sheriff Timmons and the state troopers that Grace had discovered a possible gravesite. She made no mention of the recent digging.

Timmons said he'd need to go tell the landowner about them digging on their property. But there was no house, no farm as far as Creed could see. He had noticed on the drive that there were miles of pastures and fields without a building in sight. Also, he realized this was the sheriff's county. Most likely, he knew exactly who owned the property and where to find them.

Through the rain-streaked window, Dunn watched from the secured back of the trooper's SUV. Creed tried to avoid looking his way, because every time he did, the man was grinning at him.

Maggie volunteered that she and Creed would go get lunch for everyone while they waited out the thunderclouds. He caught her and Lucy exchanging a glance and a nod that told him Lucy would keep an eye on things while Maggie climbed into his Jeep.

They bumped along the dirt path, the ruts quickly filling with rain. He poked at his GPS to find out how far they'd need to go to get lunch. David City was the closest at eleven miles. He glanced at Maggie to see if she had any recommendations, but she didn't appear to be thinking about food.

Instead, she pulled out Eli Dunn's small notebook and started flipping through the pages. Finally she said to him, 'I don't like this.'

54

Omaha, Nebraska

Tommy Pakula was at the Douglas County Crime Lab when he got the call from Ms Gabriel at Project Harmony. His mind was still trying to wrap around what one of the techs had just told him. Pakula didn't know a thing about dive tanks but when the tech took the apparatus apart at the top of the tank and showed him, Pakula could feel the knot twist in his stomach.

'There's no way,' the tech told him, 'for these pieces of plastic to find their way inside here on their own. To be honest, I don't even know what they are, yet. I'll break them down and find out, but I know they don't belong here.'

'Could they come from some sort of corrosion? Or something like that?'

The tech shook his head. He pinched one of the clear pebbles and brought it out. There had to be almost a dozen of them inside the gadget that connected to the top of the tank. He gestured for Pakula to give him the palm of his hand, and he dropped it in the middle. It felt like a hard, plastic bead.

'So these could be the reason why the air wasn't flowing from the tank properly?' Pakula asked.

'They definitely would make it difficult to breathe. Even if the diver opened up the airflow, these little devils would still be rattling around inside. Sort of like clogging up an air filter. You'd still be getting air. Actually, your tank would be registering that it had plenty of air, but you'd be sucking in hard just to breathe.'

So Pakula was trying to figure out how and why someone had tampered with Ryder Creed's dive tank when Ms Gabriel called.

'Konnor has asked to speak with you, again,' she said. 'He's starting to remember.'

This time when he arrived at Project Harmony, Gabriel was waiting for him.

'I must warn you,' she said. 'He's been battling these memories. The drugs his captors were giving him helped repress his memories. Without the drugs, we expected this to happen. We've been working with him, but this morning he said he needed to talk to you.'

'What do you suggest I do?'

'Listen. Try not to prod.' She led them through the halls, and now she stopped ten paces away from the door. 'Just remember, some of his memories might not be real.'

'What do you mean?'

'We don't know what drugs he was given. Some of them could have been hallucinogenic.'

Pakula dragged his hand over his shaved head and released a heavy sigh. He'd come up empty-handed and had no clue where Eli Dunn had moved the rest of his victims before the raid. He suspected that the drug dealer named T-Rock might know, but of course, the man wasn't willing to share.

Pakula had even checked on Eli Dunn's mother, Eleanor. The director of the long-term care facility told him that the woman's dementia would probably make it difficult for her to tell Pakula anything about her son when she didn't even remember she had a son.

He was growing more and more frustrated. The days were ticking by. He knew if he didn't find a trail soon, those kids would be gone. Maybe they already were. They could be half-way across the country by now. Konnor might be their only hope.

The boy was waiting for him in the same spot, even the same chair. This time the kid actually smiled at him.

'Hello, Konnor,' he said as he took his chair.

He looked better but on closer inspection, Pakula could still see the sunken cheeks, the dark circles under his eyes. However, there was a sparkle that hadn't been there last time.

'I'm starting to remember some things,' he told Pakula, and he sounded anxious to share.

'That's great.'

'There were four of us in the house before the police came,' he said. He furrowed his brow like he wanted Pakula to know he was serious and ready to get down to business. 'I was the only boy. There was a woman. Older. Long brown hair. The other two girls were around my age. I think. I don't know for sure. They had long brown hair, too.'

Pakula was thinking about what T-Rock had told him. That Eli Dunn had a 'type' that he liked. Long brown hair was one of the details.

He listened and let Konnor talk. The kid didn't remember anyone's name. He said they weren't allowed to use names or even really talk to each other. Sometimes there were others that came. Once there was another boy, but he didn't last long.

'He made Eli mad and the next day he was gone.'

That was all Konnor said about the boy.

Pakula wanted more details about the 'fix-ups'. That's what Konnor called them, but he saw that the boy was terribly uncomfortable even mentioning them or the men. When Pakula asked if he might recognize some of them, Konnor told him that he mostly closed his eyes.

But then he started telling Pakula about the hotel. Once a month. The same hotel. The fourth Monday of every month.

How did he know what day, Pakula wanted to know. Most of these kids were kept in the dark about what day of the week it was.

'I heard Eli say once. And then I tried to keep track.' Konnor hung his head, his chin tucked against his chest. He went quiet for so long Pakula worried that he shouldn't have questioned the boy.

'I stole a calendar,' Konnor finally admitted. He looked up and smiled when he said, 'I was hoping that some months didn't have four Mondays.' The smile slid off his face, and he dropped his head again. This time when he went silent, he was finished.

No more memories for today.

55

Nebraska

Creed wondered if Maggie was putting too much stock in Eli Dunn's scribbles.

'I'm trying to find which one of these drawings is today's site. He was so proud of how he drove that car onto the frozen lake, and yet this time,' Maggie said, 'he shrugs like he has no idea where the gravesite is. Like there are so many bodies he can't possibly remember them all. I keep looking at how many drawings he has in here. If each one is a burial site, there could be dozens.'

'You want to know what I think?'

'Yes, of course.' She turned to face him, as much as the seatbelt would allow.

'I don't think this is playing out the way he hoped.'

'What do you mean?'

'Have you noticed the way he looks at Grace? I don't think he expected a K9 to come along on his scavenger hunt.'

He glanced at her and could see she hadn't given it any thought before.

'He gives minimal information each time. Insists that we don't even get to know where we're headed until late the night before.' He checked on Grace and in the rearview mirror he saw she was watching him with her ears pinned back. He knew she didn't like the drumming of the rain above her and the flashes of lightning. 'It's okay, Grace. Go ahead and lie down.'

Maggie readjusted and reached back to pet the dog.

'I've been expecting him to ask about your connection,' Maggie said. 'I saw him craning his neck to get a look at your Florida license plate. I thought perhaps it was you that put him on edge. I never considered it might be because we brought along a scent detection dog.'

'Earlier when he pretended he couldn't narrow the search, he raised his wrists like he was suggesting he might remember more without the handcuffs.'

'I did notice that. It's all a part of the game. From the beginning he's been playing let's make a deal.'

'I get that. But if you didn't have Grace or another K9, would you be indulging him? Maybe a little bit? This is sort of out in the middle of nowhere.'

'I can't imagine doing this search without a dog, but I suppose if one wasn't available immediately ... I'm not sure. I think I would have still waited.'

'You were in a hurry because of Brodie,' he said and his eyes met hers briefly, just long enough to see a flash of emotion, before he looked back to the windshield and the curtain of rain.

'It's not just Brodie,' she said. 'It's not just the others Dunn may have murdered. Although I must admit you've taught me how important finding the remains can be for the families to recover, to move forward. Pakula and I believe there are other kids who are still alive. There were others in his house right before the raid. He had to have moved them. Or someone else did it for him.

'I keep hoping Dunn will slip. Maybe get cocky and inadvertently give us something, anything that will help us find them.' She held up the notebook. 'I keep looking for a clue. Some place he hides them. But I'm beginning to think this was only meant to be part of his game. A bargaining chip in case he got caught.'

It was sprinkling by the time Creed's Jeep pulled into David City. The sky was still dark but the clouds with thunder and lightning had moved to the north. With nothing to obstruct the view, Creed could see them rolling and churning away with white streaks of down-pouring rain beneath them.

On the GPS's list of available fast food, restaurants and cafés, Maggie recognized a place called Runza on 4th Street. Turned out that Highway 15, the route they were on, was actually 4th Street. It didn't take long to find the green awning amongst a row of brick buildings along the street.

'The last time I was in Nebraska,' Maggie told him, 'a wildlife biologist named Amee Rief introduced me to a Runza. They have burgers, fries, chili – even cinnamon rolls – but their signature sandwich is a bread roll stuffed with beef and cabbage.'

He dropped her off at the front door so he could put in gas across the street.

'What would you like me to get for you?' she asked.

'All of it sounds good.'

'A Runza, fries, chili, cinnamon roll?'

'Yes, please.'

'Which?'

'All of what you just said.'

She smiled at him as she closed the Jeep's door, and if Creed had resolved in his mind to set aside all the physical attraction and feelings he had for her, that smile just dismantled all his resolve.

As soon as he stepped out of the vehicle he noticed the storm had reduced the temperature significantly. According to The First National Bank's digital sign, it was fifty-two degrees. It had been in the seventies earlier.

He filled up the gas tank and went inside the small convenience store. Earlier he'd noticed some of the wounds Dr Avelyn had so patiently and expertly patched up were weeping through the bandages. It looked like this place had a little bit of everything.

'Can I help you find something?' the clerk behind the counter asked.

'I need some bandages. Basic ones are fine. Doesn't need to be pretty.' He smiled and showed her the dirty gauze wrapped around his forearm.

'We have a whole section of "it doesn't need to be pretty". Next aisle over.'

He glanced at her nametag. 'Thanks, Danine.'

He found what he needed, grabbed a couple bottles of water and was headed for the cash register when the newsstand by the door caught his eye. Newspapers, let alone newsstands, were a rarity, but it was the front-page photo that drew his attention. He recognized Sheriff Timmons even without the man's signature ball cap and dressed in a suit. He had his arm wrapped around a woman. The headline read, CHARITY BALL TO BENEFIT VICTIMS. Maybe Creed was wrong about Timmons. It looked like he might be one of the good guys who practiced what he preached.

Creed added one of the newspapers to the rest of the items he put on the counter.

'You know Sheriff Timmons?' he asked Danine.

'Oh yeah. Butler County Justice Center is just up the street. Sad news about his wife.'

'I didn't hear about her.'

'Just found out she has MS. Both of them were planning on retiring next year. They were going to do some traveling. Her illness will certainly change that. Where in Florida are you and your wife from?'

She caught Creed by surprise. But with a glance, he noticed she had a perfect view of the street, along with the back of his Jeep. She was sharp and quick. Both were probably a necessity for the job.

'The Panhandle,' he told her. 'Just outside of Milton and Pensacola.'

'I love those beaches. Sugar-white sands.'

'You've been there?'

'It's been too many years. You're lucky to live in such a gorgeous place.'

But Creed realized he couldn't remember how long ago he'd taken a walk on Pensacola Beach. He vowed to fix that as soon as he got back.

Danine finished bagging up his purchases then took a couple of dog biscuits from a container beside the register. 'For your cute dog.'

He realized she didn't miss a thing. He wanted to ask more about Timmons, but two more customers came in. He thanked her and left. As he drove back around to pick up Maggie he took a good look at the town, at the businesses, the justice center, the neat and clean streets. Cars and pickups parked orderly at just the right angles. There was no litter, no trash. People went about their business, not deterred by the thunderstorm and not a single umbrella in sight.

And yet, less than a dozen miles away, Eli Dunn may have buried several bodies in their pastures and fields. Creed wondered what other secrets were buried out here that no one knew about.

56

Santa Rosa County, Florida

Mrs Woodson greeted Sheriff Norwich, but she wasn't pleased to see Jason and Scout again.

'I thought your dog didn't find anything?' she asked, standing in the doorway and not moving to invite them inside.

'We wanted to check on one last thing,' the sheriff told her. 'May we come in?'

She stepped aside but she didn't take her eyes off Scout.

And why would she? Scout was dancing with too much energy, with barely enough patience to stand around beside Jason for these boring formalities. After all, he'd been cooped up inside the back of the SUV while Jason had breakfast. The open sunroof only made it worse with smells of bacon coming from the diner. Sheriff Norwich had offered her leftovers without Jason asking for them, and Scout had slurped them down in two grateful bites. But now, he was ready to go.

He recognized the house and the smells. Jason wondered if Scout believed they'd returned simply to go for another walk on the trails behind the house.

'I don't know why you keep bringing that dog,' Mrs Woodson said to Sheriff Norwich. 'I don't like him poking around my daughter's things.'

'We're only trying to help find her,' the sheriff said. 'You mind if we check the backyard again?'

Jason hadn't shared anything with Norwich, other than he wanted to see one more time where Scout would lead him.

Trust your dog, Creed had told him. He'd also said that Scout's alerts were some of the most honest of all their dogs. Creed had saved him when he was just a puppy, so Scout had never had to worry about going hungry.

All this time, Jason thought he'd screwed up. He thought maybe he hadn't trained Scout properly. What if he had confused the dog by giving him food as a reward? Creed liked to share the very real story about a K9 rescue team that alerted to an area after a massive mudslide in Washington. Crews brought in earth-moving equipment to remove debris, and rescuers worked for hours believing the dog had alerted to victims trapped under the mud. At the worst, they expected to find bodies. They never expected to find, instead, a refrigerator filled with rotting food. And all because the handler had used food as a training reward.

Scout loved food as much as Jason did, but Creed was right. Food was never an issue. Scout loved playing with his rope toy. And he loved doing the searches and pleasing Jason. But did he want to please Jason too much? They were about to find out.

He didn't mind that Mrs Woodson followed them out into the yard. Inside Jason's daypack he had brought along a tool he thought they might need if the sheriff agreed with him. Three steps out the back door of the house, and Scout was already leading Jason to the shed at the corner of the property.

'This is ridiculous,' he heard Mrs Woodson say.

Scout pawed at the shed's door and Jason opened it. Immediately, the dog raced to the battered old freezer that filled the space with its electrical hum.

'Do you have a key for this padlock?' Jason asked.

'Key? I told you there's just a bunch of frozen fish my ex-husband left. I have someone coming next week to haul this old eyesore away to the dump.'

'Do you have a key?' Sheriff Norwich asked.

'Of course I don't have a key. I made him put a padlock on it so the neighbor kids don't mess with it. He has the key. Ask him.'

Jason wasn't sure how long Mr Woodson had been deployed to Afghanistan, but the padlock looked pretty new.

'Is it okay if we open it?' Jason asked, but he was asking the sheriff.

She met and held his eyes as one of her eyebrows raised, but she looked willing to play along. Keeping her tone as casual as Jason's, Norwich asked Mrs Woodson, 'Do you mind if we take a look inside?'

'Why in the world would you do that?'

The woman was angry now. Her hands were twisting the hem of her knit shirt, and her eyes flashed at Jason when she saw him pull the tool from his daypack.

'This won't break the padlock,' Jason told her. 'So we can lock it back up.'

'Right,' Norwich said. 'That way you don't have to worry about the kids messing with it before you have it hauled away.'

The lock popped in seconds. Jason glanced at the sheriff one last time, giving her a chance to stop him. She nodded. Then he shoved the lid open.

Inside were dozens of packages wrapped in white butcher paper, but on top of them was the curled-up body of a young girl dressed only in a pink nightshirt.

57

Nebraska

After the tarps were removed, Creed watched Lucy Coy. She brought out a worn duffle bag and started removing items – gloves, several different-sized trowels and plastic basins. It looked more like she was planning on doing some gardening instead of digging up human remains. She kneeled in the mud in the area Creed had marked with the first two flags. The area where Grace had given what Creed considered a soft alert.

He suspected, but didn't say, that these sites may only yield bits and pieces or perhaps only blood. If Dunn had carried or dragged the body, and blood or body fluids escaped into the soil, it was possible Grace could detect the scent. Another possibility was if wildlife had scavenged the body after it had been buried.

Maggie stayed close by Lucy's side, assisting her like a nurse to a surgeon. The rest of them all watched from about fifteen feet away. Even Eli Dunn was allowed to be there despite needing help to stumble across the uneven pasture with his ankle shackles left in place.

Creed understood what Maggie was hoping for, but he wasn't happy about having the man this close. She wanted to watch Dunn and study every flinch or grin or blink of his eyes. As a profiler, he knew Maggie expected to gather information from his mannerisms, his gestures, his involuntary tells. Creed understood all this and yet, he hated that the man who may have murdered his sister would be able to witness them recovering her remains.

It felt wrong. It felt like one last violation.

Sheriff Timmons continued to let Maggie know he didn't agree with this arrangement either.

'He doesn't deserve to be here. He should be—' He stopped mid-sentence when he saw Lucy's fingers carefully pulling out, bit by bit, what looked like a bloody piece of fabric. Lucy waited with the item pinched between her forefinger and thumb while Maggie unfolded and opened an evidence bag.

'I'll be damned,' the sheriff muttered under his breath and took a step back as if he needed to compose himself.

Creed wanted to see Dunn's reaction, but he couldn't look away from the bloody fabric.

Usually he and Grace left the evidence gathering to the experts while they packed up their gear or waited until they were needed again. Most of the time, he'd take Grace off to the side and play fetch with her elephant. He glanced down to see if she was already feeling his dread. The dog was sitting behind him. His legs blocked her view of the gravesite, but it didn't matter. She was no longer interested. Her body was turned, her head tilted as she watched a squirrel in a nearby tree. He was relieved to find that she knew her job was finished, despite still being on the leash. Now, she was simply being a dog.

Lucy unearthed another piece of fabric, this one smaller. She shielded its identity, cupping her left hand between it and the men. Immediately, Creed suspected it was a pair of underwear. He tasted bile and swallowed hard.

By the time Lucy was finished with the secondary sites, Creed had shoved aside his physical discomfort. One thing the Marines had taught him was how to refocus his mind and energy on the task at hand, no matter how uncomfortable he was. He needed to concentrate on the here and now.

Lucy was more hesitant at the primary site. He heard her tell Maggie that she would start the process, but only to see if there was a body. If there were one buried here then she'd call in the Douglas County Crime Lab's mobile unit.

She gently brushed the crusted top layer with her gloved fingers. Slowly, she scooped small bits of dirt using only the tip of the garden trowel. Seconds into the undertaking, Lucy jerked her hand away.

Even Maggie startled. 'What's wrong?'

Despite the crumbles of black dirt, Creed could see the brown fur, matted and bloodied.

'What the hell?' Sheriff Timmons asked as he shot a glance of disgust at Creed and Grace. 'So all your dog found was a dead animal.'

58

Maggie had been watching Eli Dunn when she saw Lucy jolt back. Before Creed could answer the sheriff's accusation, Maggie put her hands up to calm everyone. She said to Timmons, 'Scent detection dogs are trained to ignore dead animals.'

'Maybe that's why the experts use real dogs,' the sheriff told her, 'instead of scrawny little terriers.'

'She didn't alert to the road kill,' Creed said in a calm tone that made Maggie check his eyes then his hands. She was relieved to see that his fingers weren't balled up into fists. She wouldn't have blamed him if he were angry, but she also knew he was used to defending the stature of his dogs.

'The scent of a dead animal is different,' he explained, 'than the scent of a decomposing body.'

'Well, she must have gotten confused.' The sheriff shook his head. 'I can't believe we wasted a whole day. If we leave now we can make it home before the next round of rain.'

While Timmons stomped around Maggie watched Dunn. He hadn't taken his eyes off the hole with the dead animal.

'There's something underneath,' Creed told them. 'It's a common mistake killers make.'

This time Dunn's eyes flicked to Creed then to Grace and back to the mound of fur. The state troopers stood silently, one on each side of the prisoner.

'Don't make excuses for your dog,' the sheriff said, pacing back and forth. 'Let's pack up and get the hell out of here.'

'He's right,' Maggie said while staring at Dunn. The man seemed mesmerized.

She reminded herself that serial killers often returned to the scenes of their crimes, sometimes even to watch law enforcement officers process the evidence. They enjoyed seeing and hearing experts talk about their handiwork, just like Dunn was doing now.

'Mr Creed is right,' she continued. 'Killers have been known to leave road kill on top of graves, hoping it'll throw off a scent dog.'

'We won't know until we look,' Lucy said and bent down, again.

'Hold on, Ms Coy,' Trooper Vegaz stopped her.

Maggie had noticed the troopers had treated Lucy with respect even yesterday at the lake. Neither Gregory nor Vegaz would allow their former teacher, the former medical examiner to help them wrap and secure the corpse. Now, Vegaz marched forward to remove the dead animal carcass.

'Just a minute,' Sheriff Timmons told him, and he jutted his chin toward Dunn. 'Let him haul away his own dead raccoon from the hole.'

'It's no problem,' Trooper Vegaz said, and he accepted the canvas gloves Lucy handed him as she stepped away to make room for him.

They'd need another evidence bag. Maggie headed to where they'd left the duffle bag, close to the first two sites. Maybe it was silly to treat the road kill like evidence, but she had learned long ago to leave nothing behind.

Her back was turned when the explosion knocked her to her knees.

59

The noise made Charlotte scramble up onto the kitchen counter. This time, she took off her socks and barely needed the chair she had left up against the cabinets. The day before, she had seen the kitten pouncing up onto the table then to the counter, and she realized if she did the same, she could see out of the small window high above the sink.

Without the drugs, Charlotte was feeling stronger despite the sick dread after reading Kristel's letter. She wondered how many years Iris had locked Kristel in rooms and closets and sheds before she sent her to the Christmas house for the man named Eli to take her away. And she wondered where Kristel was now.

Since reading the letter Charlotte found herself on edge. Every sound, every flicker of light seemed to scrape her nerves raw. The thunder and lightning had unsettled her so much that she had curled up into a corner until the kitten came to bother her. The silly creature wanted to eat all the time.

But this last noise was not thunder.

Standing on the kitchen counter, Charlotte could see up over the cornfields that surrounded the house. Far off in the distance, she saw what looked like a road. She wanted to spend all her time just looking out and watching, but her muscles began to ache, and her knees threatened to buckle, so she reluctantly got down.

She heard voices earlier. And a car engine. At first, she thought she must have imagined it, but for many years she had depended on and trained her hearing to compensate for what she wasn't allowed to see.

She'd climbed up to peek out the window and was startled to see Aaron as he got into a pickup. The sight startled her so much she ducked and almost toppled off the counter. She forced herself to look again just in time to see him drive away.

She wondered how long it would be before Aaron and the other man would come for her. According to Kristel, it wouldn't be long now. Charlotte had come up with a plan, but it still scared her. She'd even practiced a couple of times, counting to herself to see how many seconds she needed from the time she heard Aaron. She dragged the kitchen table in front of the back door to buy herself extra time. In case he used the front door, he'd need to move the heavy old recliner first.

It had to be hours ago that she had seen him drive off. But she was listening for his return. Somehow she knew he'd be coming back soon. The storm may have delayed him. And then came that loud noise.

She stretched on tiptoes, and that's when she saw movement down below. The pickup.

He was back!

She wasn't ready.

Suddenly, she heard the slamming of the pickup door.

It was happening! He was coming for her.

She scrambled down off the counter, bumping her knee and ignoring the pain. She raced to the other room and realized she was counting in her head. Already up to ten, eleven, twelve . . . she'd never done it in less than thirty-four seconds.

She heard the metallic rattle of a lock. The back door. Then the clack of the doorknob.

Hurry, she told herself, as her fingers fumbled.

A bump as the door opened against the table.

A curse. Another bump. A crack of wood against wood. Another curse and he was inside.

Charlotte watched Aaron move from the kitchen to the first room. Even if she was lucky enough for him to not see her, she was certain he'd be able to hear the banging of her heart. Thankfully, the kitten had gotten so frightened of Charlotte running and the crashing at the back door that she raced to hide under the bed. In her mad dash, Charlotte took three precious seconds to close the bedroom door to protect the cat from what was about to happen.

You'll be okay, she promised the kitten in her mind.

I'm doing this for you and for me.

Aaron stopped in the doorway and she could see him blinking. The clouds had made it dark inside the house. Not too dark for Charlotte, but for someone coming in from the outside, it would require some adjustment.

She held her breath and watched, not daring to move a muscle. She couldn't afford to flinch. But the closer he got, the more difficult it was to stay completely still.

He was taller and bigger than she remembered, broad shoulders with long arms. His silhouette reminded her of Iris, a stalking hulk that moved slowly but with stealth. He looked straight at her, and Charlotte was sure that her heart had stopped beating. Then he turned and looked behind the Christmas tree.

He hadn't seen her.

It was working.

She needed to stay calm. Wait for him to get closer.

He swung around and stared hard at the plastic reindeer in the corner. Now, Charlotte could see that his hands were empty. She was relieved that he hadn't brought a weapon.

A few more steps and he walked right past her.

She was glad that she had washed herself no matter how cold the water had been. And she had taken the scissors and cut off her hair. There was such a relief, a sense of freedom, watching all those long greasy tangles fall into the sink. Had she not cleaned herself, Aaron probably could have smelled her.

But now, she wasn't so sure he wouldn't be able to hear the pounding of her heart. Her chest ached and her lungs felt like they would burst soon if she didn't let them breathe normally instead of the short, silent in-takes.

His back was facing her. He had walked right by and hadn't even seen her sitting in the rocking chair. He didn't notice that Santa was a bit scrawnier. Nor had he noticed the pair of scissors tucked up into the cuff of his red jacket.

Charlotte pounced up and out of the chair just like she had practiced. She jumped onto his back and drove the metal blades of the scissors into the fleshy part of Aaron's neck. He bucked and howled, but she hung on. His arms thrashed about, and he reached back, clawing at her, trying to find something to grab. Blood spattered her face, but she dodged his big hands.

Then he did something she hadn't expected. He pushed himself backward and slammed her into the wall. Her head cracked so hard she heard plaster crumble and saw stars as she slid down Aaron's back. Her legs betrayed her, folding under, her knees useless. Before she could do anything, she saw the syringe.

So he had brought a weapon, after all.

He plunged the needle into her arm. Then she saw him look at his hands. And she saw the look on his face when he noticed all the blood. He reached up his fingers to where the blades stuck out of his neck. He gripped his hand around the scissors, groaned and pulled them out.

Big mistake.

Even Charlotte knew that before the blood started spurting out.

From the floor, she watched his eyes, and now Aaron knew he'd made a mistake, too. He clamped his big hand around the wound and pressed down. He wobbled, and she thought he would fall beside her. He stumbled then seemed to regain his balance.

She watched him stagger toward the kitchen while she tried to get to her feet.

She couldn't let him get out the door. She tried to crawl but her knees wouldn't cooperate. The drug seeped into her veins, keeping her limbs from working.

The door slammed.

No, wait! Aaron, wait!

Even her voice didn't work.

She heard the locks click and clack back into place.

Suddenly, Charlotte found herself hoping and praying that the man she had tried to kill would not leave her behind and go off and die.

60

The force was so strong that Creed flew backwards and was now staring up at the clouds. His chest and head throbbed. His ears were ringing. He'd gotten the wind knocked out of him, and his first panicked shout for Grace struggled to make it out of his throat.

Then he heard the scream.

Creed rolled to his side and pushed up on one elbow. Everything was blurry but he still saw Trooper Vegaz writhing on the ground not ten feet away. He was clutching a bloody pulp where his right hand used to be.

Creed wiped at the blur only to get double vision. He dragged his arm and shirtsleeve over his face. The shirtsleeve came away stained with dirt and blood.

'Grace,' he called again, twisting his neck to see over the tall grass. 'Maggie?'

There was a lot of movement around him. Scuffles behind him. He managed to get to his knees when he felt a hand on his shoulder.

'Are you okay?'

It was Maggie's voice, but when Creed looked back there were still two of her. He shook his head.

'Please help me find Grace.' He tried to get to his feet and stumbled back down on hands and knees.

'She's okay,' Maggie told him, so close now he could feel her breath in his ear. 'Stay down for a few minutes.'

'I need to find Grace.' He squeezed his eyes tight and started to crawl on his hands and knees.

'She's right here.' Maggie stopped him and suddenly he felt her hands pushing something under him.

He opened his eyes and there was the dog, her head pushing up against his chest. The billow of his shirt tented her in. She was trembling but poked her nose up and licked his chin.

'Just slow down.' He heard Maggie's voice again, but she was farther away.

She wasn't talking to him now. He blinked again and shook his head, but stayed on his hands and knees, now more as a protection to Grace. Also, he was pretty sure he wouldn't be able to stand up just yet.

He looked over at Trooper Vegaz and saw that Lucy Coy was kneeling at the man's side. She was wrapping something around his hand, but the fabric was already soaked with blood. Creed tilted his head in the direction he heard Maggie, and saw that she was standing just a few feet from him.

'Let him go,' Maggie said.

Creed leaned his weight back to sit on his haunches. He pulled Grace against him while his hands ran the length of her body, his fingers checking for injuries and blood. He put her down in the grass beside him, keeping her tight at his side. He tapped the ground and Grace lay down. She wasn't trembling anymore now that she was focused on him.

From this vantage point he could see what was going on. And finally, his eyesight was cooperating.

Eli Dunn had a gun to Trooper Gregory's temple. He was still in shackles but somehow during the explosion he had managed to grab the trooper's sidearm. Gregory was on his knees. Dunn stood behind him with an arm around the trooper's throat. It was a haphazard attempt to subdue the big man, one that Dunn wouldn't be able to maintain for long. Already, Creed could see Dunn's hand with the gun swaying away.

Maggie was in front of the two men, her hands at her sides, trying to talk to Dunn. Even with his vision slowly focusing, Creed could see the manic frenzy on Dunn's face. Instead of looking at Maggie, Eli Dunn was staring at Sheriff Timmons. The sheriff was off to his side, and almost behind them. He had his weapon drawn and was pointing it directly at the prisoner.

'Drop the gun,' Timmons shouted at him.

'You all tricked me,' Dunn shouted back.

'Let Trooper Gregory go,' Maggie told him, 'and we'll talk about what comes next.'

'No way.' He shot a look at Maggie. 'I trusted you. We had a deal. You tricked me.'

His eyes flitted up and over to steal a look at Trooper Vegaz. Then Creed could see his grip weaken. His arm slipped, and Gregory took advantage. He thumped his elbow back, knocking Dunn backwards.

Without even thinking, Creed pushed off his feet and launched his body just as the first gunshot was fired.

61

Maggie should have seen it coming. The night of the raid, Eli Dunn had set tripwires. How could she have forgotten the smell of ammonia? He had called it his alarm system, so he'd know when they entered his front yard.

He'd done it again. Tricked her. Even the magpie had tried to warn her.

Now, they'd never know how Dunn had pulled it off, because this time, instead of riding in the back of a State Patrol SUV, Dunn would be heading back to Omaha in a body bag.

She reminded herself that this was a man who was crazy enough to drive a car onto the iced surface of a lake with the sole purpose of disposing of the body in the trunk. It didn't seem like a stretch to imagine that same man planting explosives in the carcass of a dead animal and placing it on top of one of his buried victims.

She rubbed her lower back as she stood in the middle of the pasture. Maggie watched the last of the rescue units leave as more state troopers, a bomb squad and the Douglas County Crime Lab's mobile unit arrived. The last of the clouds moved out and dusk turned the sky deep blue. Floodlights and headlights lit up the pasture.

A Life Flight helicopter had airlifted Trooper Vegaz. The crew had allowed Lucy to accompany him. The rest of them:

Trooper Gregory, Sheriff Timmons, Grace and herself had minor cuts and scrapes. Lucy and Creed had been the closest to the explosion. Trooper Vegaz's body had sheltered Lucy from the blast. Creed had done the same for Grace. He had to be in pain, and still, he'd found the strength to tackle Maggie and cover her with his own body when the shooting began. She wasn't sure if Eli Dunn had intended to shoot her, but Sheriff Timmons didn't give him a second chance.

Maggie tried to convince Creed to let the rescue squad take him to the ER. She suspected he had a concussion, possibly a broken rib. But he told them he was fine. However, he didn't argue when Maggie insisted on driving his Jeep as they headed back to Omaha.

The first forty minutes they rode in silence. Maggie hoped Creed had fallen asleep. She found herself playing over the scene in her mind over and over again, trying to make sense of the chaos. It was useless. She couldn't change the outcome, and yet, all day something had nagged at her. She kept thinking she was missing something and thought she might find the answers in Dunn's notebook.

'What did he mean about you tricking him?' Creed said suddenly.

'What?'

'Just before Timmons shot him. Dunn said you tricked him.'

'I'm not sure what he meant. He said something about our deal.' She wished she could remember his exact words. But Creed was right. Dunn had accused her of tricking him. 'We'll never know. I didn't want him to go to prison and take the secret of where he'd buried your sister with him. Now, he's taking it to his grave. If Brodie isn't buried in that pasture, we might never find her.'

She glanced at him, but all she could see was his profile in the blue light of the dashboard.

'There might not even be a body buried there,' he said.

'Why do you say that?'

'It just occurred to me. Grace might have alerted to the explosives.'

'But there was blood at the first two sites.'

'She's a multi-task dog.' He reached his hand back over the console to pet Grace where she slept in her open crate. 'She's done it before. Alerted to something I didn't ask her to find. Whatever kind of device he used, I'm sure she could smell it.'

At the Embassy Suites they left each other in an exhausted silence, though it was obvious that neither one of them wanted to leave the other. They had spent the last several days together. So many hours. So many emotions. So many risks. How many times had they saved each other since they'd met two years ago?

Maggie stayed under the hot steam of the shower. She hoped it would wash away the frustration and regret along with the images that she couldn't shut off. When hot water didn't work, she switched to cold. She wasn't in bed for five minutes when she threw off the covers and found herself making her way down the hall.

She knew he'd still been awake when he opened the door only seconds after she knocked.

'I don't want to think about this,' she told him. 'I don't want to think at all. I just want—'

His kiss interrupted her. He took her hand, and she let him pull her into the room.

SUNDAY, OCTOBER 22

62

Nebraska

Tommy Pakula had left Omaha when it was still dark out. The night before when he'd told his wife what he needed to do this Sunday morning, instead of their regular family time, she told him to please be careful.

Just as the sun was peeking over the horizon behind him, he turned off of Highway 92. He found the old dead cottonwood without even searching. From the gravel road, he could see the Douglas County Crime Lab's mobile unit still parked in the pasture. He knew they'd been out here all night. The CSU tech named Haney had updated him around midnight.

Pakula had left a voice message for O'Dell this morning before he left. After what had happened the previous day, he wasn't surprised that she hadn't checked in with him. In a way, he was relieved she hadn't, because then he might have felt obligated to tell her why he was heading out here this morning. And truthfully, he wasn't sure if it would be another dead end and a complete waste of time.

Instead of pulling onto the dirt path that would have taken him into the pasture, Pakula continued down the gravel road. According to his dashboard clock, he was early. He tapped the GPS to enlarge the map, but it didn't matter, he'd already memorized where he was going.

He and O'Dell had talked about why Eli Dunn would choose to bury bodies here, almost two hours away from his farmhouse. Dunn's property had plenty of nearby cornfields and woods that would have provided sufficient gravesites. Pakula didn't need O'Dell to remind him that most killers stayed close to home or used places they were familiar with. Odds were, Dunn hadn't simply driven out here, gone up and down these gravel roads then randomly decided to dig in this pasture.

So if it wasn't a random choice, why did Eli Dunn travel this far? And if Dunn felt comfortable enough to bury the dead bodies of his victims out here, was it possible he had a place to hide the live ones? The ones he moved the night before the raid.

After he left Konnor yesterday, Pakula started racking his brain for anything he'd missed. Then he pulled out a map of Nebraska, spread it out on the conference room table and started making notes of what he did know.

He remembered the RV parked in Dunn's own barn. It had been registered to Eleanor Dunn. Her son had even used her address at the long-term care facility where she had been living for the last five years.

With the map spread out, Pakula noticed that Mrs Dunn's care facility was in Columbus. That looked awfully close to the area Eli Dunn had taken O'Dell's group. In fact, that pasture was only about thirty to thirty-five miles away.

Then Pakula got to thinking – where had Eleanor Dunn lived before she moved to the care facility? Usually people chose places close to home. So he scoured the property tax records for Platte, Butler and Saunders County, searching for where Eleanor Dunn had lived before.

Finally, he found a quitclaim deed. Five years ago, two days before Christmas, Mrs Dunn had signed the document, granting all of her property – around five hundred acres – to her neighbor.

He brought the area up on the computer so he could zoom in. On Google satellite, the stretch of land looked like mostly cornfields and pastures with only a couple of cutouts. One large farmstead had a huge house, barn, and several other outbuildings.

About a half mile away, tucked tight in between cornfields and almost invisible, was a little house that must have been Eleanor Dunn's. And back behind one of these cornfields was the pasture where Eli Dunn had taken O'Dell's search party. He had used his mother's property to bury his victims.

Pakula heard his cell phone chime and he looked to see the text from Trooper Gregory.

About ten minutes out.

Pakula questioned asking Gregory to meet him after what the trooper and his partner had been through yesterday, but he wanted to continue to keep information contained. He probably should have asked Sheriff Timmons. After all, this was the man's territory. But Timmons had shot and killed a man yesterday. It didn't matter that the man was a murderer and a human trafficker. Pakula knew from experience what it was like to take a life. Out of respect, he decided not to bother the sheriff unless he and Gregory discovered something.

Pakula found the dirt driveway and drove past it. By the time he circled back, Trooper Gregory would be here. He didn't want to draw too much attention. And he didn't want to ask permission. He simply wanted to go up to the house and knock on the door.

Maybe Pakula was being paranoid, but he didn't want anyone to know he was coming. Because there was still one other piece of the puzzle he hadn't figured out.

Why had Eleanor Dunn given her farm to her neighbor instead of her son? With a little more digging, Pakula discovered the answer. The neighbor, who Mrs Dunn had granted all of her property to in a quitclaim deed, was also her daughter. Iris Malone and her son Aaron now owned both properties.

Pakula was anxious to find out if Iris knew that her brother, Eli, was burying bodies in the pastures behind her home. Maybe she did know. And maybe she was the one helping him.

63

Charlotte realized Aaron wasn't coming back.

She'd spent the night on the floor where he'd left her, paralyzed by the drug with only her eyes able to move and her mind racing. The sun barely started to squeeze between the boarded slats.

It pained her to hear the kitten meowing in the bedroom and scratching at the door. At first, Charlotte couldn't even call out to it.

She had tried to sleep during the night. Usually, sleep had been her refuge. But the drug that paralyzed all her muscles seemed to activate the nightmares. It poked deep and far into the past, whipping up memories that she had long ago stowed away. She didn't want to remember being a little girl, so innocent and happy, skipping and reading and laughing. She didn't want to remember that once upon a time she had a mother and a father, who she thought loved her, until Iris told her they didn't want her anymore.

How could they not want her anymore?

'You were nasty. You were naughty, weren't you?' Iris' tone was so casual, so matter of fact, it was impossible to question her. Of course, she must be right.

'You have to live with us,' Iris told her. 'You'll be my little girl now.'

And for a while it was okay being Iris' little girl. Except

Charlotte couldn't play outside. She couldn't leave the farm. She could only read what Iris gave her to read.

'What about school?' she remembered asking Iris while she watched Aaron walk the long driveway to catch the school bus. 'I'd like to go.'

Looking back, Charlotte knew that was the beginning of the end. When Iris had no answers, she started applying more restrictions, locking more doors. That's when Charlotte started going from her own locked bedroom to a locked closet to the locked basement. Once she was even locked in a shed for days.

Punishment came swift and often, mostly in the form of being denied something. First thing to go was her name, then her books, then food and water, and finally light.

When you're hungry and cold and in the dark it's easy to let go of something as silly as a name. By the time Charlotte started finding the messages, the notes from the others, she knew Iris would never let her leave. That's when she tried to escape. Not just once, but over and over again, until Iris decided that was enough.

'That was your last chance.'

How many days ago had Iris told her that?

And here she was. At the Christmas house. The last stop.

If Aaron didn't come back, would she be left here to die? Would Iris come? Or would the man who sold the others come for her himself?

The drug was beginning to wear off. She wiggled her fingers, but she still couldn't roll over onto her side.

She heard a scratching sound.

'I know you're hungry, kitten.' This time her voice worked. But then she realized the sound hadn't come from the direction of the bedroom. It was followed by a click-clack.

The back door. Someone was there.

Panic raced through her body, and yet, it wasn't enough to jolt her muscles to move. She needed to hide. She had to find a weapon. Anything.

She dug her fingers into the carpet and tried to drag her body behind the sofa. What did it matter? They'd find her. And she was so tired of fighting.

When the door didn't open, she waited, held her breath and listened.

The man didn't have a key. Would that stop him?

Her answer came immediately with a crack of wood. A second crack shoved the door open.

She'd managed to pull herself behind the sofa, but now she couldn't see. She could only hear the footsteps.

'Anyone here?' a man called out.

Then he went quiet. Even the footsteps stopped. He knew she was here.

Someone else came through the door.

'There's a dead guy in the barn,' a second voice said, 'Stab wound in the neck.'

'Hello! My name's Detective Tommy Pakula. I'm with the Omaha Police Department. I'm here to help you.'

It was a trick. It had to be.

She knew Omaha was a big city, and it was almost a hundred miles away.

Now, she could hear one of them opening doors – the bathroom, the pantry. She heard scratching at the bedroom door and wanted to scream out for the kitten to please be quiet, but it was too late.

'Hello there, little kitty,' she heard the first man say.

'Leave her alone. Don't you hurt her,' Charlotte screamed as she shoved her body up. 'She's mine. Don't take her away. Please don't take her.'

64

Omaha, Nebraska

Creed wasn't surprised to wake up and find Maggie gone. She was a 'conundrum'. Her word, not his. Grace, however, was curled up on the pillow next to his. She wagged when saw that he was awake, stretched, came over and kissed him good morning.

Last night Creed was happy to honor Maggie's request of no questions, no obligations, no thinking about what it means or doesn't mean. This morning, when he didn't find even a note, he realized she was serious. But he realized something else – maybe he wasn't okay with it. Maybe he needed to know that it meant something more.

Then he checked his phone and tried to tamp down the relief when he saw her text.

Having breakfast with Lucy. Join us if you like.

He checked the time of her message then glanced at his dive watch. Forty minutes ago.

Just woke up. Still there?

He started fixing Grace's meal in a container he could seal and take down with them. She was watching him now, and he noticed she'd found her own leash. It was at her feet until she saw she had his attention then she grabbed it up in her mouth.

'I know, I know. We'll go out. Just hold on,' he told her as he added water into the dehydrated mixture, all the while glancing at his phone and hoping Maggie and Lucy hadn't already left the hotel.

Still here. Take your time.
   Already have a bowl of water for Grace.

Creed smiled and to Grace, he said, 'This is definitely a woman who knows that the path to my heart runs through you.'

When he and Grace arrived, Maggie smiled at him. He slid into the booth beside her and as Lucy greeted Grace, Maggie touched his forehead.

'We need to put a fresh bandage on this,' she said, as her fingers left the wound and caressed the side of his face all the way down his bristled jawline.

It was a bold and intimate gesture for a woman who didn't want to ask questions or talk about what they meant to each other.

He barely ordered, and Lucy was anxious to update him. Usually the woman's complexion was flawless. This morning there were dark circles under her eyes from too little sleep. Her short dark hair was spiked more than usual with the feathers of silver reminding Creed of bolts of lightning.

'The CSU team did find a body,' she told him.

Creed wanted to ask what shape it was in. Was it a woman or a girl? What color were her eyes? How long would it take to compare the DNA to his mother's sample? Instead, he held back his questions. He sipped coffee and pretended not knowing these answers wouldn't unravel the last of his senses.

'Harold Fox is doing the autopsy this morning. She was a young woman. There was quite a bit of decomposition.' Then she gave him a look of apology as she said, 'I asked the CSU techs if they were able to tell what color her eyes were. I'm sorry. They weren't.'

Creed released a sigh and only then realized he had been holding his breath.

'Thank you. I appreciate that you asked.'

'Harold was able to identify the woman you pulled from the lake. Several years ago, her family submitted her DNA sample to CODIS. Her name was Kristel Unger. She disappeared when her family stopped at a busy interstate truck stop. She was only twelve at the time.'

Lucy hesitated, watching for his reaction. He could feel Maggie's eyes on him, too. Lucy brought out a photograph and placed it on the table.

The little girl named Kristel could have been Brodie. Long brown hair, parted in the middle. She had a thin face with a bright smile. But blue eyes, not brown. Creed had never considered that there were others. Not just that they looked alike but that they been taken in the same manner that Brodie was taken.

'Pakula told me that Eli Dunn had a type,' Maggie said. 'He talked to a drug dealer who knew Dunn.'

'Drugs?' Creed asked.

'Drug dealer, pimp,' then she stopped herself.

He could tell she was uncomfortable sharing this information with him.

'I've been searching for Brodie a long time,' he told her. 'There isn't much you can say that I haven't already thought about.'

'He told Pakula that a lot of the girls looked alike.'

Just then, Maggie's cell phone started to ring. She glanced at the screen and answered, 'We were just talking about you.'

Creed watched her face as she listened. Her eyes met his and darted away. It seemed like she listened for an excruciatingly long amount of time before she finally said, 'We'll meet you at the hospital.'

65

Creed thought the woman named Charlotte looked small and fragile beneath the white sheet. A monitor droned and an IV bag hung beside the hospital bed as tubes snaked to the skinny arm. Her brown hair was chopped short and her face looked haggard. He searched for something familiar about her, but right now, she looked more like a survivor who'd been pulled from the rubble of a disaster.

He hung back and let Maggie make the introductions.

'I'm Agent Maggie O'Dell,' she told the woman. 'I'm with the FBI. Are you able to answer some questions?'

The woman looked over Maggie's shoulder and stared at Creed.

'Are you with the FBI, too?' she asked him.

He shook his head, suddenly unable to answer. He knew Maggie didn't want to give his name or admit that he wasn't one of the investigators. But he swore there was something about the woman's eyes.

Brown eyes.

Something familiar about her voice, too.

But no, that was impossible.

Maggie had warned him that he might inadvertently project Brodie's traits or personality quirks onto this woman simply because he wanted so badly to see something, anything he might recognize.

'You told Detective Pakula that Iris had taken you years ago,' Maggie continued. 'Do you remember anything about that?'

Her eyes darted back to Maggie at the mention of Pakula.

'He told me he'd take care of my kitten and let me have her back.'

Creed was surprised how in that one sentence her voice seemed to transform to that of a child's panic.

'Yes,' Maggie told her. 'You can trust Detective Pakula. If he told you that, he'll make sure your kitten is well taken care of.'

'And he'll give her back to me?'

'Yes, he will.' Maggie shifted her weight when the woman glanced back at Creed. 'Charlotte, anything you can remember would help. We know that Iris and her brother took other little girls.'

'I found their messages. I never saw them,' she said. 'We were supposed to be her little girl. I think whenever she got sick and tired of one of us, she replaced us.'

'What do you remember about the day they took you?' Maggie asked.

'It was so long ago.' Charlotte looked like she was trying hard to remember. 'It was raining. We stopped at a rest area because I had to pee. I remember there was a little girl in the bathroom. She told me her name was Charlotte and asked if I wanted to see her new puppy. She looked kind of sad. I didn't understand why she could be so sad if she had a new puppy.'

Her eyes came back to Maggie. 'I went with her. She was with her mom and uncle and her brother Aaron. They were traveling in an RV. I thought it was so neat until we drove away. I was worried my dad would be mad at me, and I wanted them to take me back.'

Then she shook her head. 'But it was too late. Iris told me my mom and dad were so mad at me they didn't want me back.' She paused, looked down at her hands and said, 'I don't want to talk about it anymore.'

Creed was holding the Polaroid so tightly between his fingers, he was sure his hand had gone numb.

When Charlotte was quiet for too long, Maggie turned to him and reached for the photo. She handed it casually to the woman, and Charlotte stared at it in mid-air. She started to reach for it with the hand connected to the tubes then readjusted and took it gently with her other hand.

'Have you seen this photo before? Or one like it?' she asked the woman.

Maggie had put white tape over the names written on the bottom. Charlotte stared intently. When she spoke again, her voice was almost a whisper.

'I remember this little girl.'

Creed felt a flutter of hope and tried to tamp down the anticipation.

'She clutched this old picture and held on to it like it was some kind of pathetic lifeline.' Charlotte's tone switched suddenly to disgust. 'I hated how frightened she was. I hated how she thought having it gave her hope. A stupid photo. I wanted to rip it up. I wanted to pretend it didn't exist.'

Maggie shot a glance back at Creed. He had to stop himself from grabbing the Polaroid away and protecting it from this woman.

Then she looked up at Creed and said, 'You're the boy in the photo.'

A statement, not a question.

He simply nodded.

The woman smiled. A first. It made her look so much younger.

'I wondered if you existed,' she said. 'Or if you were just a figment of my imagination. I tried so hard to forget about you.' Then she said, 'Your name's Ryder.'

Creed felt as if his heart had stopped beating.

'Wait a minute,' Maggie said, and she put her hand out, palm flat against Creed's chest as if she needed to stop him physically from thinking, from believing what this woman was saying. To Creed, she whispered, 'She could have could heard your sister talk about you.'

To the woman, she asked, 'Did you know the little girl you were talking about,' Maggie asked. 'The one you said was holding onto this photo?'

'I used to know her. But she's been gone a very long time.'

Creed realized this was a rollercoaster, because now he felt his stomach drop to his knees.

'She disappeared when Iris started calling me Charlotte. I think Iris called all us Charlotte, because that was her little girl's name. She told me I had to stop being a frightened little girl holding onto a stupid photo. That I was Charlotte, now. And I had to stop being Brodie.'

66

Omaha, Nebraska

Creed couldn't believe that Maggie wouldn't allow him to talk the woman any more.

'We have your mother's DNA sample. We can find out whether this woman is telling the truth,' she told him.

'How would she know my name? How would she know Brodie?'

'If she saw the original photo, your names were written on the bottom. Please, trust me. You need to wait. You've waited sixteen years, what's another couple of days?'

'*Days*?'

He was upset. He was elated. He wanted to talk and ask more questions.

'What harm is there in me talking to her?' he asked.

'Because you'll believe her, and what if the test comes back negative?'

'Then I won't have lost anything that I haven't already lost.'

But he didn't argue. Deep down he knew Maggie was just trying to protect him from another heartbreak. After all, what were the chances this woman really was Brodie?

Pakula had told them that Eli Dunn and his sister Iris Malone may have taken dozens of girls from rest areas and truck stops, using an RV that Dunn had parked in an old barn. Kristel Unger, the woman they'd pulled from the lake, was proof. The girls all looked the same. Their stories would all sound the same.

And yet, she recognized him. Or did she?

Maggie stayed at the hospital with Pakula. Creed left to check on Grace in the back of his Jeep. He'd left the sunroof open, and it was beginning to sprinkle. Dark clouds hovered above the city and matched his mood. He tried to shake it off as he took Grace for a walk at the far end of the hospital's parking lot.

His cell phone rang, and he grabbed it, thinking Maggie may have changed her mind. It was Hannah. He hadn't spoken with her in days, but somehow she always had the uncanny ability of knowing when he needed her.

'Hey,' he said.

'Hey yourself. Jason said he hadn't heard from you in a couple of days, and I realized I hadn't either.'

'Is he okay?' He'd forgotten about Jason and Scout's search for the missing teenager.

'He's hanging in there.'

'What happened?'

'You were right about Scout,' she told him. 'That dog's already a good scent dog. There was a shed in the backyard. Jason was embarrassed thinking Scout was alerting to a freezer full of frozen fish in that old shed. Turns out, that poor girl was in the freezer the whole time.'

'Damn!'

'The mother admitted she wanted to get rid of the girl. Had a new boyfriend. The girl was causing problems between them. So sad and so incredibly horrific.'

Creed shook his head. He wanted to ask how a mother could do that to her child, but both he and Hannah had seen it before. Instead, he said, 'I was having Jason train Scout for search and rescue, so the two of them wouldn't have to deal with so much death.'

'Some things you can't plan, Rye. You know what I always say, man plans—'

'And God laughs,' he finished it for her.

'So how are you doing?'

'Maybe not so good.'

'Rye, I've been worried about you. Tell me what's happening.'

'Hold on,' he told her as he opened the tailgate and lifted Grace into the Jeep. He slid into the driver's seat just as the cold rain started.

Then he told Hannah about the young woman who might be Brodie.

MONDAY, OCTOBER 23

67

Interstate 80

Outside of Grand Island, Nebraska

Maggie hadn't spoken to Creed since he'd left the hospital. She'd gotten back to the hotel late and thought about knocking on his door, but she knew if she did, they'd end up spending the night together again, and she wasn't sure she was ready for that.

This morning she left before dawn, but she sent him a text, asking if they could have dinner together. She explained that she and Pakula were checking out a hunch. Then she sent the message only after they were already on the road.

She felt like she could breathe again when a few minutes later he answered:

Looking forward to dinner. Be safe.

She and Pakula had a two-hour drive. Plenty of time to talk. She told him what had happened when she and Creed talked to the woman named Charlotte. How she said her real name was Brodie.

'This woman's been gone from society since she was eleven,' he said. 'She might not know who she is.'

Last night, Pakula had already moved Charlotte to a place called Project Harmony where he said she'd be safe, well taken care of, and she'd be able to be with her kitten.

While Maggie was protecting Creed, she also realized that Charlotte's story rang true. Pakula had told her about Iris Malone. When he and Trooper Gregory went to arrest her, they found a mantle of photos. Six little girls, all around ten to twelve years old. All with long brown hair and with the same features.

Since then, Pakula had found an obituary for Iris Malone's daughter. The girl had died almost twenty years ago. Her name was Charlotte.

'Eli Dunn probably started out helping his sister take little girls to replace Charlotte,' Pakula said. 'Then he took her rejects and discovered there was money to be made in human trafficking. I'm not sure what role the nephew, Aaron, played. We found him dead in the barn. I haven't asked Charlotte about that yet.'

Pakula told Maggie about the letter they had found in Eleanor Dunn's house. The letter signed by Kristel, who they now suspected was Kristel Unger, the woman they'd found in Lake Wannahoo.

'She mentions a man named Eli. She overheard him and Aaron talking about how much he'd be able to sell her for. She said the Christmas house was the end of the line. You should see the place. Plastic reindeer, garland and glass balls. Looked like Eleanor Dunn certainly loved Christmas. She had it all decorated right before her daughter and son had her committed to a care facility. I guess they never bothered to do anything with the house. Kept everything exactly the way it was the day she left.'

Though Pakula had found Charlotte in the house, he hadn't found the three captives Eli had moved from his own farmhouse. Maggie could feel Pakula's disappointment and frustration. But over the weekend, the boy Konnor had gained back another memory. Konnor remembered where the hotel was.

Pakula had told Maggie about Eli Dunn taking the boy and the others to a hotel every fourth Monday of the month for what Konnor called 'fix-ups.' Now, as they traveled to that hotel on the fourth Monday of the month, Maggie wondered if Pakula was grasping at straws, thinking he could still find the others.

'Iris and Aaron might have helped him, but someone else warned him we were coming. Someone who knew about the raid,' Maggie reminded him, and she had her own suspicions.

After all, Creed had been right about the dive tank. Someone had tampered with it. How was that possible when they didn't know they'd need it until the night before? Sheriff Timmons had arranged for the tank and the boat to be delivered to the lake. But the sheriff had been hand-picked for the human trafficking task force by Pakula himself. Pakula didn't want to believe the man was involved. He was well respected and had been the Butler County sheriff for decades.

When Creed and Maggie were in David City, Creed had picked up a local newspaper with a front-page story about the sheriff and his wife hosting a fundraiser for the victims of human trafficking. Late Saturday night, after Creed had fallen asleep, Maggie was wide awake, her body still remembering his touch, though she was completely exhausted. She found the newspaper in the outer room of his suite and started reading, thinking she could keep her mind from thinking about where this took her relationship with Creed. There was another article in the local newspaper. One that she saved to show Pakula.

The Butler County sheriff's department had pulled over a vehicle on Interstate 80. The routine traffic stop had discovered 120 pounds of marijuana along with an undisclosed amount of C-4.

'You said the explosive device in the raccoon carcass was likely C-4?'

'That's what I was told,' Pakula admitted. 'C-4 with trip-wires to a 4.5 volt battery.'

'Eli Dunn accused me of tricking him,' she said. 'What if he was just as surprised by the explosion as the rest of us? Or maybe most of us?'

Pakula shook his head. 'I've known Sheriff Steve Timmons for a long time.'

'He knew it was a raccoon. The carcass was hardly recognizable but Timmons knew it was raccoon.'

'Lucky guess. There're a lot of raccoons around here,' Pakula continued to defend the man. 'Besides, what would be the point?'

'He didn't want Dunn's scavenger hunt to continue.'

'I can't imagine he planned to shoot Dunn. Or that he'd ever want Trooper Vegaz to lose his hand.'

She had to admit, maybe it was a stretch. But she had planted enough suspicion that Pakula didn't include Sheriff Timmons in their plans this time.

*

The hotel was just off Interstate 80, outside of Grand Island, seventy-five miles from Sheriff Timmons' hometown. Konnor had told Pakula which hotel Eli Dunn took them to every fourth Monday of the month and always in the morning. Each time, the customers were already in the rooms waiting for them.

Pakula and Maggie came in the front lobby. Trooper Gregory was waiting at the only exit in the back. He had brought along several other troopers with him. The hotel had three stories. They had no idea what rooms were being used.

Pakula flashed his badge at the young man sitting at the reception desk.

'What's going on?'

Pakula put a finger to his lips while he yanked the telephone cord from the wall. Then he put his hand out.

'Your cell phone.'

The kid looked frightened and handed it over without another word.

Maggie didn't wait. She was already halfway down the hall, her weapon drawn. As she walked by the guest rooms she knocked on the doors.

'Police, open up,' she called out as she kept walking and knocking.

She could hear rustling behind the doors. Her voice had carried so well, she could hear doors opening and slamming above her. She continued down the hall until she reached the door to the stairwell, and that's where she waited while Pakula took up residence at the other end of the hallway.

By the end of the morning, they had made thirteen arrests.

But Maggie was startled and shocked when she saw the kids. Two of the girls were so little, so young. Both with long brown hair, parted down the middle.

Pakula had brought in victim advocates to take care of them. The chaos had quieted just as Sheriff Timmons showed up, coming in the back exit.

Maggie watched Pakula's face: surprise turned to disbelief to anger.

'What are you doing here, Sheriff?'

'I just got the message. I didn't realize we were hitting this place.' Timmons looked around and shook his head, making a good show of being disgusted.

'I didn't call you.' Pakula said.

'Well, someone did,' the sheriff insisted.

'You and me need to talk,' Pakula said, and he gestured for the two of them to step outside.

There was a lot more work for Pakula's task force, but they'd made a significant dent.

Later, Pakula would tell Maggie that Sheriff Timmons had broken down and told him about his wife's unexpected diagnosis. How they had planned to travel after his retirement. And now, there wasn't enough money for that. So Timmons had agreed to simply 'look the other way' and protect a network of human traffickers in exchange for a retirement package he said he deserved.

Eli Dunn was part of a network, connected only by messages and ads on the darknet. Dunn had never even met Timmons until the day of the raid on his farm, but Timmons was worried the man would somehow implement him. He'd found a way to warn Dunn then sabotage his outrageous scavenger hunt.

Hearing about the man's financial problems didn't come close to wiping away the image of those little girls' faces. The man's pleas had gotten nowhere with Pakula. Maggie suspected that Sheriff Timmons wouldn't be spending his retirement traveling or with his wife.

TUESDAY, OCTOBER 24

Florida Panhandle

Olivia was all packed, but Hannah insisted she have breakfast with her and Jason before she left for Atlanta. She needed to get back to the studio. Work had saved her before, and she knew it would do her soul some good now, though she was reluctant to leave. She'd gotten used to having Hannah fuss over her. Truth was she hadn't had a friend like Hannah since her mother had passed away.

She joined Jason at the table. He looked better today. The three of them had talked for hours after he'd found that poor girl in the freezer. But the whole time, he petted Scout and caressed his dog.

During her stay, Olivia had come to understand that her son was an incredible man, and she wanted to get to know him if he'd allow it.

The phone rang, and Hannah answered.

'Yes, she's here. And she's all packed.'

She smiled at Olivia as she handed her the phone.

'Your son wants to speak with you.'

She could see something in Hannah's eyes. There was something she wasn't telling Olivia.

'Hello, Ryder. How are you?'

He didn't waste any time and instead of a greeting, he said, 'We found her.'

Immediately, Olivia's entire body stiffened and her pulse began to race. She had been expecting this for years, but it still caught her off guard. How could she ever be ready to hear that the body of her little girl had finally been found?

'The DNA?' she asked, barely able to speak.

'It's a match. But she's alive.'

'Ryder, say that again?' Certainly, she couldn't have heard him correctly.

'We found Brodie. And she's alive. Hannah said you're packed. I've booked a flight to Omaha for you.'

She was speechless, and Ryder must have taken her silence as reluctance.

'Unless you'd rather wait,' he said.

She glanced up at Hannah and across the table at Jason, both of them waiting for her response.

'I can't wait to meet her.'

The Creed Series

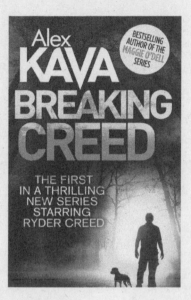

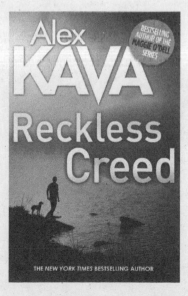